FLIGHT
FOR
SURVIVAL

Inspiration. Motivation. Plane Stuff.

"Sometimes truth is scarier than fiction"

By Karlene K. Petitt

at

Flight To Success

www.KarlenePetitt.com

FLIGHT FOR SURVIVAL

NEXTGEN IS ON the horizon with multiple threats looming. Aircraft complexity, fatigue, and training issues leave pilots open to error. Unmanned aircraft systems—drones—are flooding the airspace, creating a regulatory nightmare. Safety Management Systems are mandated to be in place by 2018, but creating a safety culture is an essential ground floor requirement.

FAA inspector Kathryn Jacobs is in charge of drone regulation, Jackie Jameson is managing flight attendant training, and Darby Bradshaw is flying an A330 for Global Air Lines while fighting for safer skies. Darby has just been offered a two-million-dollar publishing deal for her safety management book: *Fight For Safety— Inside the Iron Bubble.* Unfortunately, there are those who would do anything to stop the book's release.

The darkest realm of Global Air Lines' secret sub-culture surfaces between the pages amidst fear that the truth about what happens inside the iron bubble will come to light. When a Boeing 777 disappears, and a pilot intentionally flies into a mountain, suspicion points to Captain Bill Jacobs, hidden inside prison walls.

But the truth is never what it appears.

The worst crash in airline history plunges these three friends into a fight for their very survival.

FLIGHT FOR SURVIVAL

KARLENE PETITT

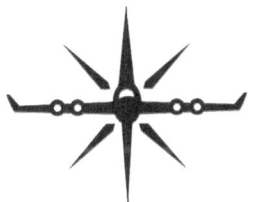

JET STAR PUBLISHING INC.
SEATAC WA

Flight For Survival is dedicated to my mom—Pat Kassner. My mom taught me to question injustice, stand up for what I believe in, and focus on what is important. Mom, your confidence, encouragement, and support continue to give me strength.

FLIGHT FOR SURVIVAL

PROLOGUE

EYES CLOSED, HE attempted to shut out the noise and irritation of passengers as they boarded. The lights were far too bright for the hour, and bags hit him as people passed. The flight attendants, with their Cheshire cat smiles, crawled under his skin as they greeted the passengers much too loudly. *Relax. Breathe. Breathe in. Breathe out.*

"You need a blanket."

He ignored the voice.

"Five thousand bucks. At least you only paid one way. You'd think they could have left one in your seat."

"I know," he whispered, eyes still closed. He refused to look left, but he knew the words rang true. Nobody cared. Nobody understood him, they never had. Yet he refused to engage with his friend. An argument would surely result in his being removed from the plane. These days all communications with his "friends" turned into arguments. He couldn't get himself removed or he would be locked up for good. This flight was his ticket to freedom.

"This is the only way," the voice said. "But you need a blanket. Ask the flight attendant. Maybe you can get her to sit in your lap. When was the last time you…?"

"Shut the fuck up!" he snapped under his breath.

"Excuse me?" a flight attendant said, stepping from the boarding door toward his seat. "Is there something I can get you sir?" she asked.

"Tell her you want a blanket."

He breathed deep. "Do you have a blanket?"

"Yes sir," she said, pulling one down from the overhead compartment and handing it to him. "If you would like to sleep sir, you're welcome to have the window seat," she said, extending her hand to the seat beside him.

He glanced left and then looked at her. "Thank you. I'm fine." She nodded and returned to the forward entrance.

"Maybe you could do her first," the voice said, followed by laughter. That insane laughter irritated him more than usual tonight. But that was not always the case. They had become friends when he was very young. Friends do not get their friends into trouble on purpose, but his friends did. Yet if he fought with them, he got into trouble anyway. There was no winning. He gave up. He gave in to a life of hell and gave control of his life to all of them.

Unfolding his blanket, he covered himself. It wasn't long until the doors were closed and the briefing was played over television screens. Nobody watched. In the past when a person gave the demo, at least a few passengers showed the courtesy of attention. He smiled. Tonight it wouldn't matter.

"Excuse me sir, is your seatbelt secure?"

He lifted the blanket for the flight attendant to see that he was strapped in, as he closed his eyes.

"Don't fall asleep," the voice said.

"I won't." And then he drifted into the clouds. White, comforting, and outlined with the glow and warmth of the sun welcoming him. Closer and closer he flew. White faded to black and a shiver crawled under his skin. Lightning flashed and thunder vibrated his seat. He pulled his blanket to his chin and he floated higher. *"Don't go to sleep,"* whispered in the wind as he pressed through the clouds. A blackened sky filled with the most brilliant spattering of stars welcomed him with open arms. A calm he had never felt before enveloped his body as he drifted toward heaven. Far, far from the chains of earth.

"Wake up!" the voice snapped. "It's time."

He opened his eyes with a start. The cabin was as black as the night sky. He held his breath as the flight attendant lifted the phone. She glanced his way, but looked right through him, then spoke into the phone. She moved to the galley and pulled two cups from the cabinet. She lifted the coffee pot and filled one cup. He unbuckled his seat belt beneath the blanket. She filled the second cup.

With lids in place, she stacked the cups, one on top of the other, picked up the phone and a faint ding from the cockpit told them she was ready to enter. She glanced over her shoulder and spoke quietly into the phone. He could not hear her words, but that didn't matter. He knew what would happen next. She placed the phone into the cradle and stepped in front of the camera outside the cockpit door. He envisioned the security of the pilots seeing her smile as they unlocked the door to their office.

He waited patiently. *One. Two. Three.* The light from the cockpit welcomed him as the door opened. He moved like a wild cat directed at its prey. Slamming into the flight attendant as she stepped through the door drove her toward the console. The captain's arm flung sideways to stop her trajectory and she fell into the first officer. Coffee flew everywhere.

"What the hell!" the captain yelled, grabbing a paper to soak up the mess.

He pulled the door closed behind him and the captain's head snapped his direction. Their eyes connected, but strapped into his seat, there was nothing the captain could do.

Without hesitation, and in one motion, he wrapped his arm around the captain's forehead and pulled it back, stabbing a pen into his throat. He had practiced the maneuver in his mind for many months, but never expected the fountain of blood. It lasted mere seconds and then shifted to a river of red, slowing to a trickle.

The shrieking flight attendant pulled him back to the moment. His eyes flashed at her and then to the first officer who sat unmoving. Then he looked back to the flight attendant who had backed into the corner like a frightened crustacean trying to hide under a rock. Shrieking. Shrieking. That God damned shrieking!

"Be quiet!" he snapped. Her screams turned to sobs gulping for air, which was more irritating than her fake smile at the door.

The voice laughed. "I didn't think you had it in you."

He smiled. He was not so sure he had it in him either. But he did. *Now what?*

"World Flight 590," air traffic control announced, "contact radar on 137.2."

"Say goodbye if you want to breathe another moment," he told the first officer. The first officer did as directed.

He reached down and turned off the radar, then the transponder, and then he glanced at the overhead panel and located the inflight entertainment system. With one press, that, too, was off. The internet was full of all sorts of information. A person could even learn how to fly if they so chose.

"What's your name?" he asked the flight attendant.

Between sobs she said, "Tiiiffany."

"Tiffany, I want you to call to the aft cabin flight attendants and tell them you are not feeling well and the pilots invited you to stay up here for a few minutes."

"Bad move. She's going to cry. They'll know something is wrong," his friend said. "Kill her now!"

"She'll be good," he said, "or she'll end up in a pool of blood."

"You're making a mistake," the voice said.

"I'm in charge, so shut the hell up!" he snapped, although his friend was probably right. He turned toward the first officer and said, "Call the back and tell them Tiffany will be back shortly." The first officer did as directed. Tiffany continued to sob.

"Good job," he said. "Now I want you to turn this beast 100 degrees left." The first officer followed directions as he pushed a button and then turned the knob. The Boeing 777 began a slow and easy left turn. He watched closely how easy this plane was to fly with a knob.

"Sweetheart, come here," he said. When she didn't move, he snapped, "Come now!"

"Tiff, go ahead," the first officer said. "Everything will be all right."

She glanced in the pilot's direction and then back toward him. He opened his arms and she hesitantly moved closer. Once she was within reach, he grabbed both arms and held her tight. "Stop crying. Now!"

"Get rid of her," the voice said. "She's giving me a headache."

She was giving him a headache also. He moved his hands to her face as he said, "There is nothing for you to worry about my dear," and then he snapped her neck. Her lifeless body slid to the floor, and he stared for too long before looking up.

"What the hell are you doing?" he asked the first officer.

The first officer was leaning right, toward the window and his hand was inside his flight bag.

Stepping on the flight attendant, he scrambled over the seat and grabbed the pilot's hand and yanked it up. "What the hell are you doing?"

The pilot held a cell phone. He tried to grab the phone from him, but the pilot fought back. In the midst of the struggle, they bumped the console and bells began ringing, red lights started flashing, and the plane began a climb.

"You fool!" he yelled, swinging an arm at the pilot, but the pilot ducked. The pilot was now out of his seat and coming at him with both hands. He moved backwards and fell over the flight attendant, and landed on his back. Arms entangled as the battle continued. He kicked the pilot between his legs and the pilot doubled over. Grabbing the headset, he then wrapped the cord around his prey's throat and pulled.

The pilot grabbed the wires with both hands attempting to pull free. "Why?" the pilot choked out.

He relaxed the cord for a moment and said, "Why what?" somewhat confused at the question.

"Why are you doing this?" the pilot asked.

"Ahh... because I can." He pulled the cord taut and snapped the life from the first officer. Laughter filled the cockpit and he joined in.

He climbed into the first officer's seat and pushed the controls forward. The plane stopped climbing. He pressed the autopilot button. Then he pushed "level change" and the plane began a descent to the altitude previously set in the mode control panel.

Now what? He had no idea.

CHAPTER 1

D
ARBY STOOD IN front of the 72-inch television, in the most exquisite lobby she had ever seen. And she had been in some pretty awesome lobbies worldwide. Beach ball sized gold and silver balls hung by red ribbons from the high ceiling. Huge swag-enwreathed windows filled one wall. Yet there was something paradoxical about the breaking news that filled the television screen in the middle of a holiday movie set.

CNN had been playing the same scene, with a search that went nowhere, for the last two weeks. Once again they managed to get another brainiac pilot on the show to say something ridiculous. She rolled her eyes. These pilots seriously needed to be brought up to date on modern aircraft. Yes, pilots could actually put on an oxygen mask, talk, and fly all at the same time.

Darby turned from the television and walked to the window, which showcased the city sprawled below. The sun was already behind the buildings and a splattering of snowflakes danced in the sky. She inhaled a deep breath at the magnitude of it all. But what was about to occur in the office excited her beyond belief.

She owned this day. Passing the 24th floor fifteen minutes earlier, she had given up trying to figure out how the hell she got here. By the time the elevator door opened, she had reminded herself that it was due to three years of focused attention on one mission—safety. Her life had been committed to solving industry problems and with Kathryn's help, and inspiration from Global Air Lines, she wrote a book. From what her agent said, it was going to be an international best seller.

Odell had his panties in a bunch over her training blog. She suspected he would need a crowbar to get them out of the crack if he were to read *Fight For Safety—Inside the Iron Bubble*. But something had to be done.

The FAA was mandating SMS (Safety Management Systems) and compliance required a safety culture. Yet as she wrote her book, Darby connected the dots creating a picture that spoke volumes—Global's Flight Operations management had no clue what a safety culture was. These pilots had missed the mark on the term *threat and error management*, too. They operated as if threat and error management meant managing by threat. Bill, Kathryn's murdering ex-husband, had once been the heart of this airline.

She turned toward the television. More than Global's processes, every accident or industry event made her question if Bill was reaching out from prison. Until he was dead and buried, nobody was safe. But she could do her part.

"Miss Bradshaw…"

Darby jumped, and turned toward the voice.

"Ms. Brooks will see you now."

Darby followed the receptionist into an office that mirrored the lobby in terms of amazing. The amazing part was the hundreds of manuscripts piled against the walls, on the armoire, and the windowsill. But it was the one sitting on the mahogany desk that made the top of the awesome list. She had written it.

"Darby, Darby, Darby," Ms. Brooks said, in rapid fire as she flew around her desk. "That will be all Cecilia," she said to her receptionist, with a wave of her hand. Taking Darby's hand, she pulled her to a white leather couch. "Sit. Please sit."

Ms. Brooks lifted a bottle of champagne and filled a glass, and then handed it to Darby. "Are you ready for the big time?" she asked, pouring another glass for herself. Darby opened her mouth to answer, but Ms. Brooks said, "Here's to you Darling." Extending her glass, Darby lifted hers and they touched glasses, binding their joint venture.

"I hope you know what you're doing, Ms. Brooks," Darby said with a raise of an eyebrow, as she sipped her bubbly.

The woman laughed. "Deloris, please," she said sitting beside Darby on the couch. "Oh, I've been doing this for a long time, sweetheart, and it's not often I get a two million dollar signing bonus for a first time author."

Darby choked on her Dom Pérignon. "Two *million*?" She grabbed a napkin and wiped up the mess she had made on the table and in her lap. When she had told Darby they had 'a deal worth two,' she had thought two hundred thousand. *Two million? Holy shit!*

"Oh, that's just the beginning," she said, patting her leg. "I've got you on the list for *Good Morning America*, *Kelly and Michael*, and *The View*. You're scheduled to do an interview with Barbara in February."

"Holy shit!" Darby said, unable to contain herself. She reached for the champagne bottle. "May I?"

"Of course, darling," Deloris said, setting her glass on the table. "This is the first time that we've got a book that will not only appeal to the traveling public, but I can see textbook written all over it for airline management, safety, and leadership. The options are endless." She lifted her glass and emptied it in one swoop. "Tell me please… because they all will be asking. What did it take write a book like this?"

Darby sighed, and thought for a second. *Good question.* "Tons of research. Common sense. Experience. And one too many needless funerals." She hesitated and then added, "And working for an airline with pilots whose egos are bigger than their management skills didn't hurt either."

Deloris grinned, and then an eyebrow lifted. "How many of those events were real? Because I'm telling you, these stories are incredible. I'm seeing at least two screen plays out of this."

"Really?" Her heart pounded harder than she had ever felt without someone trying to kill her. "Maybe I could write them."

"I'm counting on it." Deloris refilled her glass and said, "We need to talk cover. I'm thinking we'll use a photo of a Global Air Lines plane. The recognition will be fabulous!"

"I asked my Seattle chief pilot. He more or less said, uh… *hell no.*" Darby slid a finger around the edge of her glass, and looked up apologetically. "He forbade me to contact marketing."

"Don't worry about that." She patted Darby's leg again. "You leave the marketing to us." She stood. "We know how to deal with these things."

"You don't know my airline," Darby said with a grin, standing. "My union told me I could be fired for violating an order."

Deloris raised an eyebrow, and grinned. "Well, our agency has never backed a first time author like this before. But the team loved the *Iron Bubble* concept."

Glad that Deloris changed the subject, and Darby sipped her champagne in a futile attempt at calming her heart rate. She had no doubt that Odell's not wanting her to contact marketing was personal, to hell with any benefit it could be for the airline or the industry.

Deloris placed her hands on her hips and looked Darby up and down. "And look at you… Love the nails. The shoes. The hair. And the fact you are a lady pilot who flies an Airbus, will rock the world. You are going to be a star, my dear."

Darby splayed her fingers mockingly admiring her nails. She sipped her champagne, and then tossed her hair off her shoulder and curtsied. Who would have thought? The reality was she did not care about being a star. She only wanted things to change at Global. But truth be told, these were not unique challenges to her airline. She wanted a safer industry. If it took marketing and promoting her book to make that happen, she wanted a first class ticket on that plane.

Deloris laughed. "You're the package Miss Darby. With talent, too." Deloris intertwined an arm with Darby's and patted it. "Stick with me Darling, and I will take you places."

"I'm all yours, until Monday when I have to be in Seattle and sit reserve." She tossed back her champagne. "Now what?"

Deloris glanced at her Cartier watch. "We show you off. Come dear… the team would love to meet you. Our annual Christmas party is well underway, and I thought this would be a perfect time for you to meet everyone." She opened the door and extended a hand for Darby and they left the office.

Together they walked to the elevator and Deloris pressed the penthouse button, as she filled Darby in on the details of all who would be at the party. Darby's head spun with excitement and champagne.

Reaching the penthouse level, Deloris said, "Congratulations, Miss Darby. The night is yours. Enjoy."

When the elevator doors opened, her eyes widened as she stepped into the room. "Holy shit," she said under her breath. There was a band with two singers in the corner singing *Santa Baby*. Waiters mingled with trays of champagne; others held trays with jumbo shrimp, steak skewers and stuffed mushrooms. Fifty some people mingled beneath a glass roof with a fluttering of snowflakes. Never in her wildest dreams did she imagine this world existed.

Darby grabbed a plate and filled it, knowing all too well champagne on an empty stomach was never a good idea, especially with two million dollars on the table. While this was not a poker game, she was holding a royal flush. Champagne or not, she had already won the game.

She accepted another glass of champagne and wondered how the heck she would eat, and hold her plate and the glass at the same time. Life was full of challenges, and this was the kind she enjoyed the best.

"Miss Darby," Deloris said, "let me introduce you to your team."

Darby followed Deloris across the room, and the guests parted as they approached. Names flew by and Darby smiled and nodded, allowing a wink or two to slip out as she greeted *her* team. An editing staff, publicist team, and people she had no idea existed in this new world she was about to embark upon, greeted her. She set her glass and plate on a table, and began to shake hands. For some reason, Darby suspected there would be a whole lot more shaking going on tonight.

CHAPTER 2

DARBY'S WORLD SPUN from dancing on top of the world. Well, maybe a bit of champagne and kicking up her heels on the penthouse floor for three hours helped. Lying across the bed, she kicked one shoe off, then the other, and spread her arms wide, with an even wider smile.

If she had known that writing books was so lucrative, and shit ass fun, she might have done it years earlier. Darby rolled off the bed, stood, and then wiggled out of her dress. "Free at last!" she said, dropping the fabric to the floor, and headed for the bathroom. She popped two Ibuprofens into her mouth and opened a bottle of water, then tipped the bottle back until it was empty.

Tomorrow she would meet with the agency's marketing department, followed by a trip to the airport, and work her way back to Seattle. But first things first—hot bath, sleep, and upon wake-up she would order a room service breakfast.

She reached down and turned the faucet to hot, then lifted the mini bubble bath bottle and closed one eye in an attempt to read the label. Unable to read it, she dumped the contents into the water. Darby brought the Jacuzzi to life with a press of a button, and then adjusted the temperature. She then went to the other room to get her cell phone.

Once in the bedroom, she lifted the television remote and pressed the *on* button, then clicked through the stations. CNN was still on the search. She paused for a moment to see if they found anything, with the announcement of *Breaking News*. Nothing. She sighed, and pressed the up arrow until she located a music channel dedicated to the season. She tossed the remote on the bed and grabbed her cell, then headed back to the bathroom.

"Oh shit!" Jumping for the tub, Darby pressed the Jacuzzi button to *off*. She grabbed two towels off the rack and threw them on top of the bubbles creeping across the marble. "This could have been really bad," she said with a laugh. There was a reason that drinking and hot tubs did not mix.

Darby stepped out of her panties and tossed them to the counter and then slid into the warmth of the water. Chin high with bubbles, she turned the water temp down, but allowed it to flow. *Baby It's Cold Outside* blared from the other room. She closed her eyes amazed at how incredible her life was. Flying planes fed her soul, but this book thing was going to be a pretty awesome gig, especially if her words made a difference.

Sitting reserve gave her far too much time on her hands, and she had to do something with it. Kathryn was busy kicking butt at the FAA and her girls were getting older and not needing Darby around as much, and Jackie was way too serious about John. But that was a good thing. It all was.

And then there was Ray... a smile spread across her face. She would definitely call him for her kiss good night after she was tucked under the covers. The ringing phone made her jump. She glanced at the counter, debating to let it go to voice mail. *But it could be Ray.* She scrambled out of the tub, wiped her hands off on a towel, and answered.

"Darby Bradshaw?"

"This is she," Darby said, climbing back into the tub.

"We have an inverse assignment for you with a 1400 departure tomorrow."

"I'm in New York."

"Stand by."

They couldn't assign her a trip, *could they*? She was on days off and 2,500 miles away from base. She could turn it down. *Couldn't she*? Shortly after the merger, she had gone to basic indoctrination and the manager of scheduling had said if an inverse assignment was necessary, there were four reasons that a pilot could turn it down. *What were they?*

"Okay," the scheduler said, "we have you listed on flight 233 departing at 7 am. You'll connect through Oklahoma City, with fifty minutes on the ground. Your next flight will get you into Seattle at 11:15, 45 minutes before check-in for your flight to Hong Kong. Details will be in the computer on your schedule."

With eyes blinking, Darby's mouth fell open. *Is she serious?* She pulled her phone away and stared at the clock. When the time came into focus, she did a little mental math and figured she would have five hours of sleep if she dropped right now. How could scheduling do this? This was the age of FAR 117 regulating crew rest. *So much for that regulation*, she thought.

FAR 117 was the new federal aviation regulation attempting to minimize fatigue. The result was pilots could now fly nine hours as a single crew, instead of eight. More often than not, this regulation made domestic crews work more days for the same income, resulting in fewer days off to make ends meet. International regulations were a nightmare all their own for both scheduling and pilots alike.

Despite intentions to reduce fatigue, the truth was that any international pilot was going to be tired at the end of the flight due to the length of their day. Time on duty was an essential regulation, yet Global obviously found a way to work around that issue.

Darby slid deeper into the tub. Eyes closed, she attempted to activate brain cells that had celebrated a little bit too much, as she thought about how they could do this to her. How could they do it to anyone? Better yet, how she could get out of it?

Drinking—but she stopped around 9 pm, and by the time she could possibly hit Seattle, 14 hours would pass.

Kids—could not find childcare. That wouldn't work.

Could not get to the airport—might be an option.

Fatigue! That was it. She would be too tired. A chill went through her body. A crew-scheduling manager had actually said, "But don't *ever* call in fatigued. That's the other f-word around here." Dumbfounded, Darby had asked, "Even on our days off?"

Days off did not matter, as the company had to generate the same FAA paperwork whether she was working or not. The rule was—do NOT *ever* call in fatigued at Global.

Under normal circumstances she would have said no, and fought the battle at a later date. But life had been calm for the previous three years since she had stopped trying to get a flight to stay current, and gave up asking to wear her uniform to speak at schools, and dressed like a normal person. They still had not fixed the training issues, but hopefully her book would put that on a different trajectory. Train yourself at home was a way of life. A way of life for some that pointed to a grave.

Online learning was not bad. Universities everywhere offered online schools, improving efficiencies for everyone. The problem was that airlines missed the boat as to what made online training effective—interaction. If pilots could interact and discuss what they were learning, with a subject matter expert who was monitoring the virtual classroom, learning would occur. There would be great power in virtual training. As of now, this type of pilot training was nothing short of substandard.

Fitting the mold of a good pilot who kept her mouth shut was more or less comfortable. Frustrating, yes, but easy. And it gave her time to write her book.

When her phone rang again, she hadn't realized she was still holding it, or more like squeezing it with her arm hanging outside the tub. She pressed *answer* and placed it to her ear.

"Hi Sweetheart, how'd the event go?"

A smile spread across her face, and she filled Ray in the on the details of the night from the party to everyone she had met. "You might have some competition," she said with a chuckle. "I'm just saying… my dance card was filled all night."

Ray laughed. "Sounds like I'll have to *up* my cherish Darby game."

"Yup. I'm thinking that's the only way to keep you *in* the game," she said grinning. She found it challenging to imagine finding someone who was as awesome as Ray. Yet nobody was perfect and she had only been dating him for eight months, thus the jury was still out. She smiled. She was the judge and jury.

But sadly all the men she had loved managed to die an untimely death, and that fact lingered in the gray matter of her brain.

"What time are you departing tomorrow night?" he asked.

"Try morning," Darby said. "Scheduling's putting me on a flight, deadheading me in for a Hong Kong trip."

"What? The *same* day? They can't do that."

Laughing Darby said, "Oh... I'm thinking they can." She extended her legs and stretched, wiggling her red toes in the white bubbles.

"I'm on the computer, let me check. What's your password?"

"1-8-0-0- B-I-T-E-M-E."

Laughing, Ray said, "Of course it is. Why would I even have to ask?"

Grinning, Darby said, "You'll learn." She told Ray her password, and closed her eyes and melted into the warmth of the water, trying to figure out the best way to undo tomorrow's schedule.

"Here you go," he said. "Holy shit!"

"There's been a lot of that holy shit going around today. I'm thinking it's the season."

"They have you departing positive space connecting through Oklahoma City... Babe, you're going to have to move toward the airport by 5 am, that's a 4 am wake up, 1 am in Seattle. You'll be awake for hell... 13 hours before your 2-hour report. Tack a 14-hour flight onto that mess and you've got 30 hours on duty!"

"29," Darby said. *But who's counting?* "I'm not sure how they can do this with FAR 117. I wonder if it's too late to get it in the book." The wheels were spinning on how to work this into her fatigue chapter.

"Looks like they don't put you on duty until you report in Seattle," Ray said.

"Those dirty little dogs."

"You're not doing it. Are you?"

"I kind of have to," Darby said.

"When do *you* have to do anything?"

Darby laughed. "Good point." She never *had* to do anything. Nobody did. "The problems are," she said, raising a finger. "One, this is a chance to fly. Two, I haven't flown in over 8 months. Three, it's been really nice being off their radar, and I don't want to go down the path of looking over my shoulder again." Then she added, "Besides, I can sleep on the commute home and take first break. I'll be fine."

"Kiddo, I don't like it. And what about your meetings tomorrow?"

"I'll reschedule." She didn't like it either. The entire situation smelled of rat. Or stupidity. The question was, who was stupid—scheduling for assigning the trip or her for taking it?

"Sweetheart, you'd better get some sleep."

"But I'm naked and wet, and soaking in a perfectly hot bath."

"Thank you for that visual."

"I aim to please," Darby said. "When I slip under the sheets, can I call you back?"

"Of course."

Darby stood and reached for a towel, and then glanced at the time on her phone. At best, she would sleep 4 hours before her 29-hour day and that hour drive to the hotel would push her adventure to 30 hours. Ray was right again, but telling him would come with time. He was a brilliant man with a heart of gold. But what she liked most about him, besides his sense of humor, was his honesty and integrity. Ray was as honorable as they came.

Darby finished drying herself off and wrapped the towel around her body. Shivering, she pulled it tight. But she was not sure if the little hairs were from the chill in the air, or a warning not to take that trip.

CHAPTER 3

THERE HAD NEVER been a quicker rush home to jump in the shower alone in all of history. Darby had dumped her suitcase on the bed and then re-packed the cleanest of the dirty clothes. She flew to her car, backed out of the driveway, pulled out onto the street, and headed toward the airport. She glanced at her watch—her trip would depart in less than two hours.

On her flight back to Seattle, she had upgraded to first class on both legs, but did nothing more than catnap. Darby was never a good one to sleep on a plane, as she kept a sense of awareness at all times. Even with her eyes closed.

She made it back to the airport in record time, jumped on the crew bus, and was in the hallway running towards Flight Operations; fifteen minutes from parking lot to check-in. Fueled by adrenaline, she punched the top-secret security code into the door and ran to the computer. She punched in her numbers to log in, and it didn't work. She tried it again, and again. She had passwords for Facebook, Twitter, bidding, scheduling, Gmail, her bank accounts, and more. They were all running together. Panic overcame her. *Shit! Shit! Shit!*

Darby stopped what she was doing. She took a deep breath and relaxed, then typed in the series of numbers and signed in for her flight. *Ahhh.* Once the first duty was complete, she moved on into the briefing room.

"Hey guys, I'm Darby."

"John," her captain said. He stood and shook her hand. "This is Vic, and his first officer, Ted."

"Nice to meet you guys." Darby slipped into a chair, and looked over her shoulder, then brought her attention back to the crew. "Okay, here's the deal. My day started in New York this morning. Scheduling called me at 11 pm last night for an inverse assignment. Which means I've been up since midnight Seattle time, with only a four-hour nap before that.

"They can't make you take this trip," Ted said.

"Technically I didn't qualify for any of the reasons to turn it down."

"What about being on the opposite side of the country?" Ted asked. "Fatigue comes to mind."

"Yep. Global's other f-word," Darby said. "But being on the opposite side of the continent is not a legal reason to turn down the trip."

"You should call in fatigued now. That would show them," Vic said. "If they couldn't find anyone last night, they certainly can't this morning."

"But we're on high time pay," John said. "We don't want them to cancel the trip."

"Good point," Vic said. "Okay. How about Ted and I work the trip out. We'll take off and land. But you can take second and fourth breaks."

"Works for me," John said.

They had a plan. The working crew finished the paperwork and Darby glanced through the particulars—weather, fuel, alternates, and time en route—just over 14 hours. She jumped with the vibration in her pocket, and pulled her phone out and read the message, then smiled.

"Boyfriend?" John asked.

Darby's eyes flashed up from her phone. "Nope. FAA," she said with a wink. "See you guys at the plane."

She piled her computer bag on top of her suitcase, reconnected her flight bag, and then pulled her stuff out of Flight Operations and headed for the bathroom. Once inside, she parked her luggage against the wall, and took a quick look in the mirror. Not a pretty sight, and the huge yawn did not help the attractive meter, but explained so much. Unfortunately, there was no fixing this one without a couple nights of really good sleep. Instead of makeup, she turned, leaned against the counter and dialed. The phone rang twice, and then Kathryn answered.

"Hey Darb, how'd the meeting go?"

"Spectacular."

"What time are you getting in tonight?" Kathryn asked. "I want details."

"Well, that's the thing…" Darby said. "I'm kind of already home, and heading to Hong Kong in an hour."

"But…"

"It would be best if you didn't ask, and I didn't tell."

"Darby—"

"I know. I know. But I actually feel pretty good right now. The visual is another story," she said glancing in the mirror once again.

"What about two hours into the flight?"

"Hopefully I'll be sleeping."

"Dang it Darby! What the hell are you doing?"

"One, being a company person," Darby said raising a finger. "Two, keeping myself out of the chief pilot's office." The second finger went up. "And three, reminding myself what the inside of the plane looks like," she said raising the third finger. "Besides, I'm not taking off, and I get second break. *And* when I get to Hong Kong, I'll sleep for 16 of my 24-hour layover." She raised her thumb, "And maybe I'll get to fly my plane before it becomes a distant memory."

"I don't like this," Kathryn said. "Not one bit."

"I know, Mom. But it'll be the last time I ever do this. I swear!"

Kathryn was not really *her* mom, but she did work with the FAA. She was the head of the Seattle Flight Standards Office, and the mother of 15-year old twin girls. She was not only a single working mother who put her dumbass husband in jail for life, but she was Darby's best friend. There was absolutely nothing that Kathryn would not do for her friend.

Darby hated putting Kat in the position of knowing too much, but she could not lie to her. Which caused a few stressful moments balancing the boundaries of their FAA and pilot friendship. But it worked. Now all Darby had to do was figure out how to stay awake long enough to do the walk-around.

CHAPTER 4

KATHRYN SHOOK HER head and sighed as she set her phone on the counter. She had thought her daughters would turn her hair gray, but the truth was that Darby was in first place on that project. There was no way Darby should be on a plane working a trip, since she had been on the other side of the country less than 24 hours earlier.

She flipped through her pad of paper until she found a clean page and wrote —*Global Air Lines. Crew Scheduling. Fatigue.* She ripped the page out and pinned it to her bulletin board. Pulling a hand through her hair, she wondered how to approach this one diplomatically.

They must have run out of crewmembers. Unless Darby was trying to fly in order to avoid working over the holidays, or get her landing so she wouldn't have to go to Oklahoma for bounces. Maybe she picked up the trip on her own?

No.

She knew Darby better than that. Besides, how would Darby make the commute back to Seattle with oversold flights during holiday travel? She wouldn't. The only way she could make a last-minute connection to Seattle would be with positive space. This was definitely scheduling's doing.

Kathryn pulled out a chair and sat at her kitchen table, and tapped her pen on the paper. She glanced at the note on the bulletin board. The federal aviation regulation, FAR 117, outlined strict rules for airlines to eliminate fatigue. The unfortunate thing was—one fix did not fit all. That rule ended up creating far too much inefficiency for the international arena, and increased fatigue in the domestic system as pilots ended up working more days for the same pay.

How her coworkers thought the practicality of increasing flight time from eight to nine hours with a single crew would reduce fatigue was beyond her. But she had been so busy dealing with the UAS, unmanned aircraft systems, for the FAA, she didn't have the opportunity to provide input. With that said, it was beyond her how a scheduler could knowingly put Darby on a flight across the country, bypassing all safeguards of safety. Thinking Darby would be qualified for a long-haul flight, or any flight as far as that went, was absurd. She stood, and pulled the note off the bulletin board and added—*safety culture*. Darby's book could not be releasing at a better time.

Kathryn flipped through pages to the guest list and stared at the names for her Christmas Eve party. *Jackie and John. Linda and Niman. Darby and Ray*—she smiled. Just about when Darby gave up on dating, the kindest man came into her life. As the head of maintenance at Global, he understood the industry and he was able to travel on airline passes. He also owned a small plane and brought the love of flying back into Darby's life. Then there was *Tom*.

Placing a hand to chin, her finger involuntarily tapped her cheek. She was not so sure she was ready for a relationship, especially with the twins so young. But then who was she kidding by blaming the twins. Another year and they would be driving and dating, too. Maybe Darby was right and she was just avoiding men because of Bill. Either way, it didn't matter. Tom was good for her.

Tom was nice. But they were nothing more than friends—with benefits, that is. Kathryn smiled at the thought of her being naughty this Christmas. Besides, his ex-wife was taking the kids with her new husband on a holiday vacation. Of course he should join them. He knew Darby and Jackie, and would fit in nicely with the group.

Kathryn drew a heart around Jackie and John's name. A smile filled her eyes. She had never imagined they would end up together. He was her former employer from the NTSB, and Jackie was Darby's and her best friend.

John had thrown himself into work sacrificing a personal life, and Jackie had lost the love of her life. One's passion, and another's loss, brought them together. They all still missed Greg. But time healed, and people moved on—if they chose to.

Then there was Linda. Kathryn was so proud of her. Linda's husband had killed hundreds when he crashed his plane, but her drive to heal the mentally ill pulled her into school. Three years later she held a PhD in psychology, and she had met Niman, a neurosurgeon, during her residency. Kathryn was excited to meet him, as they were just returning from Tahiti—married. She added Francine to the list, Linda's daughter who would be home from her first year at college. The girls were as ecstatic to see her as Kathryn was. This would be a wonderful family reunion—the best Christmas ever.

Kathryn added Chris to the list. Jackie's son was growing into the image of his father. Her eyes moistened with the thought that Greg was not around to see him become a man. Swiping a tear from her cheek with the back of her hand, she chided herself. Holidays always brought emotion, for so many reasons.

She tipped her wrist and looked at her watch. She had less than two hours before she had to pick up the girls from the mall, and she wanted to get some shopping done herself.

She glanced at the list of names, and then at the dining room table. Eight adults and four kids—it would be tight, but they could make it work. She flipped the page, and found another blank sheet and put the pen to paper—*Prime Rib. Asparagus. Potatoes. Wild rice. Lettuce. Lemons… Dessert—something chocolate for Darby.* She had four days to think about it. She turned to the next blank page and wrote—*gifts.*

Staring at the blank page, she bit the end of her pen. She wanted to get something special for each of her guests, but was not sure what that might be. Tapping her pen on the paper, her mind whirled with many options. But instead of writing, she closed the pad and thought, *spontaneity is going to be my friend.*

This year she would enjoy her afternoon and wander the mall, and actually enjoy her day off, allowing the perfect gifts to jump off the shelf. She stood and pushed her chair up to the table, and then pulled her jacket off the back of the chair and slipped it on. She dropped her phone into her purse, threw her purse over her shoulder, and grabbed her keys off the rack. As she opened the door, her phone rang. She pulled the door closed behind her, and then dug for her phone. A call on Saturday was never a positive start to the weekend.

"This is Kathryn," she said, heading toward her car.

"Did you see the news?"

"No. I was just heading out…"

"Turn on CNN. Then call me."

Seconds later her key was in the keyhole.

Kathryn was the head of her division, but it was Bernard who pulled all the strings. He was also a man of very few words, and only called her cell phone with bad news.

Despite Kathryn overseeing drone regulation, any time there was an accident or industry event with a major airline, Bernard threw it on her desk. With the door finally opened, she flew inside and tossed her keys and bag on the kitchen table. Once in the den she grabbed the remote and pressed *on*. Switching to channel 44, her eyes widened. She dropped to the couch and stared.

Her phone rang and she jumped. "Hello," she said, not removing her eyes to look at who was calling.

"You watching?" Bernard asked. Clearly not waiting for her to call him back.

"I am. What happened?"

"The plane descended into the Alps. 1700 feet per minute."

"Aircraft type?"

"A320."

"Any maintenance issues?" She asked.

"No."

"Communications?"

"Normal. Until they began the descent. Air Traffic Control called repeatedly. No response."

"This was intentional," she said more to herself.

"Talk," he said.

"Someone had to give that plane direction to descend. It would not have left an altitude on its own. In an emergency they would have turned away from the terrain. Not to mention the lack of communication. Unless they inadvertently preprogrammed a descent, and the weather was down and didn't see…"

"It was clear."

"Okay then," Kathryn said, sucking a breath as she viewed what was left of the smoldering plane on the side of the mountain. "Someone in that flight deck did this."

"Can you come in?"

She glanced at her watch. "I'll be there in twenty."

Kathryn dialed Jackie's number.

"I was just going to call," Jackie said breathless. "Did you see the news? What happened? I can't believe another disaster in one month!"

"Can you pick the girls up at the mall at 2:30?"

"Of course. John's on his way to the office too," Jackie said.

"I'll be back as soon as I can." *Soon* was a nebulous term when there was an accident.

"This is not the way to start the holidays."

"No. It's not." Kathryn picked up her purse again, this time with a knot in her gut. First a disappearing plane, and today, a controlled flight into terrain, or CFIT as the industry called it. CFIT did not mean intentional, just controlled. She hoped it was anything but on purpose. But the thought of Bill slithered through her mind, and a chill cut through her body.

Two accidents in one month. This could not be happening again.

CHAPTER 5

JACKIE SAID GOODBYE to Kathryn, and opened the calendar on her phone. Chris would be out of his movie twenty minutes before the girls would be ready to be picked up. She glanced at her watch. They could have a hot chocolate while they waited for the twins—a little, and much needed mother-son time. He was growing up too quickly and the days slid by, as they ran in two different directions. If he ever died in an aircraft accident, she would never survive.

Her eyes shifted back to the television, and she dropped to the couch and watched, trying to calm her breathing. 188 bodies. Children. Families broken. Gone. Her eyes moistened as memories of Greg came flooding back and stabbed her heart.

The Greg she knew before the crash was in the foreground with his laughter and his kindness. The life they had together, even during the airline struggles and pay cuts, was the best time of her life. But the charred body with a bandaged head he had become after the crash moved into that picture. All it took was one tear to break free and the rest followed. Sobs took control. *Why? Why did this have to happen?* She wept for what felt like forever. But in reality it had been fifteen minutes.

Sucking a deep breath and grabbing for a tissue, she knew one thing—sometimes death was the best option. She blew her nose, and then grabbed another tissue, and dotted under her eyes. *Be strong. I have to be strong.* She had a wonderful life now, and had so much to be grateful for—a beautiful son, a wonderful man who loved both Chris and her, good friends, and a job that fit her life.

Jackie stood and moved to the mirror. She wiped a finger under each eye, and pulled a hand through her hair, and then fluffed. Then her eyes shifted back to the crash site reflecting in the mirror. Two crashes within one month. On that first flight they did not know what happened to the plane, it just disappeared. *How could a plane that size disappear?* It could not. But it did.

Darby had told her that the plane crashed somewhere, but they would eventually find it. She also thought a hijacker took it. She was adamant that it was not the pilots doing. Jackie was not so sure. But this plane was clearly flown into that mountain, and the pilots surely were in control.

With Bill still alive, Jackie often had nightmares that he was reaching out from prison, guiding others to carry on his mission. She knew better. It was simply not possible. But dreams controlled her to the point of night terrors. With John at her side, the screaming lessened, but the visions still drifted within her subconscious.

She prayed for the day when those thoughts would be gone, and he would have no power and control over her life. Sadly, that day would only come with his death. What kind of person wished for the death of another? Not her. She would not be that kind of evil person. She took a deep breath and adjusted her collar. *Jackie, you're nicer and stronger than this.*

Turning toward the television she watched as they drew lines of the flight path into the mountain. Maybe the pilots made a mistake. Maybe they had an engine failure or something, and were trying to get through the mountains. She had to believe this was not intentional, or this might be the final thread that unraveled her.

Jackie picked up the remote and pointed it at the television and clicked. Being a flight attendant was the best job she'd ever had, until she became a mother. Greg's death pushed her back into the workforce full time, and scheduling training was a great job, but not her passion. She loved the flight crews, and missed her friends in the sky, but keeping her feet on the ground was necessary being a single mother. She pulled on her jacket.

Moving into flight attendant training gave her the opportunity to help improve safety. Kathryn and Darby made this shift happen for her, and she could not thank them enough. She threw her purse over her shoulder and opened the front door, and stepped onto her porch.

Dark clouds filled the skies, and wind whipped her hair across her face. She tucked a strand behind her ear. Trouble was brewing, and it was more than the weather.

After the merger, connecting two airline's flight attendants— one union and the other without—the challenges were many. She was not so sure about the legality of how Global counted votes to make the non-union vote a reality, but she was sure that something needed to change as to how they overloaded those hard-working men and women in the back of the plane.

Jackie was also not in agreement with the decision to brainwash new hire flight attendants during the welcome aboard luncheon, that the union was a bad thing. Not that she agreed with union politics, as look what good ALPO, the Airline Pilots Organization, did for Darby. She just firmly believed that a forward looking and caring company could establish a safe, secure, and workable environment for all. However, that should come from operational practices, and allowing the flight attendants to decide. When a company had to force the issue, it always left a bad taste.

Jackie glanced toward the sky, and then ran to her car. Global's flight attendants were pushed into inhumane hours from one part of the world to the next, with minimal rest, and had far too many different aircraft to be responsible for learning.

Thank God ground emergencies were rare. Her deepest fear was if a crash occurred, and the crew was fatigued and unfamiliar with the aircraft. She unlocked and opened the door, and then climbed in.

The plane that crash-landed on the river back East came to mind, as did Bill's plane in Puget Sound. All the flight attendants, during both landings, did a phenomenal job. However, it was hard for her to imagine having similar results after the crew had flown four back-to-back ocean crossings, and then landed in the water on an aircraft type they had not worked for many months.

Jackie pulled the seatbelt across her lap and clicked it into place. She closed her eyes and sent a prayer to the families of those lost in today's crash. Looking over her shoulder she backed down the driveway as the rain began to fall, and fresh tears blurred her vision.

Chapter 6

B ACK IN SEATTLE, after the 'fatigue' trip, Darby dragged her bags through customs and then rushed toward the train. She turned the corner just as the doors slammed shut, leaving her behind. She set her computer bag on the floor, and her purse slid off her shoulder. Watching the faces fly off to the main terminal without her pissed her off. She was so close, and then she glanced at her watch. Folding her arms, she tapped her foot.

Her mind shifted back to the families of the passengers who were flown into the mountain. When they landed in Hong Kong and heard the news, she and her entire crew had been shocked. The authorities had not confirmed but, for all intents and purposes, it looked as if those pilots had intentionally flown into the mountain. The question was, why? Boarding their flight back to the states, the crew received many concerned looks from the passengers.

If she were not the operating pilot, Darby had always stood at the door and greeted everyone, while handing out wings. To her, this was more than just giving the gift of joy to boarding passengers, but she assessed them as they boarded, paying close attention to who would be on her flight. A form of profiling perhaps, but she wanted to know. Security did what they could in the check-in process, but she was the next line of defense on her plane. This was for everyone's safety.

Sixteen hours earlier, she had stood at the door handing out wings and greeting passengers, with another purpose in mind—to assure them they were in good hands. To allow passengers to see at least one of the pilots, and give them a face of the person they would be entrusting their lives and the lives of their children to, for the better part of a day, was all that was needed.

Shake it off Darby, and go to your happy thoughts.

Flying in from Hong Kong was exhausting enough, and all she wanted to do was to go to bed—not meet with the chief pilot. She could not imagine what the heck she had done now. Then a smile spread across her face. This must have something to do with her taking the flight, so they did not have to cancel it. Finally she did something right in the eyes of Global management.

Brownie points for me.

The train arrived and she lifted her purse and threw it over her shoulder. Grabbing her computer bag and suitcase she walked onboard. Glancing at her watch, she figured ten minutes for her much-earned gratitude and then she could be on her way home for a soak in the tub and a good day's sleep, followed by girl's night. Then the next day, she would be off to Oklahoma City for bounces to become current. It had been over eight months and she still had yet to get an actual landing in the plane. The train lurched and she grabbed a post.

Doors opened and Darby slipped off the train and headed for the elevator. Yawning, she pressed the *up* button and the doors opened, and she stepped on and pressed the third floor. Once she arrived to her floor, and the doors opened, she pulled her bags down the hall, smiling at those she passed.

She arrived at Flight Operations and typed the secret code into the door. Thank God they made this code as easy as 123. They all needed something easy to remember at times like this. Entering the office, she parked her bags at the counter.

"Hi, Stephanie," she said to the secretary.

"Joel will see you now."

Joel Iverson was her local chief pilot, and a great guy. She was always glad to see him. "Knock, knock," she said, opening the door. He was so much a better option than Odell.

"Come in and close the door," he snapped.

"Excuse me?"

"Sit."

Darby hesitated, deciding if it were appropriate to be treated like a dog, and then she glanced at a chair and sat. More so because she was exhausted, but her heart accelerated a few beats stronger than normal. This was definitely not a pat on the back meeting—anything but.

"What in the hell do you think you're doing?" He said, walking behind his desk.

"I beg your pardon?"

"You were ordered *not* to contact the marketing department about that book," he said, turning toward her with fire in his eyes. "I told you—"

"But I…"

"Enough!" he snapped. "I don't have time for this crap. You were given an order and *then* this ends up on my desk."

He pulled out his chair and sat heavily. Pointing a finger at her, his voice lowered as he spoke. "You have stepped over the line this time. Nobody disobeys an order by Odell at this company. Shit rolls downhill, and this time I'm standing under it."

"But I didn't—"

"God dammit Bradshaw!" he yelled, pushing back from his desk and jumping to his feet. "You never f***ing do *anything*." He turned with hands in fists, and stared down at her.

She held his stare, then looked at a spot on the ceiling for just a moment, and then folded her arms and returned his stare. This chief pilot had *once* been a great guy, and came with the Coastal Airways merger. She thought his goal was to support the pilots.

New to Global management, he had also tried to find that letter in her file for the trumped-up social media violations to expunge it, after the three years had passed. Odell had assured her that letter was nothing, and it would die a natural death. Joel had found nothing in his search of her immediate file, but later told her that the letter *never* went away, and was lurking in a hidden file someplace in the bowels of the company.

Darby had enough and glanced at the door. It was time to go. All she wanted to do was get out of this office before she said something that she would regret. That moment inched closer. His eyes followed hers to the door, and then he picked up a draft of her book and slammed it on the desk, and she jumped.

Deloris had sent Global a copy.

"You will *not* put a picture of a Global aircraft on the cover! And you *will* remove any and *all* reference to Coastal Airways!"

"I worked there." She stood. "You don't have the—"

"I don't give a damn. We own the name."

Darby threw her purse over her shoulder, and lifted her computer bag, while searching for the most appropriate words for a time like this, but sadly they all started with the letter f. She had been working on the cursing portion of her language, and this would be a good time to practice.

"I won't use a Global plane on the cover, but you can't make me remove Coastal Airways from the book. That is *my* history."

The book included training events, which held significant meaning in the history of aviation safety, with positive examples of how to manage a flight training department, by hiring experienced pilots to manage the operation. Experience was the only way to identify potential hazards. Something that Global lost sight of. How the hell could he deny her the right to say she worked there?

"Global owns that name." He turned and sat in his chair, and with a wave of his hand, as if he were shooing off a fly said, "You're dismissed."

Darby searched for an exit statement. But none came. She reached for the doorknob.

"Do we have an understanding?"

"Good day. Sir."

Darby understood one thing—nothing at Global had changed. Apparently management had no intention of allowing the past to stay buried. But that didn't matter. Soon the entire world would know the truth, and they, along with other airlines, would have to proactively do something. Darby was willing to do whatever it took to create that change.

CHAPTER 7

DARBY PULLED INTO Kathryn's driveway and parked beside Jackie's Suburban. The kids were farmed out someplace, as this was their end-of-the-year blow off some steam party. Not kid appropriate—for a few more years anyway. She turned the engine off, but did not move to open the door. Johnny Mathis's White Christmas played over the radio and Kathryn's house glowed with a zillion white lights. She wanted to stay inside this postcard for a few more minutes.

Granted, her best friends were inside with libations, and something baking in the oven that overwhelmed her senses with just the thought of it. But with that would come the reality of her facing Kathryn's wrath because she took that trip. Two planes within the month had found their demise—one into the side of a mountain and the other was missing in action. Kathryn had good reason to worry.

Bill crept into her mind, but there was no way he could have anything to do with this. *Was there?* These had to be completely isolated incidents. Then there was Odell, the director of flying. What the hell was his problem?

Joel had the draft on his desk, but had Odell read it? Odell's first denial for her to talk to marketing came without knowledge of what was between the pages. Perhaps that was his problem. He was pissed she didn't follow an order more so than the book itself.

The song ended and Darby glanced up to the sky wishing for her white Christmas. She pulled her keys out and dropped them into her purse. This would be the first time since the merger that she would be home on Christmas Eve. She was also looking forward to her first Christmas Eve with Ray. Smiling, she thought about her wake-up call during his lunch break.

She wished she could spend the day with him tomorrow but, instead, she would fly to Oklahoma City and do her bounces—that every three month ritual for not getting any takeoffs and landings, called a 'recency.' At least this time she had seen the inside of the flight deck before the simulator event. The best part of this deal was she would be flying home on Christmas Eve for Kat's Christmas party. Granted she was on call the next day, but they could not take Christmas Eve from her.

She pulled the bottle from its bag and opened the car door. They could not take tonight either. Darby climbed out of her car and slammed the door behind her.

Pressing a hand to her heart, she said a blessing of gratitude to her friends inside this house, and to Ray and the kids, then raised the bottle to the sky and gave a shout. With a huge grin she sprinted up the stairs, did a quick knock on the front door and opened it, then bounced inside.

"Happy Holidays my friends!" she yelled, wiggling out of her coat, tossing it on a hallway chair, and heading toward the kitchen.

Kathryn and Jackie sat at the table in quiet conversation. Jackie looked her way, eyes filled with tears.

"This is no way to celebrate the season," Darby said, setting the scotch on the table.

"Probably not," Kathryn said standing, and then gave Darby a hug. "What happened to the tequila?" she whispered.

"I have to fly to headquarters to do bounces tomorrow, which means clothes stay on tonight," Darby said, trying not to think about what she did the last time they drank tequila. "But it's definitely time to liven up this party."

"How can we celebrate?" Jackie asked blowing her nose. "People are dead. Babies are lying on the side of a mountain," she choked out. "What's there to celebrate anyway?"

Kathryn walked over and squeezed Jackie's shoulder, then glanced at Darby and shrugged.

"How?" Darby asked, opening a cupboard. "By pulling three glasses from the shelf and filling them with joy," she said, setting the glasses on the table in front of Jackie.

She opened the bottle of Glenmorangie she had carried in, and poured three fingers into each glass. Sliding one in front of Jackie, she handed the second to Kathryn. She sat to the left of Jackie, who would contribute to the warping of the table if she did not turn off the tears. Darby slid a hand over the table where they hit, and wiped the moisture. This table had seen them through many adventures, thousands of tears, but equally as many laughs.

Kathryn sat on the other side of Jackie across from Darby, and sighed.

"Jackie, there is *always* going to be shit going on in life," Darby said, placing a hand on Jackie's back. "People are going to die. They will get murdered, have cancer, and die from a broken heart. There is not one person in this room who has not lived that. And none of it is fair. None of it is right. But there has to be an overarching life plan. Or what in the hell are we all doing here anyway? We might not know exactly what that plan is, but we have to trust and have faith that everything will work out like it's supposed to."

Jackie pushed her chair away from the table and faced Darby.

"Sweetheart, how we celebrate is by lifting these glasses and toasting to life," Darby said, lifting her glass and extending it. "Life is so friggin' precious, we cannot spend one moment regretting anything, or not being thankful for every moment. When shit like this happens, it's life's way of telling the rest of us to wake up and drink *really good* scotch!"

Kathryn laughed, and extended her glass, touching Darby's. "Not sure I could have said that quite as eloquently. But you're right."

"I do my best," Darby said with a wink. "But Jackie, you better lift that glass and get in here with us because my arm's getting tired."

Jackie looked from Darby to Kathryn and a forced smile spread across her face. She lifted her glass to the others. "To my friends. Thank you." Then she sipped her drink and gave that Jackie face, with eyes closed and a shudder. "What the heck is this?" she asked.

Darby laughed. "Only my new favorite scotch." She took a long sip then said, "Yummy."

Kathryn, raised her glass and said, "To my friends. Thank you for being here." And she tasted the golden liquid. "You're right, this is pretty good."

A buzzer sounded and they all jumped, and Darby laughed. "Think we're all a little on edge?"

Kathryn stood, opened the foil, and peeked at the lasagna. Darby's favorite, and Kathryn managed to make that happen on their special night each year, no matter what. Kathryn's eyes flashed to Darby and narrowed. Darby knew she was living on borrowed time.

"So, how about those Hawkeyes?" Darby said.

"Don't even think about moving this conversation down any path until you tell me what the heck you were doing by taking that trip," Kathryn said, closing the foil on the dish.

"What trip?" Both Darby and Jackie said at the same time, and Darby laughed.

Kathryn set the potholders on the counter and walked over and picked up her drink. She sipped, not removing her eyes from Darby over the brim. A talent that Darby's best friend had adopted for biting her tongue, so as not to say something reactionary. Be it coffee, juice, or even opening a bottle of water. This was her way of dealing with the girls when she needed to count to ten.

Darby was in trouble.

Kathryn set her glass down and breathed deep, and turned toward Jackie. "Darby was in New York meeting with her agent, and then—"

"Oh yeah, how'd that go?" Jackie asked.

"Great, and—"

Kathryn cleared her throat and Darby and Jackie looked her way. "As I was saying, Darby flew from New York through Oklahoma City, and into Seattle, with a 45-minute break on the ground prior to a flight to Hong Kong."

"She can't do that," Jackie said.

"Exactly my point." Kathryn folded her arms.

"Come on guys. What was I supposed to do?"

"Tell them no," Kathryn said, moving toward the fridge. She pulled out a salad and a bottle of dressing. "You were not legal to fly that trip. Moreover, you were not safe!" She opened the bottle, shook the dressing, and then poured some into the bowl.

"To my defense, I thought I could sleep on the commute."

"Did you?" Jackie asked.

"Well, no," Darby said, and sipped her courage. "But to my defense, I had planned on it. And intent is nine tenths of the law. I think. Or maybe that's possession—I'm not sure and not the point. But, by the time I got here, what was I supposed to do? Cancel the flight? Man, if I wasn't employee non-gratis before, I would certainly be now."

"You were not fit to fly, and signing that release indicated that you were," Kathryn said moving back to the table, she sat. "If we lost you, I'm not sure what we would do." Tears filled her eyes. She dabbed them with a dishtowel and shook her head, and regained composure. "But how in the heck am I supposed to deal with this now without violating your ass?"

Darby bit her lower lip. She had a good point. Then a moment of inspiration struck.

"You can't violate me because I was unable to make the right decision. I thought I would be rested, and therefore began that motion into position, of what my company scheduled me to do. Not illegal in itself, for me. However, 17 hours awake is equivalent to .05 alcohol level. Thus, I was physically impaired due to fatigue. I was legally unable to assess my own mental health."

"She has a point," Jackie said. "I always say I won't drink and drive, but after that first beer... well, someone has to pull my keys from me."

"Don't encourage her," Kathryn said, with a laugh. "Darby, I'm just worried how you could do this. If you, of all people, are able to fly under this condition, that means anyone would."

Darby knew what Kathryn meant, as she never had a problem standing up for safety in the past. "I guess I'm tired of being harassed by management pilots. I've always done the best I could and I want to be a company person, but the truth is I... I guess I was afraid of retaliation."

"BS!" Jackie said with a snap. "You're not afraid of anything!"

Darby glanced at Jackie's glass to see how much she had drunk already, and then sighed. "I know. But the truth is I'm tired of it all. I was afraid of being in the spotlight again. The previous three years writing my book, and flying have been awesome—a normal life. I just didn't want my name attached to anything again, and now…" Darby stared into her glass instead of drinking from it.

"What happened?" Kathryn asked, shifting her tone of anger to one of concern.

"It's all started again," Darby said, and tipped back her glass and emptied it.

"What's started?" Jackie asked.

"I got called into the chief pilot's office again. He jumped on my butt when I was least expecting it." Darby shared with the ladies as to what had transpired with the book and the director's reaction. "And I thought he was going to thank me for saving that flight."

"What the heck does he care?" Jackie said, with an indication of a slur.

Darby shrugged, and then grinned. "Not as much as the FAA will," she said. "I'm more worried about what Doctor Human Factors is going to say about my book."

Kathryn had just pulled on potholders, and placed her mitted hands on hips. "Okay, what did you do?"

"Research."

Kathryn raised an eyebrow, and sighed. "Explain."

"Well… I came across some doctor, with her PhD, who was the head of human factors at the FAA. She gave a brief a few months ago at a safety conference about pilots and flight skill loss, mode awareness issues, confusion with aircraft complexity, et cetera." Darby took a sip of her scotch, to savor the moment.

"And your point is?" Kathryn said, moving her mitts to the oven. She opened the door. "That's exactly what you've been concerned with," she said, lifting the lasagna from the rack. "I don't see your problem."

Darby turned her glass, holding it up to the light scrutinizing the color, while Kathryn removed the lasagna and set it on a hot pad to cool. She took another sip, waiting to assure the lasagna would be safe from being dropped.

"About six months before that event, I was doing some research for the book, and found something interesting…"

"Which was?" Jackie asked.

Kathryn pulled her gloves off, and tossed them on the counter. "What did you find? Sasquatch?"

"Close." Darby stood, and lifted the water pitcher and began filling glasses. "I found an FAA human factors report stating that there was a problem with training, and that pilots lacked understanding. And there were problems due to aircraft complexity and automation, along with pilot's loss of flight skills." She filled the last glass and set the pitcher on the counter. "More or less the exact same thing that woman said at the meeting."

"You've lost me," Kathryn said.

"That report was written *twenty* years ago, and the chair of the committee that received that report was none other than the same FAA human factors doctor that spoke at the meeting, acting as if these were new problems."

"Are you sure?" Kathryn said.

"Positive." Darby nodded. "It's all documented."

"I'm confused," Jackie said. "You're saying that she knew this twenty years ago and did *nothing*?"

"Yep."

"And you put that in your book?" Kathryn asked.

"Yep."

Kathryn laughed and pulled out a chair, and sat. "I'm going to need more of that," she said pointing to the bottle. "You know, you're going to have more than your chief pilot on your tail for this one."

"I'm suspecting nothing other than death by FAA," Darby said.

"I will be the first on the suspect list," Kathryn said with a laugh. "You are going to turn my hair gray."

"Gray is in," Darby said. "It's the new blonde."

"Nobody is killing Darby," Jackie said. "Unless she doesn't give me more of that orange stuff."

Darby laughed. She didn't have to look to know Jackie's glass was at least half empty. Jackie was more than likely already reaching her limit. "We'd better put some food into this one," Darby told Kathryn.

Darby added a handful of ice to Jackie's glass and added another couple fingers. Then she helped Kathryn set the table.

They chatted about the girls and Christmas while they worked. Darby grabbed some potholders, slid them onto her hands, and set the lasagna on the table.

Lifting the foil she said, "Man, this smells great." She tossed the foil into the garbage, and sat at the table.

Jackie pulled the garlic bread from the oven and dumped it onto a plate. Kathryn set the salad on the table and the three sat to eat.

"Where's John?" Darby asked.

"Watching the kids," Jackie said.

"All of them?"

"Yep, the girls are there too," Kathryn said, placing a heaping portion of lasagna on each of their plates.

"Man, you have whipped that boy. When's he going to make an honest woman of you and get that finger on your ring?" Darby asked, pulling the bowl of salad toward her.

Kathryn laughed. "We might be cutting you off, too."

"I have an excuse," Darby said. "Double whammy—fatigue and cheer." She scooped a large helping of salad onto her plate. "So are you inviting Tom to Christmas Eve dinner?"

"Of course," Kathryn said. "His ex-wife has the kids."

"Then he has to join us," Jackie said. "He seems really nice, and it will be fun to get to know him."

"Nice, yeah. But…"

"But what?" Kathryn asked, raising an eyebrow.

Darby lifted her water glass to her lips and drank, practicing her 'Kathryn' move, looking over the brim assessing how far she should go. Tom was nice, but she worried about what he would do to Kathryn and if he would take advantage of her.

"But what?" Kathryn asked again.

"I just don't want you to get hurt."

"You keep saying that, so spill."

Jackie's eyes were wide and her head bounced from Darby, to Kathryn, back to Darby as if she were watching a ping pong game.

"Kat… his wife left him because he played on the road just a little too much, and she finally found out. But more than that, he's such a *great* guy that he's been able to suck a lot of pilots into his get rich quick schemes. I'm just saying that I know a ton of guys who have lost their ass because of his investment strategies."

Darby lifted a large bite of lasagna onto her fork, with cheese hanging. She swirled the cheese around her fork as she said, "He's always wheeling and dealing with something. Rumor has it he's flat broke and will be promoting the age 98 rule so he can keep flying to make ends meet." Then she stuffed the bite into her mouth.

"He's told me most of that," Kathryn said nodding. "Perhaps in more gracious terms for his side. But this is not my first rodeo."

"Hell you haven't ridden a merry-go-round let alone a pony for 14 years!" Darby covered her mouth as quickly as possible, but the words had already flown out. "Did I just say that out loud?"

Kathryn's mouth dropped open and she turned toward Jackie whose eyes were wide, and then they both began laughing loud and hard.

"So true," Kathryn said with tears coming out her eyes. "But don't worry, I am taking this slow. He's my practice boyfriend. And if something comes of it, I will be careful."

"Besides, he's so handsome in his captain's uniform," Jackie added.

"That he is," Kathryn said.

So was Bill. But Darby refrained from adding that commentary as Jackie had clearly shifted moods and was working toward a festive spirit.

"You never said that I was cute in my captain's uniform," Darby said. "And now I have to wear those stupid three stripes. Four were so much more cooler," she said stuffing a bite of salad into her mouth. "That didn't sound right."

"It was just fine," Kathryn said, glancing at Darby's glass.

"I could sew you some stripes for Christmas," Jackie said.

"Okay, then give me five." Darby turned toward Kathryn, "Would wearing five be illegal?"

"Illegal no, but I'm not sure how your company would feel about that. The boys might shit their pants," Kathryn said.

"They're big boys," Darby said. "They can change them."

Kathryn laughed, and then stood and pulled a bottle of wine off the rack. "We need a little red wine for lasagna. This is still a civilized society."

As Kathryn poured, her cell phone rang. Darby jumped up, and grabbed it off the counter and handed it to her.

"Your boss. Does that man have no boundaries?"

Kathryn set the bottle down and answered. Her face paled as she listened, and nodded. "Yes sir. I will see you tomorrow morning." After she hung up she walked to the living room and turned on CNN.

Breaking News flashed across the screen. "What we are hearing now," the reporter stated, and cleared her throat. "It's suspected that the pilots may have intentionally flown that A320 into the mountains."

Kathryn sat heavily on the couch, and Darby sat beside her. Jackie just stood behind them. The unspoken words felt heavy in the air. This crash may have been intentional.

"There is no way Bill could be behind this," Darby said. "Could he?"

"Maybe a copycat case?" Jackie said, tears flowing again.

"There's only one way to find out," Kathryn said.

CHAPTER 8

RAY THOMPSON WAS finishing up paperwork before he left for the night. Whoever said management was the way to go, had been wrong. There was something to be said about going to work, and at the end of the day leaving problems behind.

When he first started dating Darby, he was afraid she would not want anything to do with him if he were an ordinary mechanic. He had been wrong of course, but he got caught up in the mess, and could not quit. He had to fix what he walked into before he would move on and give this problem to anyone else. Not that the thought about walking away was not appealing.

The nights Darby was on a trip, he managed to use the time wisely either playing with his plane, or working in the office until the wee hours. This time of year, the office won due to Seattle weather. Ray thought of Darby and their lunch, and smiled. How the hell had he gotten so lucky?

Tonight she was with Kathryn and Jackie for their annual event. He wished he could watch those three in action, but apparently it was a 'girls only' party. He smiled. There were many such girl only events in college, but somehow he and the guys always managed to sneak into the party. The girls never seemed to mind.

He had graduated from University of Iowa, with shitty grades due to too much beer, football, and girls. Then he had to grow up, and went to airplane maintenance school. In no time he found himself working at Coastal. He worked hard and made something of himself, despite strikes and replacement. Or so he thought. What he made was a huge mess. The only good thing that had happened to him in a long time was Darby. The rest was an illusion based on perspective.

The phone rang as he was pulling on his coat, and he lifted it and looked at the number, and then pressed *deny*, afraid of what he might say. He was off work and wanted to go home and have a beer. Alone. He did not want to discuss this with anyone but Darby. He closed the door and locked it. Then headed down the hall.

He was just stepping out of the building when the voice rang out from across the parking lot. "Thompson!" Ray stopped short, and turned left.

"Hey Joel, what's up?" Ray said.

"I tried to call. Why weren't you answering?"

"My battery must be dead," Ray said, continuing motion toward his car. Joel followed.

"You doing anything for dinner?" Joel asked, placing a hand on Ray's car door preventing him from opening it. "Can I buy you a beer?"

All Ray wanted to do was get home, put his feet up and watch a little television and wait for Darby. He glanced at his watch, and then at Joel's hand. *Shit.*

"Okay. Sure," he said, knowing perfectly well that this would be more than a beer.

"I'll meet you at 13 Coins," Joel said.

Fifteen minutes later they were sitting in a booth, and Ray was pulling off his jacket.

"What can I get you boys to drink?" the waitress asked.

"We'll have a couple 20 ounce drafts," Joel ordered. Then he faced Ray. "So, how're things going in the shop?"

"Fine." He'd had a long day, as they had problems getting the air conditioning fixed on one of the A330s, and he had to hit the floor to help, which actually was the best part of his day. Then he thought of Darby and their lunch, and grinned. She was always the best part of *any* day. Joel Iverson inviting him for a drink had everything to do with his chitchat with her.

Beers were delivered and Ray ordered a cheeseburger and fries. Joel ordered the soup and sandwich combo. Once the waitress was gone, Joel lifted his beer, "Happy Holidays," he said.

Ray lifted his glass and said, "Cheers." He took a long drink and held his glass in both hands, resting on the table. He stared into the gold liquid figuring out Joel's motives for bringing him here.

"Any plans for Christmas?" Joel asked.

"None." Ray had plans, but he would be damned if he would tell this man anything.

"I'm not the enemy," Joel said. "I'm just doing my job."

"Perhaps. But it's the choices in life that define us." Like he should talk. Ray sipped his beer and added, "I think you've made it perfectly clear the choice you've made."

"It's the job," Joel said. "They've turned me into a secretary. My entire day is spent dealing with sick calls, and bullshit."

"With an occasional bitch out the pilots who are trying to make the skies safer?"

"You don't get it," Joel said.

"Enlighten me."

"I'm trying to warn her so she doesn't get into trouble. Those guys in Oklahoma City don't play fair. They've got their arrows out."

"For writing a safety book?" Ray raised an eyebrow.

"That's not her job."

"Safety should be every pilot's job," Ray said, lifting his glass.

"It's not that," Joel said. He stared at his beer for a moment and then said, "I like Darby, but she's got to scrap that book deal."

"A cold day in hell for that," Ray said taking another sip. "Do you know how much she's making on that deal?" Joel shook his head, and Ray said, "Two million bucks."

Iverson's face about dropped. "Holy shit!"

Ray laughed. "You should see your face. In a little in awe of money, are ya bud?"

"Fuck you."

"Despite the payday," Ray said, "that's not why she's doing this."

"All I'm saying is she's asking for trouble."

People like Joel, or most any of the other managing pilots, would never understand. Power and money drove their every motivation. But when you had a passion to fix things, or solve an injustice, asking for trouble was a given. Running from it was not an option.

"So, who do you want to play you in the movie?"

Joel laughed, "You're full of shit. She doesn't have a movie deal."

Ray shrugged. He took another long drink of beer and returned the glass to the table, and stared Iverson in the eyes. "Here's the deal. I love this woman and I'm not the guy you're going to be pumping information from."

The waitress arrived and asked if he wanted another beer. He shook his head and said, "No thanks." When she was gone, Ray returned his attention to Joel. "And I'm certainly not going to tell Darby what to do."

"I'm just saying, I've known guys who were articulate, and intelligent. They tried to fix things in flight operations, and they're gone."

"So?" Ray said, lifting his beer. "Your point?"

The point was delayed, either because the waitress was back with the food or he did not have one. She set their meals in front of them. But when she was gone, Joel said, "She's going to screw her career if she proceeds with this."

"How?" Ray asked. "Do you know what her job is?"

"What do you mean?"

"Joel, she's a pilot. There's a seniority list. When she's ready, she'll upgrade. There's nothing you can do to her." He lifted his beer and said, "Oh, wait… maybe you can put another letter in her file, or mess with her simulator again."

"They're going to block her advancement."

"You don't seem to understand," Ray said exasperated. "Those guys screwing with her have no power over her. She's not like the rest of the climbers looking for a position. She's doing this for reasons that have nothing to do with advancement."

Joel's eyes narrowed. Ray wanted to laugh when his expression changed, as if the light bulb had just turned on. Maybe he was finally getting it.

"Darby wrote that book to create change and improve safety."

"She's got to want something," Joel said.

"Yeah, for you guys to get off her ass." Ray shook his head and stared at Joel. Was this guy for real? He sipped his beer, and then said, "So, you never pulled that letter, huh?"

Darby had told him about the letter and Joel's involvement trying to help. What he found it hard to believe was, that there were two employee files.

"It's not in her personnel file anymore," Joel said. "But they still have it in another file someplace. It's part of her permanent record. I can't touch it."

"You can't have a fucking hidden file for employees," Ray snapped.

"Don't kill the messenger."

Ray wanted to kill a lot more than the messenger. These guys had been screwing with Darby for years, and now it had started again. This time on his watch. One thing Ray knew was that if they did *anything* to her again, it would be the last thing any of them did to anyone.

Then a grin crossed his face. "Did you read the book?"

Joel shook his head, "No."

Ray smiled more broadly. "I was sitting here thinking about kicking some ass—*anyone* who messes with my lady. But the truth is, I suspect Patrick will be doing a little ass kicking of his own."

"What does the CEO have to do with her book?"

"Joel, let's just say he's going to have to hire a cleaning company for Global's Flight Operations department after he reads it."

CHAPTER 9

THANKS TO ALASKA Airlines and a ten-minute taxi ride, Kathryn made it to the Walla Walla State Penitentiary within two hours from the time she had left home. She paid the driver, and gave him a ten-dollar bill for a tip so he would wait.

She glanced at the structure before her. How the hell he negotiated to get out of federal prison to this place, was beyond her. But they wanted details and he was more than willing to talk. With information, they were willing to put him in a state prison. Kathryn never knew if he gave accurate details, but they wanted answers to close up all the holes, the easy way.

She was not so sure this was the best idea, for many reasons. But when she had told her boss the plan, he said, "Go." He did not want to leave any stone unturned. Granted, the missing plane and the suicide flight into the Alps were both international events, but they were U.S. carriers, and that was worrisome.

Kathryn suspected Bill was involved. Jackie may have been accurate that his participation was nothing more than planting the idea for others to follow his insane path. Kathryn actually had thought the copycat cases would have occurred shortly after his imprisonment. Three years had passed and with each day the possibility became more remote—then two planes within one month.

Nothing was ever a coincidence.

She walked into the lobby and gave her name to a prison guard, and they allowed her to pass through the metal detector, and then patted her down. The guards opened her purse and checked all contents. She knew the drill, and carried a pad of paper, pen, and wallet. The prison administrator waited until she cleared security and escorted her into his office. Not until they were inside his office with the door closed, did he speak.

"Kathryn, nice to meet you," he said, shaking her hand.

"Kat, please."

He extended a hand to a chair, on the opposite side of his desk. "I'm Warden Filmore, but you can call me Film." He spoke slowly, and moved behind his desk and sat heavily. "I'm sorry for your effort coming out here." He slid a folder her direction. "But nothing much is in there."

"We'll see," Kathryn said, opening the folder and scanning the pages. And then she froze. Her eyes narrowed. Bill had only one visitor in the previous three years and that was eight months ago. The name all but knocked the wind out of her. She closed her eyes, and rubbed the bridge of her nose, her heart beat rapidly.

"Do you know him?"

Kathryn startled, and opened her eyes to the man scrutinizing her. "I do."

The Warden nodded slowly. The clock ticked loudly on the wall, and Kathryn looked at the page another time in hope that the name would change.

"We have record of Bill Jacob's outgoing phone calls, but not to whom. There were only three, and they lasted ten, twelve and fifteen minutes respectively."

"Meaning more than leaving a message, he spoke to someone."

Film nodded. "One was last year, in December. Another was eight months ago, shortly after his visitor. Then the last call was one month ago." He reached over the desk and turned the page, then pointed to the obvious.

Who the hell was he talking to? Kathryn tapped the pen on the pad of paper. "Any mail?"

"No. But he has sent four outgoing letters to a post office box in Seattle, over the previous three years."

"Do you have the address?"

"We do," he said, turning the page and pointing to the address.

There was no name, only a box number. The post office was in Burien, 15 minutes from her house. *What was he up to?* Kathryn scribbled down the box number, and stuffed it into her purse. *Who was he writing?* She fought the reality of what Bill's visitor meant and if he were part of the phone calls and the recipient of Bill's outgoing mail.

Kathryn closed the file. "I guess I'd better get this over with."

"You can have as much time as you need," he said. "We'll break the rules on this one."

"Thank you," Kathryn said, standing.

He walked around the desk and placed a hand on the doorknob, but did not open it. He turned and said, "He's been an ideal inmate. No problems. No fights. The boys, they listen to him. He's actually helped on many occasions with the other inmates. They call him the Captain. Like I said, he's ideal."

Kathryn humphed. "At one time he was the ideal husband too."

"I imagine so," he said with a nod. "But he's *too* good. Calculating. Something is always working behind those eyes. In my opinion he's the worst kind of scary. Don't allow him to get to you."

Kathryn knew exactly what he meant by that warning.

He opened the door and a guard stepped forward. "Sergeant Williams will take you. Good luck."

Kathryn followed the sergeant through the many gates and hallways. Her mind whirled in confusion. How much did the Warden know? Had Bernard spoken to him before her visit? And then there was Bill's visitor. The echoing of her heels in the long hollow hallway clicked loudly competing with the blood rushing in her ears.

"You okay ma'am?"

"Yes, thank you," Kathryn said as they reached another iron door.

He opened it and Kathryn was escorted to a seat in front of a glass window. She placed a headset with a microphone over her head, and waited. Glancing at her watch, she questioned, once again, if this were a good idea. But somewhere deep inside she wanted to see him. Sick, she knew, but she had to know that he was still locked up. Ridiculous. She knew that too. But somehow seeing him behind bars was needed for her sanity.

Placing the paper and pen on the table in front of her, she stared at the blank page. Taking a deep breath she chided herself, to not allow him to see her nerves. And then he was there. He stopped short of the window and assessed her, and then his smile grew. A chill ran down her spine and flashes of that night and his attack came flooding back.

Nerves turned into anger, and she did not return the smile.

Bill sat, and placed the headset on and adjusted his microphone. "Sweetheart, you look as beautiful as ever."

"Prison's been good to you, too," she replied.

Bill rubbed a hand over his face. "Yes it has." He leaned back and folded his arms, the best he could do with his hands cuffed. "So what gives *you* the pleasure?"

"You've seen the news?"

"I suppose I have."

"The recent crash into the side of that mountain. A missing plane. I figured who else other than Captain Bill Jacobs to ask what's going on."

Bill laughed loud and hard. "I suppose you're right."

"What do you know?"

"Let's just say if I knew anything, why would I tell you?"

"Because, despite the depraved way you conducted business, I know that you cared about the industry." She lied. She was not entirely sure he ever cared about anything but himself.

Bill laughed. "There's only one thing I cared about, and that's a bit scarce in here." He grinned and then lowered his eyes to her chest and raised them back to her eyes. "Maybe we can get a private room and make up for old times."

"What do you think's going on?" She would not bite at anything he said. She had to maintain control, and not give him an inch.

Bill sobered. "I suppose pilots are crashing planes." Then he grinned.

"You *don't* know anything."

"I know what I know. None of which is your fucking business, bitch."

The Bill who attacked her and haunted her dreams with nightmares had returned.

"I knew this was a waste of time. You aren't telling me anything because you don't know shit." Kathryn spoke low and in a growl.

"Your head is as empty as your heart. And just because you take it in the ass so well, they allow you to strut around like hot shit. But you were nothing when we were married and you're less than nothing now."

Kathryn allowed years of pent up anger to flow.

"You can't talk to me like that."

"The hell I can't!" Her voice raised, and then she regained control. "I'm not the caged animal. And, as good at whatever game it is you're playing in here, you will *never* leave. The only way you will get out of this place is in a box, and we will bury you without as much as a marker." She took a deep breath, and added, "You will rot in hell."

Bill leaned back in his chair and began to laugh. "Keep thinking that darling," he finally said, when his laughter stopped and he could speak. "Bars cannot hold me. This is all a fucking illusion," he said, splaying his handcuffed hands.

"What have you done, Bill?" She whispered, but that question was more to herself than him. Knowing exactly what this man was capable of, she did not want an answer.

"The question should be, what haven't I done," he said, with a wink, and then sighed. "You can leave now. And tell your boyfriend hello for me."

Kathryn opened her mouth, but nothing came out. There was so much she wanted to ask, but when Bill was done, he was done. Her foot tapped under the counter, but her eyes never left him, nor did her expression change.

He pulled his headset off and tossed it on the counter. Guards that had been standing behind him moved in, and escorted him toward the door. She sat frozen, watching, wondering what the hell had just happened.

Before she moved from her seat, Bill stopped and glanced over his shoulder. The grin he cast her way was evil. But it was those eyes she had seen on that last night with him that scared the hell out of her.

CHAPTER 10

DARBY SAT ON the curb listening to Kathryn's prison drama. "Holy shit," was all she could interject, on three different occasions. Six hours earlier they were having a Starbucks waiting for their flights—hers to Oklahoma City and Kathryn to Walla Walla. Kathryn was already back in Seattle, and Darby was at the airport waiting for her van to the hotel.

"*Tom?* What the hell was *your* boyfriend doing at the prison talking to Bill?"

"I don't know. But I'm going to find out."

"They knew each other, so I guess they could have been friends at the airline. But still…" Darby closed her eyes and shook her head. This was all that Kathryn needed.

"My thoughts exactly." Kathryn sighed. After a moment of silence, she added, "I really liked him. I trusted him. If Bill has anything to do with this, then that means…"

"Don't go there. I know there's a good explanation buried below the bullshit factor." Reality was, there was nothing that could forgive Kathryn's new boyfriend for visiting her ex in the state pen. They both could be setting her up. The worst case would be Bill paying Tom to finish the job Bill was unable to finish—personal or professional, each equally devastating.

"My advice is ask him," Darby said, standing. "But do it in person so you can see his expression. Do it before Bill gets to him to tell him that you know."

"I talked to the Warden on the way out. They're recording all calls. Monitoring all mail. Anything that comes or goes out of there will have government eyes on it. I will know five minutes afterwards."

"Can you trust this Film guy?"

"I have to."

"So you're not going to say anything?"

"Nope."

"Okay, so we need to focus," Darby said, as the van rounded the corner. "You get some sleep. I'm going to grab my van, take a quick nap, do my bounces, and catch the first flight home. I'll be there for moral support when you skin his balls."

Kathryn laughed. "That would be nice. But my reality is attempting to be normal on Christmas Eve when we have a huge problem sitting at the dinner table."

"You don't think that Bill is doing anything other than screwing with your personal life, do you?" The van arrived and Darby rolled her bag to the back of the van and the driver threw it on.

"We can't be sure," Kathryn said. "But it was John's idea to *not* tell Tom that we know he was talking to Bill. They'll be setting up surveillance in his house while he's with us tomorrow."

"Man, this holiday just keeps getting better," Darby said. "But too bad you couldn't confront him during dinner and call it the evening entertainment."

Kathryn laughed, "You might have to be our entertainment."

"I'm on it," Darby said climbing aboard the van. "Pop the bubbly, and after my 20-hour day, you know I'll do my best."

"I do," Kathryn said, her voice trailing off.

This was not what Kat needed over the holidays. She was finally coming back to life after psycho boy Bill, and then this. "I'm really sorry, Kat."

"Yeah, me too." Kathryn sighed. "I pray to God that Bill is not reaching out from prison, and had anything to do with those crashes."

"Me, too."

DARBY FOUND HER hotel, then a bed, and stared at the ceiling. While it was 11 pm, it was only 9 pm in Seattle. Sleep should find her any minute—or an hour at the very least. She double-checked her alarm clocks. Her wake ups were set at 3:55, 4:00, and 4:10 in order to make the 0530 van to report by 0545. The first alarm would be 0155 her time. Why they had pilots on the West Coast fly the early session, she had no idea. Thank God headquarters was not on the East Coast, as that extra hour would make this fiasco twice as challenging.

Kathryn was right. Twenty hours awake after a four-hour nap, training session, and a flight home could be her demise. But the fact she was on reserve the next day, sobriety would be her best friend this holiday.

She had hoped that their girl's night and associated festivities would have allowed her to sleep longer. They would have, but after coming in from the Pacific, her body clock was a hot mess. She rolled to her side, and pulled a pillow over her head.

"Grrrrr."

Darby finally dozed off for what felt like a few minutes when her first alarm went blaring. The last time she had looked at her clock it was midnight thirty. She rolled out of bed, and dropped to the floor. Once standing, she pulled on a pair of gym shorts, socks, her tennis shoes and a sports bra. Glancing at her body, she did a double take to make sure she was not missing an important piece of clothing.

After she confirmed she was fully clothed, she grabbed her key then slipped out of her room and went downstairs to the lobby. She poured an extra large cup of coffee and then worked her way to the gym. The exercise bike was the only way she could drink coffee and get her mind, body, and muscles working at the same time. In thirty minutes no less.

Not knowing where the time went, she arrived at the training center ready to fly. As ready as anyone could be, after four hours of sleep and an *oh God too early* show time. But life was good and it was Christmas Eve. She could not wait to celebrate with Ray, Kat, the girls and her friends, and tell that ass *Tom* what the hell she thought of him. *Oh wait.* But she couldn't—she had promised Kathryn silence. This would be an interesting dinner for sure.

Darby worked her way through the halls of the training center and found the briefing room. "Ron," she said to her captain for the session, parking her bags against the wall. She handed him a candy cane. "Breakfast of champions," she said, unwrapping a cane of her own. "Merry Christmas."

"Thanks, and Merry Christmas to you too." He unwrapped his candy cane and said, "I'm not sure if this is a good time to fly, but it guarantees the rest of the day off."

"That it does," she said sticking the end of her candy into her mouth and sucking. "I'm on call tomorrow. How about you?"

"Off for two days."

"Awesome. Your family's got to love that, and…"

The captain instructor rushed in. "Hi guys, I'm Phil. Do you have your licenses and medicals?"

They handed their documents to the sim boss. He took a look and then asked, "So, who flies first?" as he handed them back.

"Your choice, Ron," Darby said.

"I'll go first then."

"Great. But I'd like to do something different this time," Darby said. "I want to do three arrivals—one in Hong Kong, the night arrival in Amsterdam, and another arrival into Seattle."

"You don't need to do all that," Phil said. "We'll just run you around the pattern and do an autoland, and then you're outta here."

"I know. But I haven't flown an arrival for over 8 months, and we don't normally fly in the traffic pattern on the line," she said, with a wave of her candy cane. "These events in the pattern don't do anything for competency, they just fill a proficiency square."

"I don't mind staying," Ron said. "That actually sounds like a good idea, and kinda fun. I wouldn't mind doing that myself."

"Thanks," Darby said, and then looked back to Phil, whose mouth was open, and eyes glazed—from the hour or her request, she could not be sure.

"I was planning on the 9 am flight out of town." He sat on the edge of the table. "That's not what we're supposed to do." He looked at his watch. "Shit," he murmured. "It's Christmas, don't you guys want to get home?"

"My flight leaves at 11. Ron lives in town. When's your next flight?"

"Noon."

"We could have you out of here by 10 and you'll get that without a problem. But you're the boss," Darby said. "Whatever you want." She never had much choice, but it also did not hurt to ask. Besides, these guys *were* paid for a four-hour session.

His eyes did not blink, but she was the master of stare-down and they were only on three potatoes. She could go for as long as he wanted, but priceless simulator minutes ticked by.

"Excuse me," a voice spoke from behind her, followed by a rapid tap on the door, and they all jumped. Her head turned toward the open doorway.

"Yes?" Phil said sharply to the intruder. "Can I help you?"

"I need to speak to Darby Bradshaw before she leaves town."

"And you are?" Darby asked, with an eyebrow raised. This man was dressed way too nice for this hour of the morning.

"Jack Andrews," he said. "I'll be at the airport in the chief pilot's office waiting."

"Are you a chief pilot?" Darby asked.

"Assistant."

"What's this about?" she asked.

"I am not at liberty to discuss it."

"You want to see me on Christmas Eve?"

"That was *my* thought exactly." He glared, and shoved his hands deep into his pockets and Darby's eyes glanced down at the movement. She grinned at the location of his pockets, and then thought about how often guys had stared at her chest while talking to her. Perhaps it could be a fun turn of events for women to give a little back and crotch watch while the ladies talked to the guys. Might be interesting to see what came up.

Damn I need some sleep. Her eyes raised to his, with a smirk still on her face, which he may not have appreciated as he was watching her. His face held a new red hue that hadn't been there before.

"*What?*" she asked. She bit her lip to fight off the laughter at his expression. "Okay, let's just step into the hall and get this over with now."

"I was told to bring you to the office."

"Do you always do what *they* tell you?" Darby stuck the candy cane between her lips. She was beginning to think 'they' at this airline was like the great and powerful Oz. But she never knew exactly who was behind that curtain. Nobody took responsibility.

He glared, and then said, "Don't be late." He turned, and left as stealthily as he arrived.

"What the hell?" Ron mumbled. "You must have done something pretty bad to pull a manager in on Christmas."

"I didn't do anything," Darby said. Folding her arms, she tapped her foot. A total Kat move, but it worked. Her taking that trip slipped into the gray matter. Could she actually be violated for taking it, even though scheduling assigned it? At this point she wasn't sure. But she *was* sure that she was way too tired for their games.

These guys were beginning to piss her off. First she busted ass to make the trip work for the company. Then she got her balls busted for wanting to promote the airline on her safety book. And now she was being called in on Christmas Eve. This was officially three strikes, and this time she was not going to take their bullshit. If they wanted a fight, she was on.

"So," Phil said, his voice startling her, and she turned toward him. "Your flight was at noon? You still want to make this a full session with a detour to your hanging? I'm game if you are." His Cheshire cat grin displayed his great pleasure of getting his way.

Darby's eyes narrowed. Once again, this was not the best time to give up swearing. She stuck her candy cane into her mouth and sucked.

CHAPTER 11

AFTER THE TRADITIONAL flights around the pattern with two landings, followed by an autoland, Darby was complete with her recency. The hell if that made her a better pilot, but she was legal. They checked the box, and that was good enough for the Feds. Darby and Kathryn would definitely continue *this* discussion when she returned. If one thing needed to be revamped in the modern world of computer aircraft, it was they needed a better way to stay proficient than the current process. Something she discussed in her book in great detail.

Darby worked her way to the chief pilot's office, and glanced at her watch. If she could keep her mouth shut, she could be out in fifteen minutes. She entered the flight operations area and the few sorry souls heading out for their Christmas trips lingered. She looked around the room, winked at a pilot that had his eyes glued to her as she entered. He grinned and turned back to his computer.

Darby found Jack's office. "Hey, I'm here," she said. But it was not Jack in the office.

"What the hell are you doing?" the man said.

"Excuse me?" Darby said, staring at someone she had never met, sitting behind the desk.

"You've stepped over the chain of command one time too many!"

Darby dropped her bag, placed her hands on hips. "What are you talking about? I go to my chief pilot for everything I do. And I follow the flight operations manual!"

"*I* am your chief pilot," he said flatly.

"No you're not. Joel is."

"I'm the regional chief pilot."

"So you're my chief pilot's boss?"

He nodded and said, "Yes."

"Then if I went to you, wouldn't I be going over the chain?"

"Don't play with me," he said standing, his bulk towering over her. Her eyes went from eye level up two feet, and Darby cranked her neck to look up.

She gave him a once over, then folder her arms. "Okay. No playing with you. Got it." She grinned and then winked, which appeared to move him just a bit. "This is going to be a dumb question, I'm sure. But if I had no idea who you were, how exactly did I know to report to you? Besides, I'm based in Seattle. Joel Iverson is my chief pilot and I have been ordered to go to him. Nobody else."

What in the hell did these people want? She didn't even know who this guy was, and yet she was suppose to report to him?

"As far as you're concerned, I am the only person you report to."

"Do you have a *name?*"

"Captain Hughes."

What is it with these guys who take management roles and think the world should know who the hell they are, because they'd been assigned to a position? Darby was tired of this, but she was even more tired of them screwing around with her. They had backed off for the previous three years, and now it was as if her book had been thrown into a hornet's nest.

"So, Captain Hughes, it's nice to meet you," she said, extending her hand. "What brings you to the Oak City chief pilot's office?" She winked.

Glancing at her hand, he shook his head and made some guttural sound and sat behind his desk. "You're supposed to be reporting to me."

"About *what* may I ask?"

"This damn book shit."

"Book *shit*?" An eyebrow raised. Her book was suddenly gaining a great deal of attention. "How would I know to report to you if A, I had no idea who you were before a few minutes ago, and B, I had no idea my agent was going to call the marketing department?"

"You know now."

She bit her lip assessing the man in the suit, who clearly wanted to be here as much as she did. She handed him a candy cane. "Truce?"

His eyes smiled. "No thanks."

Darby set the peace offering on the desk and slid it forward. She pulled another from her bag and unwrapped it, and slid the candy between her lips, and sucked gently, not removing her eyes from his. Damn she loved the holidays. She pulled the cane from her mouth and licked a finger. He shifted in his seat and glanced at his watch. She smiled, and then glanced at hers.

Captain Hughes cleared his throat. "Going forward, you will come directly to me."

"But the flight operations manual says I'm supposed to contact corporate communications for outside activities, and then *they* talk to Wyatt for a thumbs up or down. Whom, I believe is a couple levels over your position. So wouldn't I be violating the chain of command if I went to you instead? Sir."

She returned the phallic symbol to the most appropriate place, her mouth, and did not remove her eyes from his.

"*Everything* you do comes to me," he said. "I don't want any surprises."

"Your boss came down on your ass and you didn't know what he was talking about with the book? Huh?"

No reply was answer enough.

"You can't blame me for that," she said.

"Maybe not, but I sure as hell can monitor you now."

This had Odell written all over it. Darby had given him the benefit of doubt, when he was a chief pilot. She took one for the team three years earlier, and allowed Odell to throw her under the bus, believing that keeping him in place he would be a powerful force to support the pilot group.

Some force he's turned out to be.

He sure as hell moved up that chain of command, but support was for one person only—himself. He moved from union leader at one airline, to the CEO's right hand man at the other. An interesting career progression in any book. His lust for power, however, came with an ethical sacrifice. She wondered if he ever had any ethics or sold them along the way. While that behavior didn't work in her book, it certainly made for an interesting chapter.

Word on the flight line was that it was Odell who sold their medical rights in the last contract that the company tried to shove down the pilots' throats, attempting to play with their sick leave policy. The truth was that the company did not try to shove it down their throats, but it was the union driving that action.

Her union actually promoted that Global should have full access to all their medical records, contrary to HIPAA laws. That action was not in anyone's favor. She had been vocal, and worked to make sure the release of records would never happen.

The pilots voted down the contract—the first time in the history of Global Air Lines. Her eyes narrowed assessing the big guy. Was this about her involvement with the contract? Or could it have been the ugly past rearing up?

The director of training and fleet training captains were both dead, and Bill was in the state pen, but all that did was leave holes for other vermin to slip into. Or maybe it was fear of what may come from her book that was about to be released.

"Do you read Kindle or paper?" she asked. She would give him a copy of the book. He had not been around during most of the excitement, and this could bring him up to date. She could also help him to understand and learn about SMS and safety culture. But with his delay in response, she asked, "Do you read?"

He laughed, one of those uncomfortable laughs. "I'm too busy to read." Darby's eyes widened. A management pilot who did not read meant only one thing—he was not keeping up on industry issues.

"Who's our SMS guy?" Darby asked.

"Our social media person?"

Darby eyes widened, and she stared for a moment allowing that information to settle into the room, and her brain. He was a regional director and had never heard of SMS?

"SMS is safety management systems."

"Uh, uh, the safety guy is Baxter, I think."

Darby raised an eyebrow. Global was in more trouble than she thought. They had a moment of stare down. She won.

"That's all," he said. "You've got your marching orders. I would suggest you follow them."

Darby didn't move. She stuck the candy cane into her mouth and just stared at him. Her mind whirled a zillion miles a minute, bouncing into areas she had not visited for a long time. She had given these guys far too much credit. But the reality was, they were way over their heads—clueless, perhaps.

They also would never change, until the culture changed. There would be only one way to get this airline pointed on the right flight path, and she had to do it. If she didn't, nobody would.

CHAPTER 12

DARBY CLIMBED ABOARD the elevator from the chief pilots' office, located deep within the airport basement, and pressed the button to the gate level. Okay, his office was only one floor down, but it seriously felt like hell all the same. And she had demons crawling on her back from their talk to prove it. She had to figure out how to shake it off.

The doors opened and the elevator spewed her into the terminal—the real world among the chaos of holiday travelers. She stood for a moment, watching as they rushed to their gates. There was definitely a different vibe in the air up here. Everyone was smiling, laughing and carrying bags filled with gifts. There was only one thing she could do at a moment like this.

She glanced left and right, and then removed her hat. One more scan of the immediate area, and she stuffed it into her flight bag. *Hat police be damned.* She removed another from her suitcase and pulled it on. *This should do it.* Glancing at her watch, she calculated if she could make Starbucks and navigate the line within 20 minutes, and still make her gate and board before the rest of the passengers.

"Much better," a man said as he stepped in front of her.

"Excuse me?" Darby said.

"The hat," he said gesturing to her head. "I like it better than the other."

Darby grinned. "Hopefully my chief pilot will too."

"You look so Ho, Ho, Ho," a woman said, stepping up beside the man, with a huge smile.

"Thanks. But if I were standing on the street corner I might take offense to that," she said wagging a finger at the woman.

The woman's eyes widened, and then she laughed hard, as did the man. Then she turned to her husband and said, "Sweetheart, they'll be boarding first class soon. We should get to the gate."

The man turned toward Darby and asked, "Will you be flying us to London today?"

"Nope. I'm a passenger today." She hesitated and then added, "Looks like I'll be sleeping with the passengers to Seattle instead."

"I love this airline," the man responded. "Global pilots definitely take *doing whatever it takes to make first class passengers happy* to the next level."

Darby grinned as warmth filled her cheeks. "I guess that didn't sound very good, did it?"

"Sounded great to me," he said grinning.

His partner in crime smacked him on the arm, and said, "Yeah, I bet it did." She laughed and turned toward Darby, "Merry Christmas." Then she pulled him by the arm across the concourse toward their flight. He looked back and he gave Darby a wave that she returned.

Holiday travelers were awesome. She remembered her goal, as it immediately became fueled with a huge yawn. The extra oxygen, while appreciated, was not enough. She needed caffeine. She was also thankful for the mood shift as she joined this holiday party. But, she needed to do one more thing to get this party going.

She pulled her iPhone out of her purse, plugged in the ear buds, and scrolled through her playlists to Christmas, and pressed play. *All I want for Christmas is You* played, and a smile spread across her face with the thought of Ray. She glanced at her watch—coffee first, and then she would call. She adjusted the white ball on her hat, and gathered her stuff and headed down the concourse.

She joined the holiday party as songs played in her head, which were much better than voices, rattling on about the management pilots at Global.

An airline was an interesting business model. The federal aviation mandated management in flight operations to be type-rated for one reason only—they would have insight and experience of what was happening in the aircraft that would assist them in making better and safer decisions. However, as airlines grew, and decisions became more complex, these pilots needed management experience, which most, if not all, in these positions did not have.

Those that came from the military may have had a resume with leadership positions listed. However, clearly indicative of Global management pilots, these people were old school, chain-of-command do-as-I-say managers who lacked understanding of true leadership, or came from the cockpit when the captain was king, and held all the power.

Unfortunately, management positions were filled based on friendship and alliances, not performance. If Darby could describe it best, it was as if they were a pack of wild dogs. The dominant dog would only allow those into that pack that would follow orders and do the top dog's dirty work.

Darby's heart lifted once again when the Starbucks sign hung directly across from her gate. *Yes, there is a Santa*. But she hesitated, waiting for a family to cross her path battling bags, a baby in a stroller and three children, as they worked their way to their gate.

She was not helping matters as the children were in awe of her uniform. Darby glanced up at the ball dangling from her hat, and realized it was the red hat part of the uniform that captured their attention. Worked for her.

"Merry Christmas," Darby said. "Where are you flying to tonight?"

"Grandma's," a little girl around the age of five said.

Her brother, who was an inch taller, said, "And they have snow."

The smaller boy hid behind his brother. The kids' mom and dad cleared passenger traffic, parked the stroller by the gate, and then stood to the side watching Darby with the children, grinning.

"Awesome! Okay… I want you to wear these wings to Grandma's house," Darby said, kneeling. She pulled a handful of wings out of her purse, and began pinning them on the children. Four more children approached and she pinned them too. "Now, I'm going to give you each a candy cane." Darby opened her flight bag and pulled a bag out, and reached inside. "But these are airplane candy canes. So, I want you to give them to your Mom or Dad, and ask if it's okay to have them when you fly."

She stood, glancing from her watch to the Starbucks sign. "Time to fly!" she said, and waved to the kids as she walked out of site. She loved Christmas. But it was not really time to fly yet. It was time to fly to Starbucks.

Within minutes she reached her goal. The line was only ten deep, and moved as slowly as she had expected, but nobody cared. Not even her. Today was Christmas Eve and everyone was in a great mood. And she was literally feet from her gate.

Her mind shifted back to wondering what the deal was with Global management pilots. Was it as simple as they were just shitty managers? Or was there more? Global was known as the military airline. Yet, not even the military managed like they did at Global, anymore. Times had changed, and processes had been put in place for a reason.

Besides, there was no way they all had read her book, yet. Deloris only sent one copy, and that was two days before. And Hughes confirmed he did not even read. She began to doubt if any of them did. But when she was brought into the office about her blog years earlier, the assistant chief pilot had not read the post, and yet he was not short for words on the negative impact to the public.

These guys were tasked with running flight operations of the largest airline in the world, and yet they were in a tizzy about a safety management systems book. Granted, Global's performance may have been the poster child for what *not* to do in the book. But for the most part, the airline was de-identified in the construct of stories, and only those living inside that world would know that the stories all came from Global.

This curiosity had bounced around her brain since her first verbal spanking, to no avail. There were always curiosities in life, and this was definitely one of them.

"Love the hat!" the barista, said. "What can I get you?"

Darby had been staring at her, deep in thought, but without seeing. With her words, Mary's name tag came into focus. Darby smiled and pressed *off* to cancel the music.

"A Venti double cup sugar free gingerbread latte please."

"You got it! Can I get you anything to eat?"

"How about an orange scone. Holiday carbs don't count, do they?"

"Not on Christmas Eve," Mary said. "After your discount, that'll be $6.89 please." She reached into the cabinet and selected the largest scone on the shelf, and stuffed it into a bag, then set the bag on the counter. Grinning.

"I thought coffee was free today," Darby said, handing her a credit card.

"Oh, sorry, that's tomorrow. Santa *never* comes early." She winked. "Sometimes I do."

Darby laughed. "You did not just say that." She pulled a twenty-dollar bill out of her wallet and put it in the tip cup, and picked up her scone.

"'Tis the season for naughty and nice," she said, handing Darby's credit card back to her.

Darby knew that all too well, and was glad there were more like-minded people in the world. "Merry Christmas."

"Wow! Thank you!" Mary said, seeing the size of her tip in the jar. She looked like she was going to cry. "Okay, tomorrow coffee is free!"

Darby laughed. "Yeah, yeah, I bet you say that to all the pilots *leaving* town."

"Only the cute ones," she said, with another wink, and was on to the next customer.

Sliding down to the pick-up zone, Darby wondered if that girl had actually just hit on her. This day was filled with surprises, and it wasn't even noon. Within minutes her coffee was up, and she slid the cup into a sleeve. She glanced back at Mary, who was throwing her charms to the next guy in line. That girl knew how to work a counter.

Pulling her bags over to the window, behind the podium to her gate, she parked them and sat on top of her suitcase. She pressed the phone icon to find her favorites. First on the list was Ray.

"Good morning love," he said.

"Hey, how'd it go yesterday?" She asked, and then took a sip. Ray was the head of Global's maintenance department, and he had been under the gun to get inventory under control. A problem he inherited, and one he was trying to clean up.

"We got everything worked out. I hope," he said. "Shelves are still pretty lean."

"So how do you fix planes without parts?"

"Good point," he said, with a chuckle.

"Dispatch will help. If it's legal, they'll talk us into going," Darby said, followed by a huge yawn.

"Did you get any sleep last night?" Ray asked.

"Not much, but I can catch up when they bury me." A text dinged through her phone—Neil. *Merry Christmas. How's my girl today?* Darby rolled her eyes.

"Sweetheart, you need to take care of yourself," Ray said.

"I thought that was *your* job," she said, typing a message back to Neil—*Not your girl. Merry Christmas. Get a life.*

"What's that beeping?" he asked. "Are you recording our call?"

"Nope, just a man fan text."

"Well, whomever it is, tell him you're taken."

Darby typed to Neil—*love of my life said I'm taken. Bye.*

"Done. Now I'm only yours."

Ray was the most incredible person. He balanced her, made her laugh, and when she was with him, she felt like she mattered to the world. Neil had been her boyfriend from another time, under majorly false pretenses. They had both moved on, but every so often he sent her a message to keep that connection alive. History was a powerful thing. She forced Keith out of her mind, doubting she would ever get over him. But she did love Ray despite his not replacing Keith.

The interesting thing about the power of the heart, there was always room for more love.

"How'd training go?"

"Fine. Super short as always. Then I had a chitchat with a chief pilot. Not just any chief pilot, but some regional mucky muck. Who is now *my* personal go-to guy."

"On Christmas Eve? What the hell was that about?"

"I'm not exactly sure," she said, and then filled him in on the details.

"There's something amiss, sweetie, and you need to lie low. These guys don't play fair."

"*Ladies and gentleman, we'll be boarding Flight 32 to Seattle in five minutes,*" broadcasted in the terminal.

"Yep, that's what they want me to do, get on my knees," Darby said, with a laugh. "But they're about to board my flight so I'll work on the suck-up-process plan later."

"What time can I pick you up tonight?"

Darby glanced at her watch, and tried to calculate arrival time. "I'll be at my house twenty minutes after landing. You can join me whenever it works best for you, and we'll head to Kathryn's around five."

"If I'm doing the math right, that's ten minutes for playtime, and two hours for you to get ready for dinner."

Grinning Darby said, "Oh baby, you are underestimating the power of my get ready quick skills—anything beyond thirty minutes is overkill. How do you mess with perfection like this?" she said, stacking her bags and wheeling them toward the boarding door. "But you, darlin', that ten minutes might be pushing *your* limits."

She stood with coffee in hand and bags in tow, next to the boarding scanner. Positive space in a uniform did have its perks to get on before the other passengers and stow her stuff.

"Challenge is on baby. My ten minutes to your thirty," Ray said, with a smile in his voice. "Be safe, sweetheart, I'll see you soon."

Be safe. She had always been safe, so she thought. But the reality was that nobody boarding a plane had that choice. Safety was one thing beyond the passengers' control. They were all victims of what went on behind the scenes at any airline, and their lives were in the hands of whoever was in control of the plane. But with the advancement of automation, she was beginning to wonder if even the pilots were losing control—the subject of her next book.

Sadly, the industry was also marketing drones with technology to eventually replace pilots. But humans were always involved with technology, and when a human was involved, error was possible. At least with pilots, they had a vested interest in the outcome of the flight.

Safety culture and safety management systems were the new buzz words in the airline industry, as the industry prepared for NextGen. Pilots would be responsible for separation between other aircraft, operating with more complexity, and flying with reduced separation between aircraft. If pilots did not fully understand how to manage all systems in their automated aircraft, she feared the worst would happen when something broke. And something always broke. Airlines had to redesign training programs—there was no other way.

Fight For Safety—Inside the Iron Bubble, told it as it was. Hopefully if the public knew the truth, and she could provide airlines with economical ways to problem solve, then change would occur.

She glanced up to the television, as CNN announced, *"Breaking News."* The latest crash was now confirmed—intentional. The captain had gone to the bathroom and first officer denied him access. CNN played the audio of the captain screaming, as he pounded on the door to get back in. The first officer flew the aircraft into a gradual 1700 foot per minute trajectory to their death. Darby thought of Brian.

Her first love, Brian, had crashed into a mountain in Cali during the early age of automation. Only his crash was anything but intentional. He had been a victim of a human factors fiasco with the implementation of automatic aircraft and substandard training. But the same would occur, for similar but different reasons, when the NextGen changes became fully implemented. Change always disrupted any system. When introduced to an aircraft, the results could be catastrophic if proactive systems were not put in place.

Darby stared at the television with the other passengers. The official news was nothing other than a kick in the stomach. One pilot flew that plane into the mountain. The silence in the terminal holding tank was more eerie than the news of the suicidal pilot. Now that news confirmed this crash was intentional, and the captain had been locked out, she feared, more than ever, that Bill was involved.

Scanning the faces in her gate area she saw a mixture of fear, disbelief and horror. It was like a snow globe that settled all the flakes to the bottom, with frozen people. Silent and unmoving, the energy had left the room. She felt like the enemy in her uniform.

Turning to the agent, who was also engrossed in the breaking news, she asked, "Do you mind if I get this crowd back into a holiday spirit?"

The agent looked at Darby. As if her words slapped her back to reality, she glanced at the room, and nodded.

Darby picked up the microphone and began singing. "You better watch out, you better not cry, better not pout I'm telling you why... Santa Claus is coming to town... He's making a list and checking it twice, gonna find out who's naughty and nice, Santa Claus is coming to town."

Everyone had turned from the television the moment the first words came out. Not only at her gate, but nearby gates as well. And then someone began singing with her, and then another and another.

"He sees you when you're sleeping, he knows when you're awake, he knows if you've been bad or good so be good for goodness sake!"

Some people were crying, yet still singing loud and off key. Darby was the leader of the off key club, but they were back with the day of jolly. The children in the gate were jumping and laughing. Darby gave the microphone to the agent, and then offered the little ones each a candy cane, with parent's permission of course. She learned the hard way from Kat—mother's rules rule.

After holiday cheer was handed out she asked, "Do you mind if I slip on?"

"If I could upgrade you to first class, I'd do it."

Darby laughed, "Wow. And, it's not even Christmas." She scanned her ticket and slipped through the door with passengers still singing in the gate area.

CHAPTER 13

DARBY SLID INTO her window seat and buckled in, then set her purse on the floor and kicked it under the seat in front of her. She pressed her forehead against the cool glass, and glanced up to the crystal blue sky, and then at the bodies scurrying on the ramp.

Guys in fluorescent yellow vests were loading the plane at the adjoining gate. The handlers were laughing and enjoying the season, not aware of the breaking news. Yet, an accident never impacted a person as much as those who had loved ones involved. Then it became part of their life.

Darby had lost far too many people she loved as a result of airplane crashes, as did Kathryn. Together, they would make a difference in the industry—Darby inside the airline, and Kathryn on the regulatory side. But there was no denying the reality that they both faced equal, but complementary challenges.

When passengers began flowing down the aisle, Darby turned and watched them pass. She sipped her coffee. She smiled and nodded, as passengers looked her way. Many thanked her as they passed. She could only imagine their fear. Not knowing who was in the flight deck and what was happening up there. Worse yet, if their flight would end in a similar and fateful manner.

The reality was, there was always a crazy person out there and no industry was exempt. Everyone just had to do their best to set up processes that would keep the bad guys out of the flight deck and off the aircraft. But when those bad guys were the pilots, that changed all the rules.

Passengers' lives had always been in the pilots' hands. Just as any driver's life, on the freeway, is in the hands of the person driving 60 miles per hour in the opposite direction. But today was Christmas Eve—the season of love. Not a time to think about death by airplane.

Darby had lost too many loved ones over the years. She had warned Ray that his life would be in danger if he became involved with her. He had said, "I'm going to die one day. I would rather live a moment with you, than a lifetime without." She was not sure if that was the best line she had ever heard, or if he really meant it, and had told him as much. Without removing his eyes from hers he had replied, "I'm willing to face death while you figure it out."

"Excuse me," a man said as he bumped her arm sliding into the middle seat. "Was that you singing?"

"It was," Darby said, with a blush.

"A pilot huh?"

Darby glanced at her shoulder to confirm the stripes were still there. "Yes, sir. I am," she said, and then tipped back the remainder of her coffee.

"I hope you fly better than you sing."

Darby's laugh found coffee spewing out her nose.

The woman taking the seat on his other side said, "You're an ass!" She pulled a napkin out of her McDonalds bag and handed it to Darby.

"Thanks," Darby said, taking the offering and wiping up her mess.

"I'm just saying she was off key."

"That was the best song I have ever heard, and you're a dick, so sit there and shut up the rest of the flight," the woman said, daggers emitting from her eyes, as she buckled into her seat.

Darby liked that lady, and enjoyed the ensuing discussion as she cleaned up the mess. She wiped the seat in front of her. After the man got his butt chewed from the lady to his right, he must have realized he might not be making brownie points with the line of discussion, so he fell silent, as did she.

"I'm sorry I said that," he finally said. "I didn't mean anything by it."

"That's okay," Darby said. "The only place I really sing well is in the shower. But then I don't think your wife would appreciate if you heard me there."

He glanced to his ring and played with it a moment. "She left me."

"I'm sorry," Darby said, and she was. But with an attitude like his, she knew why he got dumped. And yet, maybe he had the attitude because of the dumping. It was Christmas and he was alone. Nobody ever knew what was going on inside another's head, or in their life to pass judgment.

"I'm a good singer in the shower too," the woman next to him, said. "But I would never find myself dead in a shower with you." She folded her arms.

"Okay kids, peace offering," Darby said with a laugh. She handed them each a candy cane. "Suck on these. When they're gone, you can come out of your rooms if you talk nice to one another." Both passengers laughed, as did all within earshot.

"Are you a mother?" the woman asked.

"Nope. But I've been learning from the best."

"She can be my mother," a voice behind her seat said, and the guys beside him laughed, too.

Her job of joy was done. But the dead in the shower comment stuck as Bill slithered in with memories of the attack. She opened the magazine to see what movies they were playing for the month. *Intern. Everyone's Fine.* There was also an advertisement for the movie *Joy* that would be playing in January. She could hardly wait. She was also thankful she had already seen the listed movies. If she attempted a movie today, she would most definitely be missing some plot points. She turned her attention out the window once again.

Forcing herself to think happy thoughts, instead of thinking of Bill or Hughes, Darby pulled Ray back into her mind. Then she thought about the evening ahead and how she would deal with Tom. Her mind drifted from past to present, to her relationships, and then to her Hawaii Christmas, and tears filled her eyes. Then the thought of Ray forced those tears and images away, and she relived her and Ray's many special moments.

Darby's forehead was pressing against the window as Mt. Rainier came into view. Ray owned a plane and had flown her around Mt. Rainier on their first date, and then took her to the Bend airport for lunch. But sadly the diner was closed, permanently. There was no lunch, but they met with the airport manager and actually contemplated opening it.

Timing in life was everything. If they were at the retirement portion of their career, they would have moved there, opened the diner and worked it together. Maybe one day.

She felt the plane turn and her ears pop, and she realized the mountain's position was shifting. They should be passing the mountain to the right and well above it. But the plane was now in a rapid descent, and turning left. Turning toward the mountain! *What the hell!*

The guy next to her was quietly chatting to the woman beside him, and she was giggling. Darby whacked his arm. "Look!" she shouted. But he ignored her. He was too entwined with the woman. Darby repeatedly pressed the flight attendant call light. But the cart was in the aisle in back, and there were people lined up to use the restroom.

She pressed her face against the window as the mountain grew, and now loomed above their altitude. That mountain was every bit of 14,000 feet! They should not be that low. Heart racing Darby fought with her seatbelt, and after she unbuckled it, she climbed over the two seatmates and jumped into the aisle.

Once in the aisle, Darby flew forward and yelled at the flight attendant, "Help! We have to get into the cockpit!" The flight attendant's response was tears.

Darby picked up the hand microphone and called the cockpit, but no answer. There was only one reason—they were incapacitated.

"What's the code to that door?" Darby demanded. More tears came in response. Darby took a chance and typed in the code from her plane, not sure if it were universal among fleets. Within seconds the green light gave her access. She pressed open the door and froze.

The pilots were very much alive. Captain Bill Jacobs was in the left seat and Tom was in the right. They both turned her way and smiled. The mountain blanketed the windows.

Jolted by the impact, Darby opened her eyes with her heart racing. They were on the runway in Seattle. She looked at her watch, and could not believe she had slept the entire time. Never again could she say she never slept on an airplane.

Running a finger under her eyes, she yawned the cobwebs away and glanced at the two sitting beside her. They were chatting, just as in her dream. The man's ring was no longer on his finger. Darby smiled and turned on her phone.

Three messages—Ray, Kat, Ray. She smiled and stuck ear buds where they belonged, and listened.

Ray—"Hi Sweetheart, welcome home. I've got a couple errands to do, so I will pick you up at your house at four, and we'll head over to Kat's right after that." So much for their 30/10 challenge. But she would appreciate the time alone to get some things done, and still needed to wrap Kathryn's gift—her annual Christmas puzzle.

Kat—"Hey Darb, welcome back. Will you bring champagne for the holiday toast? And remember… do *not* say *anything* to Tom. Also, did you see the news this morning? Just makes me think… Okay… never mind. See you as soon as you can get here. I will put you to work. Love you!"

Ray—"Don't think for one minute you are getting off the challenge. I am certain that I can go as long as it takes you to get ready." Laughter. "But that's only because I know you can get ready in 20!" More laughter. "Yes, I do think I'm funny. Remember, good things come to those who wait." Darby smiled.

CHAPTER 14

D ARBY YELLED, "TURN!" Ray snapped back to present time and cranked the wheel, and pulled into the parking lot. Once they were not moving, she asked, "Where were you just then?"

"Sorry, just work stuff. Complications." He patted her leg. "But enough of that. I *am* with you, no place else. Besides, we're off for a couple days and Global will not be part of our holiday."

"One of us might be off a couple days," Darby said. "Technically I am off for the night. Back on call tomorrow." She reached for his hand and squeezed. "But, we have tonight! And the open board is empty so there are no unassigned trips. There are also three people ahead of me on the list!"

"English please."

"There is a Santa." Darby chuckled. "We get to spend Christmas together!"

He lifted her hand and kissed it. "I'm looking forward to that."

He jumped out of the car and ran around to get her door, but she was already in motion. She would never be one of those women who just sat waiting for the door to be opened. But, she loved that he was right there beside her.

He closed the door behind her, and asked, "Tell me again why we couldn't go to the grocery store to get champagne?"

"Oh, Ray," she sighed over-dramatically. "I have so much to teach you about the art of drinking."

He laughed and wrapped an arm around her shoulders and pulled her close, then kissed the top of her head. "Yes you do."

They worked their way into the hustle of the liquor store, obviously the *go to* choice for last minute holiday gifts. Darby had been glad to have the time alone to get some gifts wrapped, but the shower was not nearly as much fun without Ray. However, had he been waiting for her, there was a high probability they would be late for dinner, or miss it all together. Had she gone horizontal, for even a moment, she would still be sleeping.

"Where were you this afternoon?" Darby asked, turning the corner to the champagne aisle. Her eyes opening wide at the selection.

"What do you think of this one?" Ray asked, lifting a bottle of Bollinger, with a ninety-dollar price tag.

"Oh… so James Bond. Nice," she said. "We'll need four, it's a big crowd."

"James Bond?" Ray pulled a second bottle and placed it into the shopping cart.

"Watch a Bond movie, you'll see." Darby set two more bottles into the cart.

"You have way too much time on your hands," Ray said, taking control of the shopping cart.

"Goes with the job. And a fringe benefit I must add."

There had been times she had oodles of free time, and the reason she was able to start her training blog. But since she began writing, every moment was sucked up and eaten by her computer. She had fed it regularly and at all hours of the night to make her book a reality.

They worked their way to the front of the store, and were three deep in the line, when Ray asked, "Do you think we need chocolate?"

"Oh my God, I knew there was a reason I loved you." Darby laughed. "But seriously, do you actually need a verbal response to that question?"

"No ma'am, he said," selecting a box of gourmet chocolates from a stack at the end of the register, and then grabbing a second box.

"So, you never did tell me what were you doing this afternoon," Darby said. "Everything okay?"

His ignoring her question the first time that she had asked did not go unnoticed. That was not his style. Something was up at work, and the fact his work was tied to hers she wanted to know what was going on. His world impacted hers in more ways than one.

"Just a lot of pressure to keep parts to a minimum on the shelf, and lower inventory."

"So nothing's changed," Darby said. "Is that making the juggling act a bitch to handle?"

"It's not that," he said, setting a bottle on the counter. "It's just that…"

Darby helped to unload the basket waiting for him to continue. When he didn't, she said, "Maybe if your shelves get in line, they'll get off your ass?"

"I don't know if that will ever happen."

"Which part? Shelves or ass?"

"Both," he said, pulling out his credit card.

"Put that away," she said, handing her card to the clerk. "This is my gift for Kathryn, and I'll wrap up the chocolate for you." She stepped close and looked up, batting her eyelashes. "I was so busy I forgot to get you anything for Christmas," she lied.

"You are my gift," he said, wrapping his arms around her and pulling her close.

"Damn!" the clerk said to Darby, "I want what you're having for Christmas."

Darby laughed. "Maybe Santa will deliver your own down the chimney this year."

"Oh Lord! Now that would be special," the woman said. "But I don't know how happy my husband would be about that."

They thanked the woman and headed out the door. Ray placed a ten in fake Santa's bucket, as they headed to his car.

Once the treasures were placed in the backseat, and they were buckled in, Darby turned toward Ray, and touched his leg. "I'm not sure what's going on at work. But I do know something has been bothering you for months, and seems to be getting worse. I have one question."

"Shoot."

"In the worst case scenario is it going to kill me or anyone else?"

He hesitated, as if he were actually searching to find the answer to that question. "I don't *think* so," he finally said, with a smile.

Raising an eyebrow, Darby said, "Okay, then. Here's the deal. We'll go with the 'don't think so' as a high probability that nobody will die. And if there's a chance, then whatever it is, after the holiday, you'll tell me and we figure out how to fix it so death doesn't happen. Unless of course, it's the director of flying, and my personal chief pilot." She grinned.

"Trust me. I've got a few to put on that plane too," Ray said.

"Okay. It's a deal. Whatever it is, nobody has died yet. So let's not think about it tonight." Darby leaned over and kissed his cheek. "But, you *will* make a New Year's resolution to resolve whatever it is, the first of the year."

"A resolution?" his eyes went wide and he made a scared face. "Oh man!"

Darby laughed and slugged him. "Don't be such a wimp. I'll help you. It's super easy—you just decide what you want to do, and do it."

CHAPTER 15

DARBY AND RAY were the first to arrive, so Ray parked on the street to leave room for the other guests. As they climbed out of the car, Jackie and John drove up and parked in the driveway.

"Merry Christmas," Darby yelled! She ran up and hugged Jackie with all her might and gave another hug to John. "I'm so glad you guys are here. I was totally afraid Kathryn would put me to work, and now I have help."

Jackie laughed, lifting a bag of golden wrapped gifts from the car. "Hi Ray. Merry Christmas."

Ray approached, holding the box with champagne and chocolate, and kissed her cheek. He adjusted the box, and shook John's hand.

Darby tucked an arm into Ray's and another into John's and sang, "We're off to see the wizard..."

Jackie grabbed John's other arm. "You can't leave me out of this one."

Walking up the driveway in a row of four, they stopped short of the path when the front door opened. Kathryn's stressed—I'm trying to throw the perfect party—face shifted slightly at first, and then it cracked, as she broke into laughter. "You are not going to fit up the path like that."

"Good point," Darby said, and yelled, "Train dance!" Darby stuffed Jackie's bag of gifts into the box, and took it from Ray. Then they reformed their line in single file, with Darby the leader. Everyone held the person's hips in front of them, and they proceeded up the path. They were all laughing so hard when they made the front door, that Darby thought she was going to wet her pants.

By the time hugs and kisses, and holiday greetings were done, it was but minutes that the women were in the kitchen, and the guys in the living room watching a football game.

"I am so glad we live in such a sexist world where the women folk hang in the kitchen," Darby said, digging a chip deep into the clam dip, then stuffing it into her mouth. "Seriously, we have the food!"

"And the champagne," Kathryn said, placing the bottles inside the refrigerator. "This is way too nice."

"Merry Christmas," Darby said. "And sorry I didn't have time to wrap. It's my paper save the trees conservation program."

"What about my…?" Kathryn said, with a wounded look.

Darby laughed. "I am so predictable. It's in the car. And 5,000 pieces this year."

Kathryn rubbed her hands together, "Oh goody."

"You're a nut," Darby said. "But you know Jackie and I will be here to help you."

"Where's Linda?" Jackie asked. "She could help too."

Kathryn glanced at her watch, "Not sure. She's bringing a guest and…"

"And she's here," Linda said, from the doorway.

"Oh my God, how did you get here? I mean… When?" Kathryn said.

"Merry Christmas," Linda said entering the room, and hugged Kathryn. "We were parked across the street watching the entertainment."

Jackie and Darby moved in for their holiday hugs, too. Linda was more beautiful than Darby had remembered. Maybe it was the air of confidence about her. Or new love.

"I think being a doctor agrees with you," Darby said. "You look really hot."

Linda laughed. "If I'd known becoming a psychiatrist would make me hot, I would have gone back to school a long time before this." She accepted a glass of wine, and sat at the counter. The girls merged into a mini catch up chitchat. They were a unique group brought together by life circumstance and death, but held together with friendship.

Kathryn's childhood friend, Greg, had married Jackie. Years later Kathryn's psycho husband, Bill, had brought Greg to work at Coastal Airlines. Darby met them all at the airline. Bill had been in Vietnam with Linda's husband. But not until Bill's manipulation of all their lives, killing hundreds in his wake, including Linda's husband, and Greg, did they find Linda, who subsequently moved to Californian to study psychology to help others. They talked often, but it had been three years since they had last seen her.

"I was watching the news at the airport this morning," Linda said. "I... that accident... it feels like..." and she stopped with tears in her eyes.

"We're all thinking the same thing," Kathryn said. "But this could be a copycat nut case, or just someone who really needed help."

"John says it may be months before they know," Jackie said.

"He's a good guy, I'm really happy for you," Linda said. She and Jackie had formed a bond as Linda sat at bedside with Jackie during Greg's hospital stay, and was there during and after his death.

"We need to go meet this mystery man," Kathryn said. "Where are my manners?" She wiped her hands on a dishtowel.

"No rush," Linda said. "There will be time for that. But now, I need a little more wine." She held out her glass, rotating the stemware as if she were admiring the color.

"Holy shit!" Darby yelled. "You got married! Look at that rock!"

All eyes flashed to the ring. And Jackie and Darby spoke at once—*when, why didn't you invite us, how did you meet…*

Linda raised a hand. "I met him at the hospital doing a residency. He's a widower too, and we had our weddings. So Niman and I flew off to Las Vegas and got married after the Thanksgiving Day weekend and then to Tahiti for a quick honeymoon."

"Why was he at the hospital?" Darby asked, raising and eyebrow. "He's not one of your mental patients is he?"

Linda laughed. "Sometimes I wonder, but no. He's a neurosurgeon. Fixes brains from another angle."

"I am so happy for you," Jackie said with tears filling her eyes.

"Don't cry sweetie," Linda said, wrapping her into a hug. "This is a good thing."

Jackie grabbed a napkin and dabbed it under her eyes. "Oh, I know. I am just so truly happy for you."

"Kat, why aren't *you* surprised?" Darby asked, eyeing her. Then clarity hit and she said, "You knew!"

"Only for a week. I promised to keep the surprise intact."

"Secrets, secrets," Darby sighed.

"Only for Christmas. Now it's time to meet this new addition to our family," Kathryn said. "Think he can handle us all at once?" She grinned placing a hand on Darby and Jackie's backs.

"Oh, he's been looking forward to this for a long time. I've told him all about you."

"Only the good stuff, I hope," Darby said, feigning concern.

"But of course."

Then Darby turned toward Kathryn. "Speaking of good stuff, where's your beast? Is he still coming?"

Kathryn gave Darby the eye. "He'll be here soon."

"I'm not even asking," Jackie said, with a wave of her hand, as if to wipe away what had just been said. "You two can tell me about the *beast* comment later. Today's about holiday joy and celebrating Linda's and Niman's wedding. Let's go meet him!"

CHAPTER 16

DARBY WAS THE first to enter the living room carrying a platter of warm Brie covered in raspberry sauce, surrounded by crackers. John, Ray, and Niman were watching CNN, which was replaying the episode she had seen that morning in Oklahoma City.

"Excuse me… is there a doctor in the house who will write me a sick note?" she said, setting the platter on the coffee table. She picked up the remote and changed the channel back to the football channel.

"In light of what is transpiring in the airline industry," Niman said, "one simply employed with an airline might constitute a note on grounds of mental instability."

Darby broke out in a hearty laugh. "Oh, you're not only handsome, but smart too." She spread her arms for a hug. "Darby Bradshaw… and welcome to the family."

He hesitated, glancing at John and Ray, and then with a huge grin, hugged Darby.

"Merry Christmas," he said hugging quickly and then pulling back. He adjusted his tie that was still meticulously straight.

"Now that you've met the famous Darby," Linda said, entering with a bottle of wine, "I want you to meet Kathryn and Jackie."

Darby bowed at the *famous* comment and then went to the bar and poured herself a Diet Pepsi. For holiday principles alone she added three cherries, then squeezed a lime wedge and dropped it into the glass. She had been up since 2 am, after arriving from an international trip the day prior, and if she had anything to drink she might just do a face plant.

Besides she was technically on call at 8 am Christmas morning. The first departure on her plane did not go out until noon, but she was looking forward to some much-needed sleep. She was even planning to help the process with a double-dose of melatonin—her go-to sleep aid.

She raised an eyebrow at Ray to see if he wanted a refill, and he smiled and nodded. She bounced over, retrieved his glass, smelled it and returned to the bar. Rum and coke—his favorite. When he wasn't looking, she used Pepsi instead, added a lime and returned it to him.

"Thank you, sweets," he said, took a sip and smiled. "You will *never* convert me."

She chuckled, "Never say never." Just then the front door banged open.

Jennifer, Jessica and Francine bounced in, in the middle of a vibrant discussion that only teenage girls could pull off. Chris quietly followed, with a smirk.

Jennifer and Jessica were Kathryn's twin daughters, and Darby's adopted nieces who were now fifteen years old. Chris was Jackie's son and less than a year younger than the girls. Francine was Linda's daughter and four years older than the girls, and a lifesaver, too, as she made a great chauffer for the kids.

"Hey ladies," Darby said.

Jen and Jess squealed simultaneously and ran to her arms. They were her height now, and almost knocked her over when they slammed into her. Darby jumped up and down squealing, mimicking them. Everyone laughed.

"Okay, girls," Kathryn said to all three of them, "it's time to settle down."

"Oh mommmm…" Darby said, and then added "Hi Frankie! How's college?"

"It's still super fun," she said pulling off her coat.

"Where'd Chris go?" Darby asked Jackie.

"Game room," Jackie said, motioning to what used to be Bill's office. "Video games are his life these days."

"I've got a fire going in there, and Elf is ready to play," Kathryn said.

"That's my *all-time favorite* movie," Frankie said.

"Mine too," the twins said together. Then the doorbell rang.

Beast, Darby thought. Kathryn opened the door, and sure enough Tom was standing there. Darby moved back to the bar and busied herself by adding an ice cube to her glass. Not sure she could keep her tongue, she needed a bit of distance. Ray looked her way with question, and she mouthed, "Later."

"Good to see you," Kathryn said.

Yeah, right, Darby thought.

He was carrying a stack of large wrapped gifts. "Here you go girls," he said handing them each a bright red box.

"Can we open them mom?" Jessica said.

"Please, mom!" Jennifer added. As if there would be any other answer.

Just like him to bribe the kids to get at Kat, Darby thought. Chris was back in the room watching from the doorway.

When Kat smiled and nodded, the girls dropped to the floor in the entryway and ripped paper off the packages. Darby's eyes went wide and darted to Kathryn, whose eyes flashed her way. Darby raised an eyebrow and Kathryn sighed, and slowly shook her head.

"Oh my God!" Jessica yelled. Jennifer was already busy reading the box.

"Cool!" Chris said, now standing over the girls. "Drones!"

"I have one for you too, buddy," Tom said. Darby rolled her eyes.

"Okay you guys, here's the deal." Darby said, stepping forward. "These are not toys." Francine began to laugh. "You, young lady, are going to be on my naughty list," she said wagging a finger at her, but laughed too.

"Yes they are," Chris said, holding his box in awe.

"Okay. You win," Darby said. "These *are* toys. But they are grown up toys, and come with some huge responsibility. We're going to get you B4UFLY apps on your phones that show you where you can fly, and where the hot zones are, so you can see all the regulations."

"They have an APP for drones?" Jackie asked.

"They've been working on it for a while," John said. "More regulations are around the corner, too. An animal the FAA is not sure how to manage."

"Give me a break," Kathryn said, grinning. "This job gives me all the responsibility without authority where it counts."

John knew the insurmountable job Kathryn faced, and was pulling her chain. The truth was, the complications with drone regulations were many, and each time a plane crashed Kathryn was pulled away. The two recent events would put her nine months behind what needed to be done with unmanned aircraft systems.

"Won't be long until we take out a plane with one of these," Darby said, and Kathryn gave her the death-ray look, that meant one thing only—*Don't say that in front of the girls.*

"Sorry," Darby mouthed.

"We don't have phones," Jessica said. "How will we get the apps?"

Kathryn gave Darby the eye, and said, "We can upload that APP into my phone."

Darby grinned, hoping she could survive this holiday.

She had bought the girls iPhones for Christmas and added the service to her plan. Something she probably should have cleared with Kathryn first. However, the twins were fifteen and way behind the times for normal high school girls. Kathryn was seriously going to scar their development. It was her job to make sure they survived their teen years. Tom buying them drones might actually make her gift easier for Kat to digest. Maybe having that ass around might serve a purpose, after all.

"These are pretty neat," Jackie said, kneeling beside Chris.

"Thank you," Kathryn said, to Tom. "But this is way too much."

"No it's not!" Chris said, holding his box close to his chest.

"They're kids and it's Christmas," Tom said, leaning in for a kiss. Kathryn turned her head toward John, and Tom's lips landed on her cheek.

"Tom," John said, extending his hand. "Good to see you again. I'd like you to meet our friends Niman and Linda."

Way to go John, Darby thought. Kathryn used that moment of distraction to move away, and help the kids gather the paper off the floor. "Francine, do you want to sit at the table with us, or eat with the kids and watch the movie?"

Francine grinned, "I think I better supervise the kids."

Kathryn wrapped her into her arms, and whispered, "I wish I could join you."

Darby leaned in and whispered, "Me too."

"What are you three whispering about over there?" Ray asked.

"Who us?" Darby said, placing a hand to her chest. Then laughed. "We'll never tell."

"Girl stuff, and I'm sure non-consequential," Tom said, handing Ray a cigar. "Merry Christmas."

"Excuse me?" Darby said. "Baby, it's *all* consequential. And, if you can't remember that, you could stick a post-it-note on your butt cheek, and that way before your head goes up your ass you can read the memo."

CHAPTER 17

DARBY'S COMMENT FLOATED by with a good laugh by all, even Tom, and she refrained from adding to her disdain for the man playing with Kathryn. They visited for another thirty minutes, and then settled into their seats for dinner. After salads were finished, Darby helped Kathryn clear the plates, and carried them to the kithen.

She and Kathryn returned to the dining room. Darby was carrying a platter of prime rib, followed by Kathryn with the potatoes, when her phone rang. *Seriously?* She set the platter on the table and dodged around Kathryn, then dashed to the entryway, dug through her purse and answered her phone.

All the people she loved were in this house, and there was only one person who would be calling—scheduling. "Merry Christmas," Darby said, in place of hello. The only appropriate salutation at a time like this.

"Is Darby Bradshaw in?"

"Is this a crank call or just obscene?" Darby asked, wondering if she should laugh or cry at the totally inappropriate call.

"We have a trip for you," the scheduler said, with a laugh.

Of course you do, Darby thought. "When?"

"Tomorrow, 10 am report. You'll be flying to Amsterdam, Mumbai, and back to Seattle."

Definitely an obscene call, Darby thought.

With a "Happy Holidays," Darby tossed her phone back into her bag and turned toward the dining room. All eyes stared her way.

"And?" Kathryn said.

"Tomorrow. Amsterdam. Mumbai. Amsterdam. Seattle. 10 am report," she said returning to the dining room.

"Oh sweetie, I'm sorry." Ray stood and pulled her into a hug.

Suck it up buttercup, echoed through her mind, as she pushed away from Ray. Hoping tears wouldn't spring from her eyes as she pulled out her chair and sat. "But we have tonight."

She was so tired. If it wasn't the international arrival from one ocean crossing followed by a flight in the opposite direction, or the *oh-God early* bounces in between, it was the stress of management getting on her case about her book. There were only a few people who had a right into her private life, and Global management pilots did not have that pass. But they did have the right to send her on a trip. Besides, somebody had to do it.

"You've been out a lot, in the last few days," Jackie said. "How are you even legal with FAR 117?" Darby smiled at Jackie's knowledge. Dating John had its privileges, as did managing training scheduling.

"They know the rules, but sometimes I wonder," Darby said, glancing at her watch. The problem was the illegal deadhead to the Hong Kong flight. Had that deadhead been on paper accurately, not only would she have been illegal for that trip, but it would have made her illegal for the flight tomorrow.

"Eight hours from bottle to throttle. Since I won't be flying at 8 am, I can share in the holiday toast the proper way." She looked at the Kathryn. "Race you to the kitchen."

There was no race, but when Kathryn and Darby returned, they were each holding a bottle of champagne. "There is more where this came from," Darby said. They popped the corks, and filled glasses and then took their respective seats.

"May I?" Darby asked, and Kathryn nodded.

Darby lifted her glass. "We are so fortunate to have this feast on the table, warmth in the fireplace and love in our hearts. Our children are safe and happy under the same roof. It's moments like this that we should *never* take for granted. Merry Christmas. I love you guys."

"Merry Christmas," Kathryn said. The salutation was repeated around the table as glasses clinked.

Within minutes, plates were filled, and multiple conversations overlapped, and then Niman asked Darby, "How do you enjoy flying to Mumbai?"

"That's our nicest hotel in the system. But you can't drink the water, or take a bath."

"Which is an issue for Darby," Ray said placing a hand on her back.

She could not agree more. Bath time was her ritual before bed.

"Why can't you take a bath?" Jackie asked.

"If you can't drink it, you shouldn't be soaking in it," Darby said.

"Good point," Linda said, pouring au jus on her prime rib.

"And they've got good drugs for super cheap down there," Tom said.

"Black market?" Niman sliced his beef, and took a bite. "Kat, this is delicious."

Tom chuckled. "I never thought of it that way. A doctor comes to the hotel, and you can get anything at a fraction of the price. Like Viagra, 2 bucks for 30 pills."

Kathryn and Darby exchanged a glance, and Darby laughed. "So Tom, now I know where you get the reputation with the ladies—Mumbai."

"What? I don't need that stuff." He stuffed a bite of beef into his mouth.

"Is that legal?" Niman asked. "I mean to bring them back to the U.S.?"

"Everyone does it," Tom said, with his mouth full. "Darby, can you get me some Provigil when you go down?"

"What's that?" Jackie asked, scooping another spoon of potatoes onto her plate. Darby wondered the exact same thing.

"A narcolepsy drug," Niman said. "They don't have much data on side effects."

"Oh hell, it's safe," Tom said, with a wave of his hand. "They've been using it in the military for years to send pilots out on solo missions, and keep them awake for days. They've never had a problem."

"They have data alright," John said. "But it's confidential."

"Why do you want it?" Kathryn asked, glancing at Darby. "You're not legal to fly with it."

"Just thought I'd give it a try on my days off," he said. "Besides, it's out of your system within 24 hours."

"How do you know?" Darby asked. As if they had run blood tests 24 hours later. He was seriously a problem for Kathryn.

"My flight surgeon told me as much."

"So you do take it," Darby said, raising and eyebrow.

"I plead the fifth," Tom said, with a grin. "But let's just say it's $3,000 a box for a three-month supply and insurance does not cover it."

"Okay, then," Kathryn said. "How's married life?" she asked Niman and Linda.

"Couldn't be better," Linda said. She reached out and squeezed Niman's hand. He lifted hers and kissed it.

"Wait," Darby said. "Three grand for a box of pills? And how much in Mumbai?"

"Ten or twelve bucks, I think." Tom said, filling his champagne glass.

Darby covered her glass when Kathryn lifted the bottle to refill the other glasses. She switched to water, despite her having many more hours to go for legality. She needed a good night sleep, and alcohol would not help. It never did. Besides, just because it was legal, did not necessarily make it right.

"I read you turned down the contract," Niman said, touching the corner of his mouth with a napkin.

"First time in history," Tom said.

"The sick-leave management process was… um, problematic," Darby said. When all eyes turned her direction with a variety of expressions, she began laughing.

"I missed the joke," Niman said, and Linda grinned.

"No joke," Darby said. "These people are not used to the refined language of Darby Bradshaw. They were expecting me to say something more profound like, it sucked the big one."

"I, for one, am impressed," Kathryn said.

"What's with the change," Jackie asked. "Not that I don't like the refined you, I just don't get it." She sipped her champagne, but did not remove her eyes from Darby.

"Since the book deal, I was told that I would be spending a great deal of time in front of the public. And it was only a suggestion, but I might have to clean up the language for the media." Darby popped an olive into her mouth. "How'd I do?"

"Excellent," Kathryn said. "But I think the public will love you just the way you are."

Darby smiled. "If I get a chance to market it, maybe."

"Why couldn't you?" Linda asked.

"I was called into the chief pilot's office again. Twice now, for the same subject. My book has got their panties in a bunch."

"What's it about?" Niman asked.

"Safety management systems, called SMS, and safety culture. Think of a management book, with an airline safety focus highlighted with leadership tips." Darby cut a slice of meat, and stabbed it. Then she held her fork out as she added, "Some pretty bad stuff that my company doesn't want to be associated with." She winked, and then slipped the fork between her lips with the best prime rib she ever had. "Niman is right, this is awesome."

"Why would they care?" Linda asked.

Darby shrugged. "Many reasons, and they are all in the book."

"I'm just wondering if good old Global is back to their old games," Kathryn said, exchanging a glance with John.

"Games?" Niman said. He sipped his water clearly watching the exchange of looks between the ladies. Darby could tell that this man did not miss much. "Hard to believe airline management would have time to play games with the level of responsibility at hand."

"Ego," Darby said.

"Ego is the most powerful controlling force of the human psyche," Linda said.

"And pilots are the worst." Kathryn glanced at Tom.

"Excuse me?" Darby said, grabbing Kathryn's attention, followed by a wink. "Some pilots," she added, holding up a hand to hide the finger pointing at Tom, who happened to be oblivious. He was lost in another world somewhere.

Kathryn laughed. "Except for those pilots at this table, I might clarify."

"Ego or not, there is one thing I know for sure," Darby said. "The Director of Flight Operations has a hard on for me, and it's *not* the good kind."

Ray laughed choking on the bite he just stuck into his mouth. Then said, "Don't worry sweets, I have the good kind for you."

"You did *not* just say that in front of everyone, did you?" Darby asked, feigning shock.

"Not sure." He looked around the room and asked, "Did I just say that out loud?"

Kathryn laughed first, and the rest of the guests joined in—everyone except for Tom.

"So, I may have just given the Global boys another reason to not like me," Darby said.

"Which is?" Kathryn asked, shaking her head with a smile.

"This afternoon, well... I kind of wrote a letter to my personal chief pilot."

"Captain Hughes?" Ray asked.

"The one and only." Darby sipped her champagne, and then said, "I told him I felt like I was being harassed, and that I should be able to follow company procedures like every other pilot. I also said that I didn't think the rules they set up for me were legal let alone followed Global's mission statement. *And* if I wanted to talk to marketing he did not have the right to tell me 'no', even if it was an order from Odell."

"Aren't you worried about getting a line check?" Jackie asked.

Darby chuckled. She was, but some things were worth the risk. "Oh, they assured me they don't do things like that at Global." She emptied her champagne glass. "Besides, I never fly, and no check airman will ruin their Christmas to harass me on this trip," she said with a wave of her hand.

Kathryn raised an eyebrow.

"I'm sorry," Ray said. "But these guys are a bunch of dicks, and you need to be careful, sweetheart."

Darby could not agree more, but what could she do now? Her book was definitely rubbing them the wrong way. A smiled spread across her face, and she chuckled. "Well, we all know the problem dealing with dicks, the more you rub them the bigger they get."

CHAPTER 18

RAY WAS THE designated driver, despite Darby having cut herself off after one glass of champagne. She was beyond normal fatigue, her brain hurt. Her hair hurt. Glancing at her watch, followed by a little mental gymnastics, she figured she had been awake for 21 hours, less her nightmare on the plane, and her eyes hurt too. She unbuckled her seatbelt, and moved closer to Ray's warmth.

"Tell me again why you are going into the office on Christmas morning?" Darby asked, laying her head on his lap, she tucked her legs up on the seat and curled up like a kitten. *More like why won't you go with me on my trip tomorrow,* she thought.

He stroked her forehead with one hand, and turned the wheel with another. "The place will be empty and I have a bunch of paperwork to catch up on. Besides, with you gone, I'd just as soon keep busy."

"Oh," Darby said, as her eyes fell closed, wishing she could stay home and celebrate Christmas morning with Ray. Or that he would drop everything, and come with her on the trip.

Ray jiggled her. "Sweetheart, you'd better sit up and see this."

"What?" she said, startling awake, but not wanting to move. Nothing could be better than snuggled into Ray's lap. She dozed into the darkness.

"It's snowing." He jiggled her again. "You'd better not fall asleep. I've got holiday plans."

She pulled herself up to see the magic of Christmas fall. "It *is* snowing! Oh wow. I thought you were kidding so you wouldn't have to carry me inside," she said, rubbing her eyes.

"I'll carry you anywhere sweetheart," he said, turning the wipers on as the few flakes turned into a full-blown winter storm.

"This wasn't forecast was it?" she asked, pressing her face to the side window.

"Put your seatbelt back on, the roads are already slippery."

"Yes sir." Darby saluted. "And don't kill my car."

Within minutes they were pulling into her driveway that was covered in a white blanket. Snow blew sideways across the front window, and the howl of wind cried beyond the warmth of the car. Ray pressed the remote and opened the garage door and drove inside, then shut off the car. He closed the garage door behind them, but they could still hear the wind.

"Thank God I don't have to fly in this tonight."

"Well, if it doesn't clear up tomorrow you should call in sick." He climbed out of the car and opened her door. "Tired and flying in a snowstorm, is not a good mixture."

"I'm sure it will blow over by tomorrow," she said, stepping into the house.

Darby did not feel good about the trip. Being pulled in so many directions, with accumulated fatigue, was not something anyone should be flying with. There was so much on her plate with the battle about her book, her illegal deadhead, the recent crash, Bill, Tom, and those damn drones. Everything was piling up, and she hoped she would not break.

"That was a wonderful party," he said, following her. "You've got great friends."

"*We've* got great friends," she corrected him, as she headed through the kitchen with him in tow. "So now that you have me here, what *are* you going to do with me?" She asked turning toward him with a grin.

"I'm going to put you to bed," he said touching her cheek. "You've had a long day, and you'll have an even longer day tomorrow."

"What about your holiday plans?"

"Did I say they were here?" he grinned.

Darby smacked him on the arm, and he laughed.

"Ow!"

"Ah, don't be such a baby," she said and glanced at the stairs. "But I'm going to need some major willpower to make it up those tonight."

"Did I tell you my middle name was Will?" He said scooping her up. "Yes, Raymond Willpower the third."

He held her close and kissed her gently on the lips. Then he looked up the stairs, and grimaced. "Man, we might have to put you on a diet after the first of the year."

Darby laughed and said, "Ha. Ha."

She rested her head on his shoulder, and closed her eyes working to forget the last man who carried her up these stairs. She breathed Ray in. *God, I love this man,* she thought.

He climbed the stairs, and walked through her bedroom and into her bathroom. "Gear extension, you're coming in for a landing."

She giggled as he dropped her, feet first to the floor.

"Okay, now wash your face, brush your teeth and do whatever that girl stuff is that you ladies do. But don't be long."

Darby saluted. Then she followed orders and within minutes she was make-up free, with minty fresh breath, and wrapped in her fuzzy pink robe turned inside out. Returning to her room, a dozen candles flickered and danced upon the walls and ceiling, and something Christmassy and jazzy emitted from the stereo. Ray had pulled back the comforter on her bed, and sat with a towel wrapped around his waist on the edge, wearing a Santa hat.

"Holiday massage," he said, holding up a bottle of oil. "Now get that cute butt of yours over here," he added patting the spot next to him.

Darby complied and moved directly in front of him. She untied the belt and allowed the robe to fall open and drop to the floor. Her eyes held Ray's. Light from the candles danced within his dark eyes, and he smiled with such love, she shivered.

She moved closer and placed her hands on his shoulders, and leaned over and placed her lips upon his. A chaste kiss at first, then their lips merged into a full-blown love affair. In the heat of the most passionate kiss of her life, she climbed into his lap, and wrapped her legs around him, not coming up for air in the process. He pulled her close and her legs squeezed tight, and her body stirred, melding to his. His hands worked their way down her torso and found their way to her butt, and he squeezed.

She tilted her head back and moaned.

"So, young lady," he said, "have you been a good girl?"

Grinning she said, "Never as good as I hoped to be, but always better than I was."

Ray broke into a hearty laugh. "I'm going to have to think about what that exactly meant." He stood with her still wrapped around his body, turned and deposited her into the bed. "Now roll over."

She complied, and lay face down, her arms fell to her side and she worked her face into the pillow until it was just right. Ray trickled oil down her back, over her butt, and down her legs. The warmth caressed her body and then his hands went to work kneading the softness into her skin. Slow. Firm. Down her torso, and the length of her legs he moved. His hands worked their way back up her legs and squeezed her butt, her hips, her back…

With a jolt, she awoke as he rolled her to her back. Not sure how long she'd been out, her eyes attempted to focus.

"It's okay sweetheart," he said in a soothing voice. "Just relax." He bent down and kissed her gently on the forehead, and then on one eyelid, and then the other, and then her lips. She purred and smiled, but her eyes were too heavy to remain open, and she melted into his touch.

CHAPTER 19

TOM STOOD OUTSIDE the Argosy Cruise terminal on Pier 55, downtown Seattle, and stuck his hands deep inside his jacket. He pulled a hand out, glanced at his watch, and then stuffed it back into his pocket. The snow dumped with the fierceness of a storm Seattle had not seen since 1967. He shifted from foot to foot to find warmth, and then pulled his hands from his pockets again. One hand brushed snow from his head and the other glanced at his watch. He pulled the paper from his pocket and read the address. He looked up at the building, confirming he was at the correct location.

He had been waiting 15 minutes. This better not be a bullshit waste of time. Thinking about Kathryn he smiled, and then his mind shifted to Bill. What the hell had he got himself into? He was playing on dangerous ground, but if he played his cards right, he would…

"What do you want?" A voice said through the crack in the door.

"I've got a meeting with a Mr. D.," Tom said, turning toward the sliver of light. The door opened wide and Tom entered.

"Follow me," a man said, already walking away. Tom followed down a long, dimly lit, corridor. The man opened a door at the end of the hall and said, "Up there," with a nod.

"Thanks," Tom said to the back of a head, as the man quickly retreated down the hallway. He watched the man take position at the door he had entered, but he was nothing more than a shadow in the hall.

Wiping his nerves on his pants, he glanced up the stairs and then sucked a breath and began the climb. This was the only way. He had made some bad investments—not only his money, but also money from many of the pilots. What the ex did not take, he had lost three times over. He could have had a ten-dollar insurance policy, and be worth more dead than alive. He was stuck. Stuck big. Now with IRS on his ass, he would probably end up in prison.

Kathryn would be part of his escape plan, but there were two problems—he really liked her, and he didn't trust Bill. He reached the top of the old wooden stairs, and tapped on the door, and then opened it. At the far end of the room was a table, with a single light hanging from a cord above. There looked to be a person sitting at the table, but it was difficult to see with the haze of smoke filling the room. It also appeared there were people in the shadows, one to each side of the desk. Just outside the glow.

Tom approached, squinting to bring the man into focus.

"What the hell do you want, that has brought me out on Christmas Eve?" the man asked, and then sucked long and hard on his cigar, seconds later he added to the haze that drifted like a low-hanging fog. A chill filled the room.

"A two-and-a-half million dollar loan," Tom said, with a slight crack in his voice.

Two ticks of the clock were followed by roaring laughter, not only from the man behind the desk, but those standing beside him. Laughter echoed from the hallway below. Then as quickly as the laughter began, it stopped. Silence ticked by. Tom shifted his weight from one foot to the other. The smoke parted and Tom's eyes narrowed. He had seen this man before. *But where? Who the hell was he?*

"You're a fucking airline pilot. Why would I loan you anything?" he asked, his eyes piercing Tom's. "I've looked at your financials, your insurance won't cover half your debt," he said throwing a stack of papers. They scattered to the floor.

My financials? How the hell? Tom glanced at the documents on the ground. His life lay in ruin in more ways than one. He had nothing to lose. More than likely nothing would be gained, but at least he could extend his life for a few more days.

The man reached for a bottle on his desk, and poured two fingers into a glass, and then tipped it back, and set it on the desk. "Tell me why the hell I'm not wasting my time here tonight."

"*Limitless.*" Tom said. The man behind the desk gave a nod and Tom continued. "The movie, *Limitless*, the drug. Super brainpower. What if I told you that it was real?"

"I'm listening."

Tom held out a box. "This has a retail value of three thousand dollars—a three-month supply. I can buy this for twenty bucks a box." Granted it only cost him $10 in Mumbai, but Tom could make a little on the side too.

The man's face came clearly into focus and he realized why he felt like he knew him. He looked like that actor... De Niro.

Puffing on his cigar, the man lifted the bottle of Glenmorangie, but this time he filled two glasses, instead of one. He nodded to one of the glasses and Tom lifted it.

The man extended his glass. "Looks like we're doing business together."

CHAPTER 20

RAY'S HANDS MASSAGED her breasts, and then drifted south sliding down her hips. He followed his hands with a trail of kisses, and found his way between her legs. "Oh," she moaned relaxing into him, inviting and wanting more. She wanted nothing but Ray. His touch. His love. Everything he was willing to give and all she was willing to take… Darby came hard and screamed, and then sat upright. Dazed, alone, and naked.

Wondering where the night had gone, she yawned. Her alarm cried from the nightstand, and the wind howled from beyond the pane. She was not sure if it was her scream that awoke her, or the alarm. She climbed out of bed, pulled on her robe, then grabbed her cell phone and killed the alarm. She padded to the window. The sun shown bright, and snow drifts piled high everywhere she could see. At least a foot of snow dumped through the night.

Glancing at her bed, it appeared she had been the only guest that night. But when did Ray leave? *Why?*

Slightly irritated for his not being there, she yanked her belt tight. Then heard the front door close. She turned toward the window again. Ray's car was in the driveway. "Coffee. I need coffee," she grumbled to herself and headed downstairs.

When she reached the top of the stairs, Santa stood at the bottom holding two Venti sized Starbucks. "Merry Christmas." He stared up at the vision of the most beautiful woman in the world, whom he loved more than life itself. He would risk anything, even driving to Starbucks in the middle of a snowstorm for her.

"Oh God, I love you!" she said, flying down the stairs two at a time.

"I'm hearing that a lot these days," Ray said, with a smirk. "I'm thinking it's the hat." He handed her a cup, and she sipped the creamiest, sweetest cup of coffee she could have imagined, laced with chocolate no less.

"Step one complete. Caffeinate you." He extended a hand. "Step two, breakfast."

She took his hand and followed him into the kitchen. French toast grilled, bacon sizzled, and orange juice had been poured. He pulled out a chair for her, and she sat, and then tucked a leg up under her. He moved to the stove, but her attention focused on a box sitting on the windowsill—a small box wrapped in gold with a matching bow on top.

"Here you go sweets," he said, placing a plate in front of her. Knowing damn well she had seen that package, but not saying a word. He set a plate for himself on the other side of the table and sat. "So how'd you sleep?"

"Like heaven on earth," she said, playing his game, and ignoring the package. "I had the most incredible dream. But I'm not sure what part was a dream or reality." She sipped her coffee, her eyes sparkling over the brim. "Did you stay?"

"Nope. You were quite the date. You fell asleep in 4 minutes flat," he stuffed a bite of French toast into his mouth. "A record for you, I might add."

"Seriously?" she said, not sure if she believed him or not. "Well... I'm just saying, after two minutes I gave up."

Ray laughed. "You needed sleep, more than me staying, and molesting you for two minutes, let alone through the night." He loved her with all his being, and sleep was what she needed.

"*I'm* not so sure about that," she said, glancing at her phone to figure out how much time she had until report.

"Okay my love, I'm going to get out of here so you can get ready," he said sliding his chair back from the table.

"But..."

He grinned, "But what?" His eyes flashed to the box and hers followed. He reached over and lifted it, and then turned it as he stared at it, growing sober as he did. "I was going to give this to you this morning, but somehow it doesn't feel right since you are flying off." He stood and placed it on the top of the refrigerator, and then turned. "We'll do Christmas when you return."

"That's closer to New Year's Eve, than Christmas," Darby said.

"All the more reason to celebrate." He extended his hands, and she took them. He pulled her to her feet, drew her in close and held her tight, then as quickly as he pulled her in, he stepped back. "Now go get ready for work and I'll see you soon."

Ray had something he needed to take care of, and it could not wait until the New Year. Despite Darby's plan, if he could manage it without her knowing all the better.

Darby felt tears spring to her eyes for no reason. She blinked them back and smiled. His lips found hers and they stayed that way for a very long time. Damn, Christmas made her emotional. Before she knew it, she was standing beneath hot water cascading over her body. Within no time she was standing in her kitchen in her uniform.

Ray was nowhere to be seen, but the dishes were clean and her kitchen looked better than it ever had. She glanced up to the box, and then made her way to the window. Ray's car was gone. Returning to her position in front of the fridge, she folded her arms and tapped her fingers wondering what to do.

She loved Ray, but he could *not* be planning to propose. *Could he?* They had only been dating for eight months. Of course she imagined marrying him, but they needed more time. She tucked a strand of hair behind her ear, and glanced over her shoulder. "Ah hell," she said.

Standing on her tiptoes she pulled the box down and removed the lid, and peered inside. Her jaw dropped, and mouth fell open. The biggest diamond she had ever seen filled the box. She slapped the lid closed as quickly as she could, and placed it back on the fridge.

"Damn, damn, damn," she muttered.

Darby speed dialed Kathryn, but no answer. Then she dialed Jackie—she did not answer either. She called Linda, and then one of the twin's new cell phone, and then the other. Nobody answered. Where were they? She had to talk to someone. What the hell was she going to do? She glanced at her watch. "Oh shit!" She had less than 30 minutes to report. *Where the hell did the time go*! She was going to be late for check in, and they would really have something to be on her holiday ass about.

CHAPTER 21

DARBY RUSHED INTO Flight Operations and logged onto the company computer. She punched in her numbers to log into her profile, but it didn't work. She tried it again, and again. Panic overcame her. *Shit! Not again!*

She stopped what she was doing. *Breathe,* she told herself. After a few moments of terror, she accessed her profile and checked in for her flight. She had made it with two minutes to spare.

Once she was confident she would not be violated for being late, Darby glanced around the room. Flight Operations was eerily quiet. She went to the briefing table where another first officer sat playing on his computer.

"Hey, I'm Darby," she said.

"Hey," the guy said, with a glance her way.

"Are you going to Amsterdam?"

"Yep."

"Where's the paper work?"

"Captain took it to the plane," he said, clearly annoyed with her interruptions. "I'll be out soon."

"Okay," Darby said, glancing at her watch. "Are you flying first?" When she received no response, she shrugged and headed out the door. She pulled her phone out of her pocket as she headed toward security, and dialed Kathryn again. At the beep she said, "Merry Christmas Kat. Ray is going to propose. I don't know what to tell him. Need to talk. I'll call you from Amsterdam."

Darby worked her way through the security line, politely cutting as flight crews could, and then put all her stuff through the conveyor belt and walked through the scanner. It beeped.

"Please wait here," the inspector said, directing her to a pair of yellow feet on a floor mat.

"Raise your hands."

Darby complied, but kept a watchful eye on her stuff as it came out the other end of the conveyor. The guy was glued to the video screen and his eyes widened as her luggage passed through. "Alert!" he yelled. Two more people ran towards him and this time all eyes narrowed at the screen. One man looked her way, then back to the screen, shaking his head.

What the hell did she have that was so suspicious? Darby had no idea. Yet with arms raised she was feeling every bit a criminal.

"Ma'am, come with me," a woman said.

Darby dropped her arms and walked to the conveyor belt.

"Open that bag," she said.

Darby complied, and the woman dug through her clothes and pulled out a rather large vibrator. "That's not mine!" Darby spat. "What the hell?" And then she began to laugh. *Ray*. Paybacks were hell, and she would get him.

"Are you telling us these bags have been out of your control?"

"Never," Darby said.

"Please power that up."

"What?"

"We need to confirm that it's not a," she lowered her voice and whispered to Darby, "a bomb."

"Seriously?" The woman placed a hand to her gun, and Darby lifted the thing up, but had no idea how to turn it on. She gave it a close inspection and then found the button. A loud buzzing emitted, as well as a vibration. When nobody blew up, they allowed her to turn it off.

"Does that thing have lithium batteries?" The guy doing the initial screening asked.

"I don't know."

"Lithium batteries catch fire," the woman said. "They're illegal on airplanes."

"Complete meltdown," another TSA agent commented, with his hand on hips staring at the vibrator shaking his head. There were four agents now staring at the poor lifeless thing lying in her suitcase.

Darby appreciated their concern for her vagina, and the safety of the plane. She put them all at ease and said, "No, there are not lithium batteries in there. I think it's solar charged."

"Ahhh, good," one man said. "But why didn't you go through the Known Crewmember line?"

That was a good question, and she had absolutely no answer. Known crewmember was where crewmembers with an ID, and who were registered in the computer system, could pass through security without having their items inspected and their bodies abused. They were criminal-free in that line.

With this crisis averted, she closed her bag and was soon walking through the terminal toward her gate. Wondering if they would come to get her because, with all the excitement, they forgot to pat her down after she beeped. That thought was short-lived when she saw Starbucks.

"Merry Christmas," Darby said. "May I have a Venti Mocha with a shot of raspberry syrup and topped off with lots of whipped cream?"

"Absolutely," the barista said. "You can pick up your drink over there please." She pointed to the end of the counter.

"How about some money," Darby said, waving a credit card.

"It's Christmas," the woman said, with a wink. "Enjoy, and have a Merry one."

"Wow, thank you." Darby replaced her credit card, and stuck her wallet back into her purse. She placed a twenty into the tip jar and walked to the end of the counter and her drink was waiting with her name written on the side, no less. She glanced around looking for Ray.

Someone was setting her up, and this had Ray's name all over it. She eyed her free coffee, and decided that she didn't mind if she were being set up.

She stuck the cup into a sleeve and worked her way to the gate. When she arrived, they were already boarding, despite that the flight wasn't due to leave for another hour and twenty minutes.

"We want to leave early," the agent said. "Nice hat," the woman said.

"Thanks." Darby pulled her bags through the jetway, excusing herself between the passengers, apologizing as she went.

She worked her way to the cockpit, saying hello to the flight attendants, who all said they liked her hat. Not until she stowed her bags and went to place her hat on the hook did she realize she was wearing a Santa hat, not her uniform hat. *Oh shit!*

What would she do for the remainder of the trip? No hat was a major violation. But then, she could wear the Santa hat the entire trip. Why not? The policy just said 'hat'. And, who could violate

Santa anyway? Besides, there would not be a management pilot anywhere near the airport from now until after the New Year, unless another plane crashed.

Darby hung her hat on the hook, and turned toward the captain. "Hi, I'm Darby," she said to the man sitting in the left seat. He turned and her mouth dropped open. *Tom.* "What the hell are *you* doing here?"

"Nice to see you too," he said. "I picked this up last night. Thought we should become better friends since I'm going to be part of the family soon." Besides, he had a mission in Mumbai that needed attending to.

Darby rolled her eyes. "In your fantasy world." Oh God, she hoped to hell she could keep her mouth shut. There was so much she wanted to say to this ass, and even more she wanted to ask him about Bill. But she had promised Kathryn that she would not say a word. Dinner was one thing, but how the hell could she go for an entire trip with this idiot and keep her mouth shut? She breathed deep, and then decided she could do anything for six days.

"Is anyone depressed up here?" a flight attendant asked from the doorway.

"Excuse me?" Darby said, climbing into her seat. She was seriously thinking about working on a major depression, but that was the oddest question.

"Who could be depressed?" Tom said. "I'm flying to Amsterdam with beautiful women, and it's Christmas." Tom also planned on sleeping with as many of them as possible, since he would be on his best behavior after he married Kathryn—for a while anyway. He eyed Darby, and a smile crossed his face. Friends were always fun in bed.

Darby smiled at the flight attendant. "Why do you ask?"

"A passenger in 4A was asking about your mental state. He's kind of nervous."

It was only a matter of time until passengers began worrying in light of the crash. Darby thought of Bill, glanced at Tom, and then said to the flight attendant, "Tell him we're just fine." Then she thought better of it, and said, "I'll make an announcement."

Darby lifted the handset to the P.A. system and said, "Merry Christmas ladies and gentlemen. From the flight deck, on behalf of the entire flight crew, I would like to welcome you aboard flight 777, non-stop to Amsterdam. Our flying time today is ten hours and three minutes," she said glancing at the paperwork.

"Please know that you're in good hands today. Not only do we have the best flight attendants at our airline serving you today, but our captain has a gut like Santa and is equally as jolly." She winked at Tom and continued. "And, well, with a woman up here… we never get lost, because we're not afraid to ask for directions. So sit back and enjoy the flight. Happy Holidays!"

Darby hung the phone up and then her eyes widened, as the man standing in the doorway came into focus.

The name hanging from the lanyard was one she would never forget. His appearance had changed. He was now overweight with less hair, but there was no doubt that this was the man who had haunted her dreams for many months, if not years.

Alan Jones was the sleaze ball that had screwed with her in the simulator, years earlier. She had been warned to never get in the simulator with him. Now he was on her plane.

"What are you doing here?" Darby asked.

"Giving you a line check."

"On Christmas?"

"Tis the season."

"But they fired you out of training."

"Perhaps."

"How the hell could *you* be a line check airman?"

"Line training is another world all its own," he said, with a smirk. "I would like to see your licenses."

Chapter 22

R AY SAT AT his desk sipping cold coffee, clicking through the pages on the computer screen, tracking inventory. More like looking for inventory. One part in particular. He shook his head, leaned back and pulled a hand through his hair. Things had been difficult at Coastal within the maintenance department before the merger. They had fired all the mechanics, and the replacement group was more or less worthless. But that was the least of his problems.

He had discovered his best friend had been pulling the ultimate scam. He had been purchasing parts from a company out in Los Angeles and making payments for those parts with a company check, for parts they never received. Yet they had been added into inventory.

The Los Angeles company was a shell that did not sell parts, or anything else as far as that went. But it looked good on paper. They were invoicing Coastal, and being paid a shitload of money for nothing. When Ray found out, he had confronted his friend, who had laughed and said Ray would be involved, too, so he had better go along with it.

Ray reported him. Despite the fact that he had nothing to do with any of it, he still felt responsible. He held his position, and then was promoted during the merger. He hoped it was due to his performance—but that, too, was a sham.

He suspected someone in flight operations management was involved, but he could not put the finger on whom. They promoted him for his silence because they thought he knew more than he did. Ray sighed and sipped cold coffee.

Now, he did not know what to do. Prior to the merger he had been under the gun to make ends meet. All he had to do was find a few extra hundred thousand dollars. He found it, with a safety net no less. The problem was after the merger Global changed their business model.

Keep the inventory as lean as possible. No parts were allowed to back up on the shelf—nothing extra, just the FAA minimum required. He pushed back from his desk, and stood. *"Dammit,"* he whispered.

It would only be a matter of time, and he had no idea how to stop that snowball from rolling downhill.

CHAPTER 23

DARBY FINISHED HER preflight, and then asked, "Are you going all the way to Mumbai?"

"Why the hell would I be on this trip if I wasn't?" Tom said. "Besides, Kat wanted us to get to know each other better." He grinned, thinking she would be his by Amsterdam.

"I knew you were a pervert," Darby said. She pulled her phone out and dialed Kathryn.

"If you think you're going to talk to her about me, you're mistaken," he said, followed by laughter that sent a chill through her bones.

She dialed Kathryn, and when the voicemail answered, she said, "Dammit!" and set the phone down with the recording going.

"What did you do to Kat?" Darby asked.

"It's not what I did to her," Tom said, "But what I have in store."

"What the hell?" Darby said, "I want off this plane."

"Call in sick now, and you're really screwed."

He had a point. Besides, as long as Tom was with her, he couldn't hurt Kathryn. "What are you up to?" Darby asked. If nothing else, she could be Kat's accomplice.

"Shut the phone off and I'll tell you," he lied.

Darby pressed *off* on her phone and put it into flight mode. "Well?" She said.

"Preflight checklist," he called.

Darby read the checklist and then glanced over her shoulder. Captain Alan Jones was already out of the cockpit, and buckled into his first class seat. She expected nothing less.

During her first recurrent training session on the Airbus, he had sat in the back of the simulator and texted his girlfriend, or his pending ex-wife. She never actually learned who was on the other end of that texting that was more important than passenger safety.

How the hell they made him a line check airman was beyond her.

DECEMBER 26, 2015

THE FLIGHT WENT more quickly than she had ever experienced. They arrived into Amsterdam and Tom took the landing. The moment she got to her room, she tried to call Kathryn, but she still did not answer, nor did Jackie or the kids. But then, it was 2 am in Seattle. She called John, but the recording wished her a Merry Christmas and said they would be back in the office after Christmas.

Darby dialed the Seattle Police Department. "I'm calling from Amsterdam. I think something has happened to my friend. Can you go check on her?"

"Why do you think something has happened," the officer questioned.

"Because she hasn't answered her phone for like 20 hours."

"I'm sorry ma'am, we cannot help you unless she's been missing for 48 hours. Please try back tomorrow."

Darby's mouth dropped open with the sound of a dial tone. When her eyes opened, three hours had passed, and she fluffed her hair and headed to the bar. Tom was center stage hosting the party.

"Darby doll," he yelled. "Come have a drink with us."

When she approached, he wrapped an arm around her and pulled her onto his lap. "What happens on the road stays on the road," he said laughing.

"Screw you," she said, pushing away from him.

December 27, 2015

"Did you have a fun time last night," Darby asked, not caring what the asshole did, but small talk with the captain always made for a better flight.

"The best," he said. "I could show you how much fun in Mumbai."

Darby rolled her eyes. "Are you seriously such a sleaze?"

"Depends on who's asking."

"Good point," Darby said. "Okay, are you here to screw me, or to get drugs?"

Tom laughed a hearty laugh, as he pushed the thrust levers to full power. "Drugs, baby. Drugs."

December 28, 2015

The next morning Darby wandered up to the crew room, to see what the locals had for sale. Tom was at the far end talking with the doctor. Negotiating more like. Tom glanced her way, and then spoke into the doctor's ear. The doctor's eyes widened and he pulled out his phone and walked to a corner of the room and began to speak with pure excitement.

One hell of a deal's in process, Darby thought. She turned her back to them, and bought purses for her six favorite ladies, and a wallet for Ray.

December 29, 2015

RETURNING TO AMSTERDAM felt like a rerun of the prior 48 hours. This time she opted to hide in her room to sleep, but sleep never found her. She still could not find Kathryn or the girls, but Tom convinced her they had gone skiing and the cell coverage was down. She was not sure why, but she believed him.

Despite the ass taking all the landings, he had been reasonably nice. Perhaps it had something to do with his carrying extra baggage and her willingness to help with the load. She knew better, but she did it anyway.

CHAPTER 24

DIRECTOR ODELL STOOD, slapped the back of his chair, and then kicked it. The chair rolled across the room and slammed into the bookshelf. He had sent orders that she was not to call Global marketing about that damn book. *That fucking little bitch!*

He was not sure who had read it. But he could not risk it being published, or Darby going on any speaking tour. This was a past that would come back and haunt him. He knew one thing—she would continue to cause him grief until she was gone.

Odell picked up the phone and called the secretary. "Can you find Joel, and send him in?"

Within minutes Joel Iverson, the Seattle chief pilot, was standing in the doorway. "How'd it go?" he asked.

"It went." Odell walked over and slid the chair behind his desk and extended his hand to another chair so Joel would take a seat. The director stepped toward the door, closed, and locked it.

Joel sat. He folded his arms and leaned back, crossing a leg. Not really sure what the big deal was. He liked Darby. He liked Ray. Besides, if there was a chance he could be in the movie, he did not want to give up that opportunity.

"We've got a problem," Odell said. "A big fucking problem and her name is Darby Bradshaw." He stood with his hands on hips.

"She'll be fine."

"Bullshit!" Odell snapped. "She didn't listen to you when we ordered her to not contact marketing. I ordered Hughes to shut her down." He walked around his desk and sat heavily. "I think corporate communications and marketing both read that fucking book. Thank God marketing tossed it on my desk."

Odell leaned back, as his right fist formed a ball. "That book cannot go out, or we're both screwed."

"I don't think we can stop publication," Joel said, leaning forward.

"No. But we can have her edit the hell out of it. Call Stan over at ALPO and have him get a message to Darby that her ass will be fired, *without* their protection, if she violates my order. Tell her we have a list of edits and she has to remove Coastal, and anything about fatigue. We'll start there."

"Consider it done. But will that stop her?"

"Hell if I know," he said, "but we've got to keep her out of the media."

"She didn't give names, and Global was de-identified," Joel said. "I'm not sure this will hurt the airline." This book would be equally as much a problem for those above Odell, but Joel didn't care. When they cleaned house, he would move up and slide into a better position. For now, he had to play the game.

"Fuck the airline," Odell said. "This is going to hurt *us*."

"What the hell are we supposed to do?" Joel asked.

The director stared at Joel. Seconds clicked passed before he said, "We have to get rid of the problem." Odell knew there was only one thing that would fix this, and it would be to help Bradshaw take her last breath.

"We could give her a few line checks. Set up training failures. Write her up, three strikes and she's out sorta thing," Joel said.

"She's got too much crap with similar events."

Odell had been the chief pilot when they tried to silence Darby. He thought they had solved the problem, and never expected during his rise to power that he would have to deal with her again. But that bitch disobeyed an order. Nobody disobeyed an order from him.

"I'm history because those assholes made me sign that letter." He stood, walked to the opposite side of the room, and placed his hands on his hips. Then he turned. "We have to get rid of her."

Joel's eyes narrowed. "How?" Was he really serious? Joel may be a climber in his own right, but doing what it took to get to the next level, that was another thing. This was an interesting dilemma, and a test of desire.

"Remove her," Odell said, and returned to his chair. "But first we focus on removing any ties in that book to Global and Coastal."

Joel had always wondered how far he could go. Today he would learn that answer.

"We'll make it look like an accident," Odell said. "Hell, we've had two accidents in the previous two months, it will just be another."

"Are you sure?" Joel asked.

"Your life or theirs," Odell said. "You make the choice."

Chapter 25

December 30, 2015

KATHRYN FOLDED HER arms, and drummed her fingers. This was a 'mother moment' that she was not sure if she were being overprotective, controlling, or just plain unreasonable. "I don't think this is a good idea." They still needed to register them.

"Mom, it's going to be fine," Jessica, said. "We've got our apps, and we'll fly low over the beach and won't get near the airport."

"I promise to keep an eye on them, Mrs. Jacobs," Francine said.

"We'll be fine," Jennifer contributed, placing a hand on her hip. She glanced at Chris and rolled her eyes.

"Don't be rolling your eyes at me, young lady," Kathryn said, exasperated.

Tom had been wrong in giving the kids drones, especially with all the controversy and her responsibility at the FAA attempting to regulate them. Besides, how he could afford them was beyond her. She wanted to help him get his finances under control, not be a contributing factor.

When Kathryn's phone rang, Jennifer said, "Saved by the bell. Love you Mom. Bye."

"Stay away from the airport," she yelled, as they were heading out the door. She pressed *answer* and lifted her phone to her ear.

"Have you heard from Darby?" John asked.

"No, why?" Kathryn glanced out the window. The kids were laughing as they climbed into Francine's car.

"The FBI is meeting her plane upon arrival today."

"Why?" Kathryn turned from the window. Her eyes narrowed. "What would the FBI be doing with Darby's flight?" Giving her full attention to John, she sat at the kitchen table.

"They've been watching airline crews buying stuff in Mumbai for months. Hell, they've been watching them for years. Drugs, products, etc. So far, just personal use so they've looked the other way—until now."

"Darby wouldn't..." Kathryn said, with a wave of her hand relieved that everything would be fine. She stood and pulled a cup from the cupboard.

"I don't think so, either." He cleared his throat, and said, "It's the captain."

"And?" Kathryn said, filling her cup with coffee.

"Tom is the captain. And he's carrying drugs. Lots of them."

Kathryn's eyes widened. "No," she said, as her cup overflowed. She set the pot down and grabbed a towel. "He was scheduled to fly the Hong Kong trip," she said wiping up the mess.

"He traded trips and went on Darby's pattern."

"What the hell's going on?" Kathryn said, more to herself than to John. She pulled the paper off the bulletin board and set it on the table, and sat.

"The million-dollar question," John said.

She wrote *Tom* on the center of the page, below Global. Then added the word—*drugs*. She tapped her pen on the table and then wrote *Bill*. She drew lines between them. Her mind shifted to the girls, and those damned gifts. She wrote *drones* and drew a line back to *Tom*. Then added a dollar sign.

"Kat, you still there?" John said.

"Yes… It's just…"

"It's just that Tom's bringing a couple million dollars' worth of drugs into the country for one of the biggest drug cartels in Seattle."

"Are you sure?" Kathryn asked. She found this conversation unbelievable. But then, nothing surprised her anymore. The fact that Tom had money to buy expensive gifts for everyone now made sense. She wrote *cartel* under the word *drugs*.

"Feds have been watching this cartel for years. When Tom's report came in, they made a connection. Darby being on that flight could implicate her."

"Her mere presence shouldn't implicate her."

"They have videos of her carrying his bag onto the aircraft in Mumbai."

"That doesn't mean…"

"I know," John said, with a sigh. "Tom could be setting her up." He could also be setting up Kathryn. But John would not tell her as much, as she had far too much to worry about.

"Could Bill be behind this?" Kathryn asked, placing a hand to her forehead. She closed her eyes and then squeezed the bridge of her nose. Her imagination had been running wild for days between that suicide pilot investigation and Tom meeting with Bill, and then the gifts. *Why hadn't Darby called her to let her know Tom was on her flight?*

"I wouldn't put anything past Bill. You'll need to find the best attorney you can," John said. "Meet me at the airport when the plane arrives."

"What time do they land?" Kathryn asked, looking at her watch.

"Two hours."

"How am I supposed to get an attorney to meet the plane in two hours?" Kathryn stood and headed for the stairs, then climbed them two at a time.

"The entire crew will be in custody for 24 hours, regardless. You won't need anyone until tomorrow."

"That's comforting," Kathryn said, rushing into her room. She slipped out of her sweatpants. "I've got to get out there. She'll need to know that we're here for her."

"She'll know," John said. "But we've got another issue."

"Which is?" Kathryn asked, digging through her closet. She pulled a pair of slacks off a hanger. She did not need to be on National television in sweats with the kind of press this would draw. Her boyfriend and best friend smuggling drugs would certainly put her in a precarious position at work. She would become the topic of her office gossip. Not that she cared.

Bill has to be behind this, she thought, pulling on her slacks. He had to be setting up Darby.

"Ever hear of Mr. D?" John asked.

Kathryn froze, "*That's* who Tom was carrying for?"

"Yes. Where are the girls?"

"With Francine and Chris, playing with those damn drones."

"Have them stay with us tonight. I'll get security stationed outside our house." John would also have security outside Kathryn's house, as she was equally as much a target.

Kathryn's heart raced, as she grabbed a blouse off the hanger. "Should we get them now?'

"No. Let them have some fun," John said. "But when the news breaks, Christmas vacation will be over for everyone."

"Have you called Ray?" Kathryn asked, sitting on her bed. She pulled on a sock, and grabbed for the other.

"No." John said. "Could you?"

"Coward."

"Smart," he countered.

MR. D. STOOD on the end of the pier, listening to the seagulls cry as they flew overhead. He sucked deep on his cigar, and then blew. He did not turn when footsteps approached, flanked by two sets of eyes watching his back.

The man stood behind him about two feet and said, "There's a small problem, boss."

"So I've heard," Mr. D. said. "How long have you known?"

"Shortly after departure from Mumbai."

"Will he talk?"

"He's a pilot."

Mr. D. mouthed his cigar, and then sucked. "Can you take care of it?" he asked, still staring out over the bay.

"Consider it done."

"Good. Then there doesn't seem to be a problem now, does there?" He took one final drag and tossed his cigar into the water below.

CHAPTER 26

D ARBY GLANCED AT her watch. Ten hours and she would be home. She could ditch the asshole, and tell Kathryn everything he had been up to. Tom taxied onto the runway.

"Global 42, cleared for takeoff runway 18 Right."

Within minutes, Darby called, "Climb check."

"Complete," Tom responded. "By the way, do you think the kids liked the gifts?"

"I'm sure they did," Darby said, pressing the autopilot button to *on*, and turning her attention toward him.

"Good. Got to keep the brats happy."

"How could you afford those anyway?"

"They were a gift."

"From who?" Darby asked.

Tom laughed. He would be damned if he told her. Besides, she would never understand.

Darby's mind flew in all directions bouncing off the corners of her brain. Who the hell would have given drones to Tom? Maybe Bill, but logistically how could he have pulled that off? He couldn't.

Within no time it was Darby's turn for a break. However, despite an all-out effort, she did not sleep. More than the noise of the first class service and the scents of meals cooking in the ovens, nothing felt right and she could not turn off her brain. The gifts Tom gave to the girls, Bill, Tom being on her flight, and her not being able to get ahold of anyone at home was all wrong. She tossed and turned the entire time.

Back in the flight deck, Darby glanced at her watch. They would be landing in just over an hour. Tom sipped the last of his coffee she had brought him, engrossed in a magazine as he turned the page. The other first officer, Jeff, was on his break.

"Can I get you another coffee?" Darby asked. Pressing buttons on her watch, she placed the time back to the Seattle time zone.

"I've had enough. Thanks," he said, eyeing her.

Shivering from the temperature, more so than his look, she reached overhead and turned up the heat in the flight deck. And then she selected the conditioning button on the ECAM control panel to check the temperatures in the entire aircraft. All were in the low 50's.

"What the heck?" she said. "Both hot air trim valves are closed."

"Why didn't we get an EICAS message?" Tom asked.

"Hell if I know," Darby said, reaching for her quick reference manual. "More than that, why haven't the flight attendants been dinging us?" she said, flipping pages. "Okay, it doesn't say anything but 'information only'. But I'm not sure if this addresses if *both* are failed, or not."

"Don't worry, we've got an hour until landing. I'll keep you warm."

Darby rolled her eyes just as the flight attendant call light flashed with the associated chime.

"Flight deck, this is Darby."

"We have a really sick passenger back here," she said. "He's been vomiting all the way from Europe. We just found out."

Tom picked up his microphone and said, "This is the Captain. See if there is a doctor on board. We're also locking down the cockpit."

"Okay," the flight attendant said. "And it's really cold back here."

"Yeah, we're trying to fix the heating system," Tom said. "Let me know if you get a doctor."

The aircraft alerting system, somewhat like text messaging, dinged and a message popped up from dispatch. Darby printed it, and read. "Global, park at the customs ramp. Passengers will be bussed off, and crew is to remain on board."

Tom turned white.

"Don't worry, they probably want your drugs," Darby said, knowing he was thinking the same thing.

"Shut the hell up!" Tom snapped, and then the flight attendant called again.

"We've got a doctor with the passenger. He's on oxygen. How long until we're on the ground?"

"Fifty minutes or so," Darby said. "Let me know if we need an ambulance."

Darby glanced at Tom, his color had returned, but now he was sweating. This time Darby laughed. She knew exactly what was wrong with him. "Don't worry, if you survive, we'll get you a cell with Bill." She began typing a message to dispatch about the sick passenger.

He glanced down and said, "Tell them we need to go to a gate."

Then the master caution light flashed and a bell rang. She pressed the light to silence the bell. A list of messages began filling the EICAS and the thrust on the left engine went from cruise power to max thrust, and then fell back to climb power, and then increased to cruise, again.

Then an amber message that the oil was clogged displayed, and fuel flow went to red line, and then dropped to zero as the engine rolled back. The red master warning light illuminated, as did the engine fire button. Lights flashed, bells rang and then all engine displays on the left engine indication were replaced with amber X's. This time Tom pressed the light cap to silence the noise.

"What's going on?" Tom snapped. "Do the ECAM procedure!"

There were many messages, but she started at the first on the list, which directed her to shut down the engine. Thrust to *idle*. Engine master switch to *off*. She pressed the fire switch. Tom acknowledged each movement, confirming that she had the right switch, with a head nod, while he talked to ATC.

"We've got an engine fire and are descending early. We want radar vectors to Boeing Field," Tom said.

Darby was confirming the steps in the engine failure checklist and said, "Boeing? Why the hell do you want to go to Boeing?"

The airports were 10 miles from each other, SeaTac had all the services they needed and all passengers would be at destination.

"Global 42, cleared to descend to Flight Level 220. Cleared direct to Jackson."

"Let's get Jeff up here," Darby said.

"We're locked down for the medical." Tom snapped. "We can't."

"You're the captain. This is an emergency and you have the authority."

"I said NO!" he ran a hand over his face and wiped it on the front of his shirt, and then held it there for a moment.

"Global 42, Boeing's long runway is closed. We'll vector you into SeaTac. Are you declaring and emergency?"

"Affirm," Tom said, placing a hand to his chest, again.

"Global 42, descend via the GLASR Nine arrival. Expect ILS 16 Left."

Darby responded to air traffic control and then said, "Tom, are you okay?" He was sweating like the pig that she knew he was, hoping she had not gone too far. She did not want him to die. Prison would be so much more fun. "Let me take the plane."

"I'm fine," he snapped, just as the autopilot kicked off, followed by the autothrust disconnecting. "God dammit!" he said, and then called, "Descent and approach check."

Darby read, "Altimeters," and double-checked both. He didn't respond, and the airplane began a slow climb as the speed bled back. "Airspeed!" she yelled.

Tom was not moving. Darby kicked his hand off the thrust and pressed the 'takeover the plane' button on her stick. The airplane announced, "Priority right." Yet, his hand was still on the control stick. Darby got the plane back on profile and speed.

Crossing Jackson at 12,000 feet, ATC said, "Turn left to a heading of 220, and descend to 7000. Altimeter is 29.82."

"Left 220, and leaving 12,000 for 7000," Darby responded. "Be advised, I think my captain is dead."

"Not a good day for Global 42," the controller said. "We've got equipment standing by. Contact tower. Good luck."

Darby called the tower and reported emergency aircraft, and then dinged the flight attendant. When she answered, Darby said, "Get Jeff to come to the flight deck. Immediately!"

"Okay," she said, "I'll see if I can find him."

Darby extended the flaps and pulled the power back manually to fly flaps-one speed. Then she pulled flaps two, and squeaked back her speed, the aircraft bouncing with the turbulence made control difficult.

She was contemplating entering a holding pattern until Jeff arrived, but the fuel was lower than she felt comfortable with. Especially with Boeing field being closed. She needed to get this plane on the ground.

"Global 42, turn left heading 190, descend to 4000 feet. You're cleared for the ILS 16 Left approach. Cleared to land. Be advised, winds are 200 at 35 knots gusting to 40."

Darby responded to ATC as she reached for the gear and selected *down*, and then moved the flap lever to three. The plane bounced wildly, and Tom's hand clung to the stick. His eyes wide open, but he was not moving. Jeff had yet to arrive.

Darby glanced at the total fuel. They only had 10,000 pounds, in spite of the gauge indicating only minutes before that they would be landing with 13,000.

She did not have many options. She needed to land, whether Jeff came up or not. She rehearsed the missed approach procedures as she intercepted the localizer and then the glideslope, just in case. She read and responded to the landing checklist, out loud.

Her plane was cocked into the wind, and coming at the runway at an angle. Between the wind and the failed engine, she battled control of the massive aircraft. She had never been trained for a 40-knot crosswind, let alone with an engine failure.

Seconds later the airplane jolted. Bells began ringing and lights flashed, as the right engine failed. "Oh shit!"

She was on short final without power and the plane was falling like a rock. "Dual Engine failure," she said, to the tower.

"Global, state your intentions."

"I'm comin' in. My intentions are to live!"

Darby created a trajectory to the airport, and wished to hell she had followed through and taken those glider lessons. She held tight and pulled back on the stick to make the runway.

Without engine power she would not have stall protection, or would she? She thought about raising the gear. But then she was not even sure if the gear would come up without engine power. What about flaps? Hell if she knew. A moment of panic grabbed her senses. She could not remember *anything*. But she knew how to fly.

"Come on baby, you can make it," she said to her plane.

CHAPTER 27

JACKIE HANDED LINDA a cup of tea and sat on the couch beside her. CNN was on the television. They were watching *Breaking News* of a Global flight arriving from Amsterdam with drug smuggling pilots. Tom and Darby. The FBI was stationed at the end of the field as they waited for the 'big' drug bust.

"I can't believe this is occurring on Darby's flight," Linda said.

"Nor can I. It's hard to believe Tom would do something like this." Jackie sipped her tea.

"You're too trusting," Linda said. "I never imagined Grant could have done what he did either."

"I know sweetie." Jackie touched her friend's arm. "I kind of knew something was up with Tom. I overheard John on the phone the other night."

"About what?" Linda turned her attention from the television.

"I don't know. When the time is right, he'll tell me."

"Niman wouldn't sleep until he spilled his guts." Linda chuckled. She set her cup on the table.

Jackie placed her cup of tea next to Linda's and then turned toward her friend. She lowered her voice in a conspiratorial whisper, despite that nobody was in the house. "I have a secret weapon."

Linda grinned. "Do tell."

"Well, see that flight coming in?" Cameras were now on Darby's plane in the distance. "Darby is mush. She always knows everything because of Kathryn and John." Jackie grinned. "All I have to do is wait for her to get off the plane. Or in this case out of prison." Jackie laughed at her joke. "Then she'll tell all."

"Wouldn't John and Kathryn tell you if you asked?"

"Oh, of course they would," Jackie said, reaching for the remote. "It's just so much more fun interrogating Darby. There's usually alcohol involved, and tons of laughter." She pressed a button and raised the volume.

"*We've just got word the flight coming in has a failed engine. The right engine has died!*" the reporter said. Richard Quest was in Seattle for the big drug bust episode, and narrating the unraveling story of this arrival. "*When an engine fails on a high powered aircraft such as the Airbus A330, half the power is gone! This means the pilot must be on his sharpest game. Missing no cues he must…*"

"Oh my God," Linda said, covering her mouth.

"Don't worry. Darby's been trained for this, and there are three of them up there," Jackie said, not feeling as convincing as she sounded.

The flight had been long and Darby had to be exhausted. They all were. Besides, she had read Darby's book and knew pilots were not trained as well as they could be in these automated jets. She and Greg had many long talks about that exact issue, as well. A tear worked its way into her eye. She missed him so much. But she pulled her focus back to the television.

"I wasn't talking about the flight," Linda said. "What the hell is *Quest* doing here? This drug thing must be far bigger than I thought."

"Really?" Jackie glanced at Linda, and back to the television. "I shouldn't have been joking about Darby going to prison. What if—"

"I wouldn't worry." Linda said. "She's got a team that won't let her down."

Jackie nodded.

"We've just had incredible news. The flight limping in on one engine is having problems. Wait… Wait. Yes, it's been confirmed," Quest said. *"The pilot is dead! The pilot is dead! The pilot has officially died! Now there is no pilot on the plane, just two co-pilots. Can they handle it? We have no idea what is going on with that plane, but frankly, I for one, am worried."*

Cameras zoomed in on the Airbus, A330. The plane jerked, pitched up, and then began descending more quickly.

"What just happened?" Linda asked.

Jackie shrugged. "I don't know. But it doesn't look good."

"The plane has no engines! Without power and the dead pilot, I fear the worst," Quest said. *"This is absolutely the worst quest I've been on—from drug bust to a pilotless airliner without engines. All we can do now is wait."*

CHAPTER 28

KATHRYN STOOD IN the tower waiting for Darby's plane to land. When she heard that the plane was limping in on one engine, she worried, but when Darby said, "I think my captain is dead," a chill hit hard and wormed into her core.

If anyone could handle a single engine flight, Darby could. *But Tom is dead?* Kathryn folded her arms and attempted to force her foot to remain still, to no avail.

"Can I borrow those?" she asked the controller pointing at a pair of binoculars sitting on the table.

He nodded, as he spoke to Darby's aircraft, wishing her luck.

Kathryn lifted the glasses and found her plane. She was on profile, looking good. Kathryn glanced to the south ramp—the welcoming committee waited. A lot of good it would do for Tom. She shifted back toward Darby's plane.

The Airbus jerked, but then got back on course. But the pitch was wrong, and the plane was no longer on a proper glided path.

"Dual engine failure," blared over the radio.

"Global, state your intentions," the controller said.

What did he think her intentions were?

"I'm comin' in. My intentions are to live!" Darby said.

A smile spread across Kathryn's face, and a tear filled her eye as she watched. Her body tensed. "Fly Darby, fly," she whispered.

DARBY PULLED BACK on the stick in a final attempt to reach the runway. She was too low. The plane was sinking too quickly. Then a gust of wind lifted her plane, and her heart. Smiling, Darby had made it.

That moment was short lived when the landing gear hit the retaining wall. The plane jerked left and the nose slammed into the runway. Sliding sideways, the A330 slammed between two Alaska 737 jets in line for takeoff, pushing them over like toys as her beast headed toward the cargo ramp.

Her head jerked forward and aft, and sideways, but she was alive and did everything she could to stop the movement, smashing the breaks, to no avail. She had no brakes. The plane would not stop.

Darby covered her head with her arms and ducked, just before impact. Screams from beyond the flight deck door fought with the screeching of metal and breaking of glass. The nose of the plane pressed inward, pushing her against her seat and squeezing life out of her. Fire exploded and then she felt nothing.

CHAPTER 29

KATHRYN'S WORLD STOPPED and life went into slow motion. A surreal vision played out in front of her, as Darby's plane slammed into the end of the runway, bounced, and rolled left, breaking the left wing off. The Airbus slid across the ramp knocking into planes as if they were bowling pins. Then one explosion followed another. First one aircraft, and then the next, and then Darby's.

Bells rang, someone screamed, and controllers were barking orders at other aircraft. Kathryn could not move. She was that nine-year old watching her uncle John and her brother's plane crash. "Noooo!" she yelled. Then she was back in the tower, and it was Bill's plane she watched. No. It was Darby, and she ran for the elevator. Pounding on the button tears streamed down her face. She had been here before.

"This cannot be happening!" Kathryn yelled pounding on the elevator. Her phone rang and she opened it.

"Where are you?" John asked.

"In the tower. I'm on my way," she yelled, as the door opened and she stepped in.

"Don't go. Stay there," John said. "There's nothing you can…"

Kathryn hung up. She would do something. She had to do something. She would get to Darby. The elevator opened on the ground floor, and she ran across the parking lot to her car. But she could not find the key. Her hands trembled and her legs shook. She found her key.

The hand on her shoulder made her jump, and she turned.

"Sweetheart, there's nothing you can do," John said. "Stay."

Kathryn pushed him. But he did not move.

"Leave me alone. I have to get to her. She needs me!" She turned her back to John and fumbled with the key.

John grabbed her shoulders and turned her toward him. "No. You do not want to be there."

Kathryn hit his chest with a fist. "Leave me alone!" she cried, and then hit his chest again and again.

He pulled her into an embrace. Kathryn's legs gave out, and he held her before she toppled to the ground. He held her tight, and she sobbed.

"This cannot be happening. Darby *cannot* be dead," she chanted. Her body convulsed as she worked to catch her breath between sobs.

The scent of jet fuel, fire, and death filled the air. Bringing the night that Greg's plane crashed back into view, Kathryn pulled from John, turned, and vomited.

John stood by her side, and lifted her hair, rubbing her back. "We have to be strong for the kids."

Kathryn knew that. She always had to be strong. But who was going to be strong for her? That was Darby's job. How the hell was she going to survive this? How the hell would any of them go on without Darby? She stood upright and wiped her mouth on her sleeve. "John… she might be…"

"There's always a chance," John said, his voice cracking. Tears filled his eyes and Kathryn gave into his loss, too, and opened her arms for him.

They all loved Darby. "She can't be gone. She just can't be," Kathryn said.

"Let me take you to our house," John whispered. "Jackie will be there. She'll need you. The kids will need you."

He was right. Kathryn pulled back, but the look in his eyes was one she had never seen. He, too, was haunted from the past, taking over the present. Something unspoken, but evil drifted in the air between them, mixed with the scent of death.

"I'll drive myself."

CHAPTER 30

BOTH HANDS WENT to Jackie's mouth. She wanted to close her eyes, but she could not remove them from the television.

"This cannot be happening," Linda cried. She reached over and grabbed Jackie's arm and held tight.

"She'll make it. She has to," Jackie said gripping Linda's hands.

But the worst vision played out in high fidelity. Both Linda and Jackie lost their husbands in similar crashes. The only difference was, they did not watch the accidents unfold on television. The plane hit the runway, slammed into two aircraft on the taxiway spinning them sideways.

Jackie screamed, "Nooooo! Oh my God. This can't be happening." She stood and ran to the television, placing a hand on the screen and cried, "Darby. No. Please God no. Not Darby!" Then sobbing, she dropped to her knees.

Linda rushed to Jackie, dropped to the floor and wrapped her arms around her. She held her tight. Tears filled Linda's eyes and she, too, shook violently. Both women's nightmares resurfaced in the greatest terror they could ever imagine.

"Not again," Linda murmured.

"No. Please God. No!" Jackie cried. "This can't be happening!"

The plane finally came to a stop, explosion after explosion, and the only life was that of fire, climbing, crawling and eating everything in its path. Emergency equipment had been standing by and foam covered the aircraft. Quest's lips were moving but Jackie no longer heard anything he said. She was in a silent world looking into another realm.

"Jackie!" a voice yelled.

She turned her head.

"Kat!" Jackie cried. "Darby… she…"

"I know sweetheart," Kathryn said, dropping to the floor beside her. Crying, she embraced her friends.

With tears flowing, Linda hugged them both and said, "We have to be strong for the kids."

"And we will," Kathryn said. "John's at the site, and he'll keep us updated. This doesn't mean Darby is dead. She could survive. We'll be there for her."

The horror of Greg's charred body filled Jackie's mind, and she cried all the harder—this time for Darby.

For all those who say experience makes life easier, they were wrong when it came to death. Greg's death would never help her deal with this. Nothing would ever help her get over the vision of Darby's crash, or the thought of what would become of Darby's life if she lived.

"Mom?" Francine said. "What's going on?"

Kathryn, Jackie and Linda jerked their heads toward the entryway.

Francine, Jessica, Jennifer and Chris, stood there with mouths hanging open. Looks of fear, confusion and concern etched on their faces.

"Mom, did someone die?" Jessica asked.

CHAPTER 31

LINDA STOOD IN the corner of the emergency room waiting area, standing guard with Kathryn and Jackie. John had gone home with the kids. Between the three aircraft involved, 435 people died, and there were 42 survivors, all critically injured, without much hope. Darby was one of them. She was still in the emergency room and nobody was allowed to see her. Niman was in with Darby watching, standing by if they needed any help. He had promised to call the minute anything changed.

"This cannot be happening again," Kathryn said, dropping to the couch beside Jackie. Tears filled her eyes once again. "This is not fucking fair!"

Jackie reached over and grabbed a hand, and squeezed. Kathryn had been silent for hours, lost in her own world. Linda moved across the room and placed a hand on her shoulder.

"It's not fair," Linda said, handing her a box of tissues. Not sure what she should do, Linda told them what they all wanted to believe, "Darby *is* going to be fine."

"Darby's not going to be fine!" Jackie snapped. "Don't you get it? She is going to end up exactly like Greg!" Jackie sobbed. Linda reached for her, but she waved her away.

Kathryn jumped to her feet pulling her hand from Jackie's. "Don't say that! Don't you *ever* say that!" Kathryn yelled. "You're wrong!" She turned and walked across the room and folded her arms. She stood in front of the window as an ambulance screamed down the street, and pulled into the emergency entrance.

Linda glanced from Jackie to Kathryn. She was worried about them. She was also not sure how to manage their breakdown if the worst happened, and handle the kids too. But often when a parent breaks, the children would step up and take the role of strength. She was not sure how this would end, but she was glad she could be with them now.

She had asked Niman if he minded if she stayed a few months to help her friends. He said that he would expect nothing less. He had been a bachelor for a long time, and a few more months would be just fine. They would do whatever it took to help them.

Jackie stopped sobbing and blew her nose. "Kat, I didn't mean…"

Linda sat beside Jackie and said, "She knows, sweetheart."

Linda loved Darby, but this was different for Kathryn and Jackie. Darby was part of their family, and had been for a long time. If Darby died, a darkness would fill their souls that would more than likely become an unrecoverable sorrow. Shifting her attention back to Kathryn, she was not sure what to do. For now, just wait with them. Be there. Show them they were not alone, and be their strength no matter what the news.

Kathryn placed her forehead against the window, and then both hands followed, as if she were looking out at something. Despite Linda glancing to see what that could be, she knew the stance was more for support. Then Kathryn stood upright, placed one hand over her mouth, and the other moved to her stomach and then dropped to the floor on her knees.

"Kathryn!" Jackie screamed, and flew to her friend. Within seconds she was kneeling on the floor beside her. "I'm sorry!" Jackie cried, "I'm so sorry. Darby is going to be fine. She is!"

Linda rushed to Kathryn's side, as well.

Kathryn was sobbing, trying to catch her breath. Her hands were ice cold. Linda jumped up, and opened a cabinet against the wall, and pulled out a blanket. She moved quickly and wrapped it around Kathryn's shoulders.

"Something's wrong with her!" Jackie cried. "Help!"

"Get a nurse," Linda told Jackie.

She knelt in front of Kathryn and Jackie rushed to the reception desk. Kathryn was hyperventilating and having a difficult time catching her breath.

"Kathryn," Linda said, taking both her hands and speaking calmly, "look at me." Kathryn complied as she gulped, and fought for air.

"Kat, I want you to breathe with me," Linda said. "You're hyperventilating. You're going to be fine."

Linda made short, blowing, breaths. Kathryn followed. Together they blew, "Whoo. Whoo. Whoo."

Within seconds she had Kathryn breathing normal again. Jackie returned with the nurse, and Linda said, "We're good now." She looked at the nurse and asked, "Can we get something to relax her? I'll authorize it."

Linda and Jackie helped Kathryn to the couch, and the nurse returned with a small cup holding two pills, and a cup of water.

"Thank you," Linda said, and turned her head toward Kathryn. "Valium. It will make you feel better."

"Can I have a martini too?" Kathryn said, taking one of the pills. She popped it into her mouth. "I don't know what happened. I just..."

"Shhhh." Linda said, reaching a hand to Kathryn's head, she tucked a strand of hair behind her ear. "This is a trauma to every part of your psyche. Are you sure you don't want this other pill?"

Kathryn shook her head. "I want to be here."

"Can I have it?" Jackie asked, with tears streaming down her face.

"Of course," Linda said, standing. She handed the other pill to Jackie. "I'll get you some water."

"I'm good," Jackie said, with a slight wave of a hand. She popped the pill into her mouth and swallowed. Then they all turned their attention toward the door that swung wide as Niman walked through. Once in the room, he placed his hands on his hips.

A quick glance at Kathryn and then Jackie, he returned his attention to Linda. Their eyes locked. He did not have to say a thing for Linda to know the worst had happened.

CHAPTER 32

WHEN KATHRYN SAW the look that Niman and Linda exchanged, her vision pulled back from the room, as if she were behind a wall of glass. Watching, but not part of the hell that unfolded before her. Her world was torn apart like she never thought it could be. She had never imagined the kind of pain she felt when Greg died, short of losing her daughters. Yet she had been wrong. She was living it now.

Darby was such a huge part of her life. She had been with her through every up and down, during the birth of her babies and the death of Greg. When Bill tried to kill her, and John said Darby was dead, Kathryn never believed it. She had been right then, but now...

She turned from Niman and she closed her eyes, as a vision of the plane crash took over all her senses. Tears filled her eyes and broke free through the slits, leaking to her cheeks. Swiping them away, she prayed to God the Valium would help take the edge off soon, wishing she had taken both. Hell, she wanted the entire bottle. She needed Darby. But Niman. That look.

She was no longer standing outside, watching the scene play out. Kathryn was back in the center of hell. She opened her eyes and the room began spinning, and her ears began ringing. She covered her ears, and then the window to her world closed into darkness.

"Sweetheart," Jackie said, "are you okay?"

Kathryn opened her eyes and was lying on the floor with a pillow, a blanket over her body, and an ice bag on her head. She pushed away the bag, and sat up. She winced when touching the spot where the ice had been. "What happened?"

"You fainted," Linda said, touching her shoulder. "Fell to the floor."

"We were so worried," Jackie whispered, kneeling at her side.

"How long was I out?"

"Three minutes," Linda said. "How's your head?"

Who the hell cares about my head? Kathryn inhaled a deep breath and asked the question she feared most, "Darby? Is Darby…"

"Alive," Linda said.

"Oh my God." Kathryn felt fresh tears blooming. She had feared the worst. Yet Darby was alive. As long as there was life, there was nothing they could not deal with.

Niman extended a hand, and helped her to her feet. He then guided her to the couch. "Is your vision clear?" he asked, kneeling in front of her and shining a light into one eye, and then the other.

"I'm fine," Kathryn said. "I don't know what happened." She was stronger than this. She had to be strong. Darby was alive and she would need her. "Can we see her?"

"When was the last time you had something to eat?" Niman asked. "Any of you?"

Kathryn glanced at her friends, at her watch and then said, "For me, maybe 17 hours ago." Then she eyed Niman. Why couldn't they see her? Who cared about food? And then her heart sank, filling her stomach—Darby was burned like Greg.

She was disfigured. She would be a charred body. Blind. All the visions of Greg's final hours came flooding to Kathryn. Then Kathryn breathed deep. None of that mattered. They could do skin grafts. Keep her pain free. As long as Darby could think and talk, the world would be a better place. Darby would be sure that the world was filled with laughter and love, as long as she was alive.

"Kathryn?" Niman said, touching her shoulder.

She startled. "Huh? What?" she said, bringing him into focus.

"Are you sure you're okay?" Niman said, "We lost you for a moment."

"I'm fine. Really." Or she would be, as soon as she was standing beside Darby.

Niman stood and said, "Okay. Good." He glanced over his shoulder and said, "Let me take you all for a gourmet cafeteria midnight snack, and I will fill you in on everything we know."

CHAPTER 33

KATHRYN SAT IN a booth beside Jackie, stirring her soup and trying to find the strength to eat. Niman and Linda sat across from them. All Kathryn wanted to do was be with Darby. But the reality was, she was not sure she could handle it. Not yet. The more she thought about Darby being burned, the more horrific that vision became. She pushed that thought out of her mind. No matter what Darby looked like now, she would always be beautiful.

"Here's the deal," Niman said. "I'm not talking until everyone takes at least three bites."

Linda smiled and winked at Kathryn, and then picked up her sandwich. Jackie hesitated and then stabbed her salad, and Kathryn lifted the spoon to her lips. The warmth of the soup went down easily, and she was glad to have the moment of doing something normal. Especially since life might never be normal again.

They ate silently, and the food tasted good. Better than she had thought it would. The three-bite mandate turned into a full meal. Each of them got into the flow of eating. Nutrition they would need to get through this would fuel their bodies. Kathryn glanced between Linda and Niman, as she slid the last bite of chicken noodle soup into her mouth. She set down the spoon with a clank, lifted her napkin and wiped her lips.

"Yummy. Now spill," Kathryn said, setting her napkin over her bowl.

"Welcome back," Linda said, and Kathryn returned a forced smile.

Niman finished his coffee, set down his cup and said, "Darby is in a coma."

Jackie began crying, again. "A coma? But she'll wake up. Right?"

"I hope so," Niman said. "We don't think she's brain dead, but we can't be sure."

"What do you mean you can't be sure?" Kathryn said.

"The MRI and brain mapping are not showing anything."

"Are you saying she doesn't have brain function?" Kathryn asked flatly.

Niman shook his head. "It doesn't appear so. But then, during brain mapping, we saw activity. It was short lived. Came in a burst, then gone. But, it was like *nothing* I have ever seen before."

"So that's good?" Kathryn said, feeling hope that Darby's burst would be enough to bounce her out of this. She had heard people awoke from comas after years of silence.

"It is good. So much so, that my hospital has allowed me to transfer to Seattle. I have approval to watch Darby's case as long as necessary."

"Oh Niman," Linda said, tears filling her eyes. "Thank you."

"They may have frowned, had I told them I knew the patient. But, we need to be here," Niman said. "I've rented a furnished apartment, two blocks from here." Linda reached over and touched his hand.

Emotion overwhelmed Kathryn, that these two people would disrupt their lives for them. She placed both her hands over Linda's and Niman's and squeezed. "Thank you both so much." Their support meant more than anything she could imagine.

And Darby is alive.

"Should we worry that her brain activity stopped?" Jackie asked.

"It would be better if it hadn't," he said. "But we've identified electrical impulses leaving her brain. That's a good sign."

"So, what's next?" Kathryn asked.

"We watch for signs. Consciousness is predicated on awareness and arousal, and—"

"What? Like she's aware that we're here?" Jackie said.

Kathryn squeezed Jackie's hand, hoping that would keep her quiet so Niman could complete a thought. But the truth was, this confused the hell out of her also.

"Awareness is when we receive and process information communicated by our five senses. This process encompasses both physiological and psychological factors." Niman spoke slowly. "The psychological factor is governed by her mental process, whereas her physiological component depends upon the functioning of her brain's chemical makeup."

"But…" Jackie began, with a confused look.

"What about arousal?" Kathryn asked, "Does she have all senses?"

"Good question," Niman said. The arousal I speak of consists of Darby's primitive responsiveness to stimuli, which is maintained by what we call the reticular activating system."

"Her what?" Jackie asked.

"We all have one. The reticular activating system, often called the RAS, is more of a network of structures which include the brainstem, along with the medulla, thalamus, and a myriad of nerve pathways."

"What does this all mean?" Linda asked.

"Darby's injury has interfered with the functioning of her cerebral cortex, in addition to the function of brainstem structures." He sighed, clearly searching his thoughts before he continued. He ran a hand through his hair and said, "She looks like she's sleeping. But she has zero brain function. Other than one burst on the scan, she appears brain dead. We don't know."

"She's a vegetable?" Jackie asked.

"No," Kathryn snapped. "She is not brain dead or a vegetable! There would not have been any function if she were. You said there was function. You saw it. Right?"

"Yes, I saw it and was able to document it," he said. "That's why they are allowing me to work this case."

"For research," Jackie snapped, "You don't think she'll come out of this. Do you?"

"I'm hoping that time will heal Darby's brainstem and cerebral cortex. We don't know exactly why she's in a coma. However, the brain is a miraculous thing."

"And, she can hear everything we say," Kathryn said. "Right?"

"Some studies have identified that," Niman said.

"Good." Kathryn turned to Jackie and said, "And with that, we are not going to say anything negative in her room. Got it?"

Jackie nodded, and blew her nose on a napkin.

"We'll make a schedule, we'll take turns. We'll sit with her and make her laugh until she wakes the hell up," Kathryn said. "I'm going to need both of you. I have to find out what happened, and why. But I don't want her in that room alone."

"I'm in," Linda said. "I'm here for as long as you need me."

"Me too," Jackie said nodding. "And we'll bring the kids."

"Is that okay?" Kathryn asked Niman. "I mean, with the kids in there."

Niman looked at Linda, for help. If the situation were not so grave, Kathryn would have laughed at the brilliance of this man, and the deer in the headlights look at the mention of children.

"The kids would be good for Darby," Linda said. "But the question is if it would be as good for them."

"This is going to be hard on them all," Jackie said. "Especially for the girls."

Kathryn nodded. "But, I think not seeing her would create more fear."

"You're right," Linda said. "Let's bring them in to see her while I'm there. I'll get a feel for how they're doing with it all. If they aren't handling it well, we'll go to plan B."

CHAPTER 34

KATHRYN WAS THE first to reach the room, but she hesitated at the door. Sucking a deep breath, she found strength and walked to the side of the bed. Darby looked like she had been in a bar fight, and lost. She was bruised, a lump growing out one side of her head, stitches across her forehead, and her right eye swollen closed. And she was bald.

They had shaved her head during testing in the event they needed to do surgery. There had been swelling on the brain, but they drained it. Now they had nothing to fix, so healing would be up to Darby.

Niman was right. For all intents and purposes, she was sleeping. Despite external damage to her body, she looked peaceful. This was not fair, but Kathryn refused to cry. She had cried too many tears. Now, tears would be a waste of energy. Everything she had would go into making Darby whole, or at least comfortable. Darby's death had been Kathryn's greatest fear. As long as she was breathing there was life, and hope.

Kathryn touched her hand, and a million Darby memories flooded her mind. A life of Darby flashed before her eyes and Kathryn smiled, the first real smile since this happened. She would use everything she had to figure out why this happened.

"She looks good," Jackie said, standing beside Kathryn.

Kathryn jumped, not realizing Jackie was there. "She does," she said, touching her forehead, again.

"Thank God she's not burned." Linda stepped to the opposite side of the bed and said, "I don't know how she survived, let alone the fire not touching her."

Niman moved beside Linda, "We're all wondering that. Every other patient was severely burned. Even Tom was…" He glanced at Kathryn and she gave him a nod that it was okay. Niman continued. "He was unidentifiable without dental records. They were two feet apart."

"It was as if she had a guardian angel protecting her," Jackie said.

"She deserves an angel," Kathryn said. "Oh my God! Ray! Where's Ray?"

"The hospital was ordered not to allow anyone in this wing unless they were family," Niman said. "I've been inundated with everything, I completely forgot about him."

"That poor man," Kathryn said. "I forgot too." She grabbed her purse and pulled out her phone. Moving by the window it came alive. Two calls from John and four from Ray. She pressed Ray's number without listening to his messages.

"Kathryn?" Ray answered on the first ring. "They won't let me in. They won't let me see her! How is she? Is she…"

"She's alive," Kathryn said. "Where are you?"

"On the street, across from the main entrance. I tried to sneak into the emergency room, but they had security remove me. Twice. They said the third time I would be in jail."

"Go to the emergency room. Stand outside the door. I will send Niman down to get you," she said, looking at Niman. He nodded and quickly left the room.

"Thank you," Ray said, choking on his words. "I just…"

"I know," Kathryn said. "I'm sorry I didn't get ahold of you sooner. We just now came into the room."

"Is… is she burned?"

"No, but…" Kathryn touched Darby's cheek. "She's in a coma. Niman will fill you in on the way up."

Kathryn pressed *off* on her phone, and then held Darby's hand. "So, Miss Darby, I knew you were tired, but this is a little much. We're going to give you the 24 hours of sleep you deserve, and then I want your butt out of bed, tomorrow." Kathryn placed her hand on hips and said, "24 hours."

Linda smiled at Kathryn. "I'm thinking we should give her at least two days to sleep."

"Okay, 48 hours it is. But that's it," Kathryn said. "Darby, Ray's on his way up now. He's been sitting out in the cold for hours waiting to see you. As if you didn't know, he's definitely worth waking up for."

"I love you Darby," Jackie said, fighting back tears.

"We all do," Linda said.

"When Ray gets here, we'll go and get some sleep, and give Ray some time," Kathryn said. "We'll be back tomorrow."

In no time Ray rushed into the room. He looked like shit. Just like the rest of them. He froze, as if he were afraid to approach the bed. Kathryn moved to the doorway and gave him a hug. "Go talk to her," she said, and left the room.

Kathryn found a cot, and wheeled it into the room, on the opposite side of Darby's bed.

"Are you okay if we leave tonight?" Kathryn asked. He nodded, and Kathryn added, "We're going to get some sleep. Starting tomorrow, we're all taking turns hanging with our favorite lady."

Ray nodded, again. Tears streaming down his face, one hand moved to Darby's forehead, as the other held one of her hands to his lips.

"You may get first watch," Kathryn said, "But tomorrow you'll get some sleep. Okay?"

Kathryn doubted he heard a word she said. She glanced at her friends, and then looked toward the door. They nodded. She touched Darby's foot, and squeezed. "See you tomorrow Darby. I love you." She headed toward the door, and her friends followed.

Once outside the room, Kathryn said, "Could we all meet at Jackie's tomorrow for breakfast? That way we can get some sleep, and be there for the girls in the morning. They'll have lots of questions." Taking Linda's hand she said, "I really need your help with them."

"Of course," Linda said. "But tomorrow, you mean today, right?"

Kathryn glanced at her watch, and nodded.

"I like that plan," Jackie said. "John sent me a text. The kids know that Darby's alive, but they are all really worried."

"It's going to be hard," Linda said, "but children are more resilient than most adults."

BEFORE KATHRYN LEFT the hospital, she had to ask about survivors. After a phone call, she learned there were now only nine people involved in the crash still alive. Darby was one of them, and in the best condition as well. Which said nothing for the other patients. Far too many families would be moving into the New Year without hope. The missing plane, the flight that crashed into the mountains killing all, and now this—*why?*

She could not push Bill out of her mind. He kept working his way in, whenever she thought about the crashes.

Logistically, there was no way he could have been involved in any of this, but the knot in her gut told her otherwise. Kathryn needed to talk to John. This crash had to be connected to those other events. Or did it? She glanced at her watch—2 am. That talk would have to wait until morning.

CHAPTER 35

KATHRYN HAD CLIMBED into bed at 2:30 am, and four hours later she dropped her feet to the floor in an attempt to stomp out her nightmares. Planes crashed in her dreams and she doubted she had slept more than a few minutes. She yawned, while forcing herself to stand, and then worked her way to the kitchen to make a cup of coffee. When she opened the cupboard, she realized she had forgotten to buy some.

In Darby's mind, this would be sacrilegious neglect. But there was a 24-hour Starbucks on the way to Jackie's house. She glanced at her cell phone—6:42 am. She sent John a text—*Who's up? Going to Starbucks. Want anything?*

John's reply came immediately—*Me. Coffee. Large. Black. Text me 5 out.*

Kathryn slid into her sweat pants and pulled a sweatshirt over her head. She slipped her feet into her shoes and then tied the laces. With a deep breath she glanced at the paper hanging on the bulletin board. She walked over to it and wrote *Darby* on the page. Then she grabbed her purse and keys, and ran out the door.

Pulling into Starbucks drive-through, she contemplated getting everyone cocoa, but thought better of it. By the time everyone awoke, the drinks would be cold. So, Kathryn placed John's and her order.

The barista repeated Kathryn's order. "Okay, we've got two drinks this morning. A Venti coffee, black. And a Venti double cup raspberry mocha, with two inches of steamed heavy cream. Will that be all?"

"That's all," she replied.

Kathryn pulled up to the window and the barista said, "Where's Darby?"

Tears filled Kathryn's eyes. "She's in the hospital." Kathryn handed the woman her credit card. She had inadvertently ordered Darby's drink, keeping her alive anyway she could.

"Oh my God! You keep that," the woman said, not taking the card, but passing a cup through the window. "What happened? Is she okay?"

"Plane crash," Kathryn said, placing John's coffee in the cup holder. "But she's going to be fine."

"Oh. Thank God," she said, handing her the second cup. "Tell her we all love her, and will be sending our prayers."

Holding her coffee, she put her car into gear and pulled out into traffic. Driving down the street, Kathryn sipped Darby's drink. Nothing ever tasted as good.

Darby had been sent to Swedish due to the lack of burns. Whereas all the other crash survivors had been sent to Harborview, the normal trauma unit. Greg had taken his last breath at Harborview. This time, it would be different for Darby.

Kathryn was glad that Darby was in a different hospital. She was not sure if Jackie would be able to survive the memories of her last days with Greg, if she had to walk the same halls.

Within no time Kathryn arrived at Jackie's house, and pulled into her driveway. John was sitting on the front porch, which was good because she had forgotten to text him. The house behind him was dark. She put her car into park, and he was on his feet moving toward the car before she could get out. He wasn't wearing a coat, and snow was lightly falling. She left the car running, unlocked the passenger door, and turned up the heat.

"How's everyone doing?" Kathryn asked, as John climbed into the right seat.

She had not talked to her daughters since she had been to the hospital, afraid she would not be able to hold it together. She had conviction and strength, but still doubted her ability to contain her emotions. Something that would come with time.

"Not good. It was a late night," John said, lifting his coffee. He took a long sip, and then added, "Chris crashed… uh, he fell asleep on the couch at midnight. The girls were up until Jackie got home."

Kathryn sipped, moments ticked by with nothing but the hum of the heater. She finally said, "What the hell is going on?"

"I'm not sure. I didn't want to leave the kids, but I've got the best guys working the case." He sighed. "It appears there were some mechanical issues going on prior to arrival and Tom…" He glanced at Kathryn.

"It's okay," she said.

"From what Darby said on the radio, he died before the crash." He lifted his cup towards is mouth, but before he drank he asked, "What killed him?"

"Heart attack." Kathryn said. "It had to be."

"I'm not so sure. He was about to be brought in on drug smuggling charges, with the potential to identify one of the biggest cartels in Seattle. The fourth largest worldwide."

Kathryn's eyes widened. How did her city get the fourth largest drug cartel in the world? "Well, the cartel was not on the plane, and they had no access from the departure point in Amsterdam." She hesitated and then added, "Clearly there were problems with that plane, with two engine failures."

"We have a video of something flying into the second engine," John said.

"A bird?"

"I don't know." John reached up and turned down the heat. "But then we don't know if that engine was already having problems like the other. If it were, a bird could have finished the job."

Kathryn set her coffee into the holder. She folded her arms and stared out the window. She did not want to think of the worst, but it was hard not to. "What about the suicide crash? Any news?"

"Nothing confirmed."

Kathryn nodded. "John…" she worked hard trying to find the words. He would think she was crazy, but her gut rarely lied. "What about Tom's visit to the prison?" she asked, staring out the window. She sighed, and turned sideways to face him. "I cannot get this connection out of my mind. Tom was not scheduled for that flight. He was in deep financial trouble. He was upset about losing his pension. He had met with Bill. I'm just feeling really uncomfortable about all this."

John nodded. "Everything you said is on the forefront for me too."

"Where do we go from here?" Kathryn glanced toward the house. "How do we conduct this investigation when we are so deeply connected to all the players? Bill. Tom. Darby in the hospital. The kids…"

"Hell, Kat. I don't know."

She reached over and placed a hand on his. The black circles under his eyes indicated he had not slept either. And the pain etched within his eyes told how much this hurt him, too. This was his watch, and the people he loved were in pain.

Trying to lighten the mood, she said, "Maybe we could send them to camp." Still thankful that during Bill's events, the kids had been out of harm's way.

"When does school pick up again?"

"Three days."

"That'll help," he said. "Jackie's taken a leave. She'll keep an eye on them when they get home. I'll work the case. I want you part of it, but…"

Kathryn waited him out. 'I want you, but…' was never as promising as it sounded.

John looked into her eyes and said, "They might try to block you from this one. Your connection to Tom and Bill… There is rumbling that you might be, let's just say connected."

There was no response Kathryn could give to that statement. They were right about one thing—she was connected. But not in the manner they assumed. She was connected by life strings to the people involved in many ways. Only one of those connections she wished she could sever. *Time to change the subject.*

"We can't leave Darby alone in that hospital," Kathryn said.

"We won't."

"Not to be paranoid," Kathryn said, "but, Darby's book was going to be huge. They were paying her a ton of money to publish it. And the chief pilot, who put that letter in her file, had his henchmen call her in and order her to delete anything that said she had worked for Coastal."

"Go on," John said.

"Then they ordered her to report to the regional director, instead of her chief pilot." Kathryn tapped a finger on the lid of her cup and said, "Why would they fight her book? They've got a safety management system to put in place, training issues, and a plane that came within 30 seconds of hitting a community short of a runway."

"That incident was more than pilot error. That was a failure in their training processes, and those pilots' lack of understanding. If anything, I would think they would use this book to help bolster their airline and show they are being proactive toward safety."

But there was something that bothered her about Darby's book. Something that crawled around the background of her brain, trying to come forward. She was not thinking clearly, and not sure if she would for a very long time. Perhaps after some sleep, or after Darby was sitting up having coffee with her.

"You don't think anyone at the airline would do something to her, because of that book, do you?" John asked.

That was it. That was what had been bothering her. Darby had pointed out a huge indiscretion with an extremely powerful woman in the FAA. That woman had buried a report, or chose to not follow through on the recommendations. Either way, the results were the same. Many planes had crashed since, and hundreds of lives had been lost due to that oversight and from her neglecting to take action. How far would any of them go to protect their empire? Kathryn wondered.

"Maybe not anyone at the airline," Kathryn said, "but the more I think about it, someone else might have something to lose."

John gave her a sideways glance, and then stared as his cup, and sighed. He sat that way for longer than made her comfortable.

Kathryn finally said, "John, what is it?"

CHAPTER 36

KATHRYN STOOD AT Jackie's kitchen counter cracking eggs, dumping them into a bowl and throwing shells into the sink. She could not believe what John had told her. Somewhere in the gray matter of her brain the possibility lurked, but his words brought reality into her backyard.

"I think that's good," Jackie said, peeking in the bowl.

Kathryn startled. Then looked into the bowl and up at Jackie. "Maybe we can invite your neighbors for French toast?"

"And *your* neighbors too," Jackie said, touching her arm. "Linda and Niman will be here soon. Everyone's hungry, we'll be good."

Jackie pulled the carton of eggs away from Kathryn, and then poured some milk into the bowl. Kathryn lifted a fork and began beating the eggs and milk. John had gone to take a shower, and Kathryn tried to digest what he had told her in the car. He had to be wrong.

"Mom!" Jessica snapped.

Kathryn jumped, and then stared at her daughter. She had no idea how long she had been standing beside her. "What honey?"

"I've been talking to you."

"I'm sorry, what?" she asked, trying not to take her anger out on the kids.

"Can we go see Aunt Darby after breakfast?" Jessica asked, taking the bowl from her. She dipped a sliced of bread into the egg mixture, and then dropped it onto the griddle.

"We all want to go," Jennifer said, filling glasses with orange juice.

"I don't want to," Chris said. "Mom, do I have to go to the hospital?"

"No honey," Jackie said, setting a plate in front of him, she touched his shoulder. "You don't have to."

"You're so selfish!" Jennifer snapped. She slammed the pitcher of juice on the table, and yelled, "All you care about is yourself!" and she ran out of the room.

Jackie and Kathryn exchanged a look, and Jackie shrugged, and mouthed, "Sorry."

"Jess, you good on the griddle?" Kathryn asked.

She nodded yes, and Kathryn followed Jennifer. She found her on the living room couch. "What's going on sweetheart?" After the words left her mouth, she realized how stupid they were. They all knew what was going on.

"*Seriously?* Aunt Darby's going to die, and we're supposed to act like everything's okay. *And* there's nothing we can do!" She grabbed a pillow and pulled it into her lap and curled into a fetal position and cried.

Kathryn placed a hand on her back and rubbed. She stroked her hair. "There is something we can do," she said, more to herself than to her daughter.

"What?" Jessica asked, standing in front of them with hands on hips.

Jenny sat upright, with a look as if she were pleading for her life. Kathryn's heart broke into a million pieces. She glanced between the girls. This was too much for fifteen-year-olds. But then, they had already survived hell.

"What we can do, is get whoever did this."

"What do you mean?" Jessica said, sitting on the coffee table in front of them. She leaned in and whispered, "They said this was an accident on the news."

"I know," Kathryn said. "But John said it was intentional."

"Someone tried to kill Aunt Darby?" Jennifer squeezed the pillow to her chest.

"Or Tom, or someone else on that plane," Kathryn said. "We don't know who they were after."

"Tom?" Jennifer said with a confused look.

"He was the captain."

"See, there's always something good, out of every bad situation," Jessica said.

"Jess!" Kathryn snapped. And then fresh tears sprouted to her eyes.

"I'm sorry Mom," she said. "I didn't know you liked him that much. I was joking."

Kathryn wiped her eyes, and said, "Sweetie, these tears are not for Tom. It's just... It's just that... that was something Darby would say." No matter what happened, Darby would always be with them. She had imprinted her life on everyone in this house. "Thank you for keeping her with me."

"Focus, you two," Jenny said. "Why do you think this was intentional? Like terrorism?"

"Not terrorism," she said, shaking her head. Unsure how much to tell them, the truth was, there was not much the girls would not hear on the news. She could not hide anything from them. Except for one thing, she hoped. She only hoped their minds wouldn't be filled with terror and false facts of sensationalized media.

Kathryn made one more wipe under an eye, and then said, "Something was wrong with the computer system on her plane, and it was shutting down operational systems in flight. They had one engine remaining on final. Tom had died before landing, and Darby was doing a great job flying." She hesitated thinking about what she had seen. "But, something hit the remaining engine on short final."

"How do you know she was doing a good job?" Jenny asked.

"I was in the tower watching."

"Why were you in the tower, Mom?" Jessica said, narrowing her eyes. "You knew something was going to happen?"

"No. We had no idea. I was there because the FBI was there to arrest Tom and Darby for drug smuggling."

The girls' mouths dropped open and then Jess said, "Aunt Darby? Drugs? Might as well make her a nun too."

"But not at the same time," Jenny said.

"Exactly," Kathryn said, with a laugh. "Darby was being set up, by being asked to carry them, or maybe not. Maybe Tom really needed help. We're not sure. Then the malfunctions on the plane, followed by the crash. None of this is coincidental."

"Why set her up if you're going to crash the plane?" Jenny asked, thoughtfully. "But, Aunt Darby always said, 'it's never one thing'."

"So, what do we do now?" Jessica asked. She bit her lip, and added, "I want to kill those bastards."

"The first thing we're going to do is clean up your language," Kathryn said touching her daughter's leg. "Then we are going to find out who did this and why."

"We'll do anything Mom," Jessica said, and Jenny nodded her head in agreement.

"This investigation is going to take time, and I don't want Darby to be alone. I need your understanding when schedules get crazy. Help with the house, and keep up on your schoolwork, etc."

"Anything mom," Jessica said. "And we can sit with Aunt Darby on the weekends, and at night, too."

"We'll take turns," Kathryn said. "But mostly Darby would want you to live your life. Besides, that way you can tell her what's going on. I'm sure she'd like that."

"Can she hear us?" Jenny asked.

"We don't know for sure, but I'm counting on it," Kathryn answered. "Much research says that coma patients can hear."

"Kat," Francine said, standing in the doorway.

Kathryn turned. "Yes, sweetie?"

Francine came into the room and sat on the couch beside her. "I have a huge favor to ask. I got online and transferred to U Dub, for the next semester so I could be close by. Mom and Niman are living in an apartment, and they're yucky honeymooners," she said rolling her eyes. The girls smiled, and she continued. "Could I stay with you? I could earn my keep by driving the girls to school when needed, and help with the house, and stuff like that."

Kathryn's eyes moistened. Francine would be willing to uproot her life, and transfer to the University of Washington to help. She never felt more gratitude. "Frankie, I think that would be perfect." She mouthed thank you, and Francine nodded.

From that bratty teenager she had first met during the investigation of her father's crash, Francine had grown into a compassionate young lady. Francine had lost her dad in an airplane crash, and most kids would never get over that. Yet it was Kathryn's daughters' dad that had caused him to crash that plane.

These girls were strong. They would get through this, probably better than Kathryn. Yet the rest of the story was something she had wished John had not told her. A visual that would haunt her for years, and something that she prayed the kids would not hear on the news.

"What about our New Year's Eve party?" Jenny asked.

"Let's move it to the hospital," Jessica said.

"Will they let us party there?" Jenny asked, setting the pillow behind her. "We could decorate and everything."

"I think we have a doctor who would approve that," Linda said, from the doorway. "I'll bribe him with sex."

"Mom!" Frankie said, laughing. "I cannot believe you just said that."

"That's an Aunt Darby!" Jessica said. "She has to live. We have to make her live!"

Nobody ever made Darby do anything. Life would have to be her choice.

CHAPTER 37

JACKIE WAS SITTING on the end of the bed when John stepped out of the bathroom with a towel around his waist, and another drying his hair. He startled when he saw her.

"Hey, sweetie. How's everyone doing?"

"As well as can be expected," she said, eyeing him.

He gave her a forced smile, and then returned to the bathroom, and tossed the towel. She stood in the doorway and he pulled open cabinet drawers until he found a brush, and then pulled it through his hair.

"What is it?" he asked, setting the brush down and stepping past her, returning the bedroom.

"Something you aren't telling me?"

John tossed the other towel, and slid open a dresser drawer. He stood for a moment with hands on hips, as if he were contemplating which pair of white boxers he should choose. She could wait him out.

He pulled his boxers on, and then reached past her and grabbed the slacks that were laying on the bed. He stepped one leg in, and then the other, clearly not looking her way as he pulled them up.

John was the master of avoidance when he wanted to be. He zipped up his pants, and focused on a button, as if it were a challenge. Once his pants were secure, he glanced her way.

Jackie now stood by the bedroom door, preparing to block his escape if she needed to, and raised an eyebrow.

He pulled a shirt off a hanger, and pushed an arm through a sleeve. "You don't want to know," he finally said, pulling on the other sleeve.

"Did you tell Kat?"

"Yes," he said buttoning his shirt.

"John. Don't do this," Jackie said, folding her arms. She was tired of him going to Kathryn first with everything that happened. "You can't lock me out."

Jackie had awoken early and his side of the bed was empty. She peered out the window just as he climbed into Kathryn's car. John and Kathryn shared work, and that was all. Yet, that fact did not make her feel any better when he ran to Kathryn with *everything* that happened at work or that bothered him.

John tucked in his shirt into his pants, watching her warily. Then he sat heavily on the bed, and tapped the cover beside him.

Jackie sighed, and dropped her arms and her anger, and sat beside him. "I'm sorry. It's just that I want to be here for you, too."

"And you are," he said, holding one of her hands, "but this is just…"

"What could possibly be worse than Darby in a comma?" Jackie said—other than her dying. Words that she refused to speak out loud.

John assessed her as if he were debating if she could handle the news or if she could be trusted with it. She was not quite sure which worried him most. But if John wouldn't tell her, Kathryn certainly would.

"Tell me. Please," she finally said. "You need to trust me."

"I do. More than you know," he said. "I'm just not sure how to…" John released her hand and stood. He walked across the room and placed his hands on his hips. When he finally turned, he opened his mouth but nothing came out. Then he said, "The flight attendants never opened the emergency exits."

"But I saw the explosion. How could…"

"There were people in the windows. Alive. For whatever reason, they didn't get the doors open. Or couldn't."

"You mean they burned alive?" Jackie said, lifting a hand to her mouth, thinking she would vomit.

"Most of them. Yes."

"I knew this would happen," she said, tears filling her eyes. Her worst fear had come true. "I should have done something. I should have fought it like—"

"This is not your fault," John said rushing to her. He knelt in front of her and took both her hands and squeezed. "You were there to teach those flight attendants an FAA approved program."

John's words did not soften the pain of guilt. She now fully understood what Darby had been fighting. When people died due to reasons that were foreseen by you, yet nothing was done, who was to blame? The person who knew and did nothing was equally as guilty. Jackie cried all the harder.

She had been told that without quantitative data, the bean counters would do nothing. More or less, she gave up. Sadly, aviation safety was still reactionary in nature. Darby saw what could happen and may have given her life in attempt to fix those issues. What had Jackie done? Not enough.

Jackie had told her supervisors that their flight attendants were too tired flying between so many operational theaters—the Pacific to the Atlantic, and back again. They had too many aircraft differences to learn. Memory with minimum rest was human error waiting to happen.

"Darby didn't accept mediocrity. She fought it. I should have too."

"Look where Darby's fight got her!" John snapped, as he stood.

"What?" Jackie's eyes widened. "Are you telling me this happened because of Darby's *Fight for Safety* book?"

"I'm not sure," John said. "But this was no accident."

CHAPTER 38

R AY STOPPED STROKING Darby's forehead to wipe the
tears off his cheeks. The ladies had been gone for hours, and
he was glad to be alone. The chair he sat in could not be any closer,
without him being in bed with her. The only place he wanted to
be. With one movement, he used both his hands and swiped them
across his cheeks and then on his jeans. He wished he could stop
his damn tears. He leaned over and rested his forehead on her bed
and held one of her hands.

"How the hell can this be happening?" he whispered. "You
don't deserve this."

I don't know, Darby thought. *Nobody does.*

He sat upright and glanced at the machine at the side of her
bed. Beeping. Beeping. Beeping. He was surprised at how many
wires she had connected to her body, as they came into focus.
Wires to her head monitored brain activity. Her heart rate, blood
pressure, and oxygen flashed across the screen. Three bags of fluid,
leaked into her arms. But the only indication of life was that beep.

"How's our patient doing?" a nurse asked, walking into the
room.

"What's that?" he asked, about the bag she carried, nothing
more than to make conversation.

"Liquid gold. Her meals from now on will have a price tag of close to eight hundred dollars a bag." The nurse hooked the bag up and then patted Darby's arm and said, "But you're worth it."

That she was. Ray lifted Darby's hand and brought it to his lips and repeatedly kissed it in time with the beeps. A million kisses he would give her until she awoke. He would keep her alive with each kiss.

Ohhh. God that feels good, Darby thought. *I know how you could wake me up. But wait 'til the nurse leaves, I don't think I can visit you in prison right now.*

Ray's eyes widened. "Look! Look at that! There was a jump in one of those lines," he said. "See that?"

The nurse placed her hands on her hips, and stared. "I just don't see anything."

"It was there. I saw it. I kissed her hand and, and … there was a different pattern."

"I believe you," she said, "let me get the doctor."

What felt like forever, was actually only minutes, and Niman came rushing into the room. "I saw her machine take a different path," Ray said. "I was kissing her like this," he said, lifting her hand to his lips and kissing it multiple times. "Then that line right there jumped higher."

"That's good," Niman said. "That's a very good sign."

"Does it mean something?" Ray held her hand in both of his, and pulled it to his heart, holding onto every word that Niman spoke. He needed Darby to hear him. He needed her forgiveness.

"It could. We're recording brain patterns. If you see something, write it down. We can see what she's reacting to."

"She reacted to my kiss."

"Perhaps. We just don't know. But at this stage fluctuations are a good thing. Any difference is good." Niman pressed the call button, and said, "Please bring a legal pad and pen into the room."

Ray, I did feel your kiss. You make me fluctuate like nobody I've ever known. Darby could feel his heart, as if she were holding it in her hands. But as hard as she tried, she could not get that machine to react again. *I love you Ray.*

The nurse gave the paper and pen to Niman, and he wrote across the top—date, time, activity, and then handed it to Ray. "I want everyone to document changes."

Ray took the paper, glanced at his watch and wrote 0745. 12/31. Kissed hand.

"I'm heading home to catch a nap. If you need me, call. I can return in five minutes."

Ray gently set Darby's hand down on the covers, and walked Niman to the door. "Is she going to make it?" he whispered, his heart aching in fear of what he might say. But he had to know. He did not want to have false hope.

I can still hear you, Darby thought.

"All we can do is hope," Niman said. "She's a fighter, and if I were a gambling man, I'd bet on this one."

I am a fighter, Ray. I'm not going anywhere. If you want me, I'm here for life. I'm not even mad about that ring.

Niman left the room, and the nurse replaced another bag. She told him to get some sleep. How the hell could he sleep with Darby like this? He doubted he would ever sleep again. This was his fault. There was no confirmation yet, but his gut told him that it was. With what little they knew about that arrival aircraft, the malfunctions, and the engine shutting down had his name all over it. He as good as did this to Darby.

He stared at the woman he loved and tears began to flow again, but turned into sobs. He could not get Darby's words out of his mind, *"In the worst case scenario, is it going to kill me or anyone else?"* They frickin' joked about the low probability. After the first of the year, she was going to help him figure out what to do. He had tried to stop it on his own, but something happened. Someone accessed his computer, his inventory and that part was moved out into the system. Yet, he was still to blame.

"I am so sorry Darby," Ray choked out in a whisper.

It's not your fault Ray. She wanted to hold him. She needed to comfort him. But she could not reach out from her darkness. And she was so tired. The pain in Ray's heart stabbed hers. His was the only pain she felt, but as she drifted into darkness the pain subsided, and she felt good. Better. Maybe *not* fighting the darkness would not be the worst thing.

CHAPTER 39

KATHRYN DROVE DOWN the ramp at the hospital, and pulled a parking ticket. Lights from the car behind blinded her, and she adjusted the mirror. Then she drove around and around the garage, going deeper and deeper. Her radio turned to static the deeper she drove underground, mirroring her brain. She passed by many blank stalls for one reason only—she would park on level D for Darby.

She had taken the girls to the hospital at noon, to see Darby for the first time. They had done well, but were surprised at how she looked. They had brought her music, her bear, and flowers. As much as Kathryn tried to prepare them, there had been no way other than seeing her in person.

She was thankful that Ray stayed during their short visit, so that the girls would feel okay to leave Darby. They would need to digest the reality of the new Darby. Kathryn took Linda, Jackie, and all the kids to a late lunch, where they attempted to address the kids' questions. Chris was silent during lunch. Later they went to a movie.

Kathryn couldn't remember the name of the movie or anything that happened. Her mind was focused on Darby and the crash the entire time. Running all possibilities through her mind, she ended at the same place—nowhere. But there wasn't much she could do for a day or two anyway. Then she would visit the crash site. Read reports. Visit Global. She could begin to put this puzzle together, and figure out what had happened.

They had pulled the aircraft and all parts into a hangar at the end of the field. Global owned that hangar, which made her a bit uncomfortable. John felt the same, and assigned 24-hour security to guard against anyone that was unauthorized accessing the area, as well as observing those who were authorized to be there.

Reaching her floor, she pulled into space D 13 and shut off the car. Linda and Jackie were shopping with the girls for party supplies at the local grocery store. She glanced at her watch—8 pm—she hoped they would take their time. Opening the door, she heard a car approach. She closed the door, slid down in her seat, and hid in the dark.

The car drove slowly past, and continued down the ramp, and around the corner. Kathryn's heart raced. She was being paranoid, but there were far too many parking spots for anyone to pass without reason.

Once the lights were out of sight, Kathryn grabbed her purse, opened the door and ran to the elevator. She stabbed the button multiple times, and when the door opened, she flew in, slamming into the figure inside.

"Ma'am, are you okay?" The security officer asked.

"Yes," she said. "Parking garages at night make me nervous." Then she told him what happened, and he agreed that was odd behavior and would get her into the hospital and investigate further.

When Kathryn arrived at Darby's room, and poked her head in, Ray was sitting on a chair, leaning on her, sleeping. She stepped back out to the nurses' station. "How long has he been like that?" she asked.

"Two hours or so. Dr. Niman said it was okay to leave them be."

Kathryn nodded. She quietly walked into the room and picked up the pad of paper and carried it out to the lobby. Almost every two hours, Ray documented some kind of spike. Always when he was touching her, or talking to her.

Darby was with them. Somewhere in the darkness, she was still there.

"Kat," Niman said, and she startled. "Where's the team?"

"Gathering party supplies," Kathryn said. "What do you think of this?"

"Pretty standard for the body," he sighed.

"Then why are you—"

"It gives Ray something to do," Niman said, with a lowered voice.

"So it's not real?"

"Not necessarily." Niman glanced through the sheets, "I've been tracking the responses myself, and they are very real."

"I'm confused."

"The responses are real, but the power comes when people can see improvement and change. It gives them hope."

Hope was a powerful thing. She also understood the power of activity. Giving a panicked person a task would give them something to focus on and the panic would subside. Doing something always got a person out of her own head. Studies also indicate that doing for others could remove depression.

However, she had never thought about giving tasks for those waiting. Then she remembered Jackie's behavior doting over Greg during his last few days. Tucking, fussing, always doing something—her survival mechanism.

"That's a good idea," Kathryn said, "Let's keep hope alive for everyone."

"Do you have any?"

"Who me? Hope?"

She had not had a moment to think about hope. At first, all she could think about was life without Darby, but she couldn't imagine that picture. She wasn't even sure if she wanted to live in a world without Darby. But the question of hope, if Darby would be okay, had never actually crossed her mind.

"No, Niman. I don't hope," Kathryn said. "I know. I *know* she will be fine."

Kathryn spoke with such conviction that she surprised herself. But she spoke the truth. She would get through this because she *knew* Darby would be fine. She also knew she would figure out what happened and make sure it never happened again.

Kathryn glanced toward the room. As long as there was life, Darby would be fine. No, she didn't need hope. She had faith.

CHAPTER 40

DARBY'S SUPPORT TEAM poured out of the elevator and Kathryn and Niman exchanged a smile. The noise was overwhelming, but filled with love. Within no time they were in Darby's room decorating for the party. She was not so sure this was a good idea, as they were all running on adrenaline. Nobody had much sleep since the crash. Yet there was no time like New Year's to celebrate that Darby was alive.

Kathryn held the back of the chair while Jessica taped strings of silver tinsel to the ceiling. The nursing staff might not be pleased with tape all over the ceiling, but it looked pretty cool.

Jessica tied three helium balloons to the bed railing, and then two more to Darby's monitoring equipment. Ray leaned back in a chair with his arms folded watching the zoo. Linda and Francine sliced cheese and put crackers onto a plate, and Jackie opened a bag of chocolate kisses. John was home with Chris.

Chris had never gone to see his dad in the hospital, and the reality of Darby there would paint a picture he did not want to invite into his dreams. Kathryn got it, as did Jackie.

Jennifer jumped off the chair. "Aunt Darby, your room looks fabulous, if you want to wake up and take a look, you won't be disappointed."

"She's right Aunt Darby. You've officially got the most awesome room in the hospital," Jessica said, pulling a chair up to the side of the bed.

Kathryn glanced at her watch. They had three hours until the New Year. "Okay, who's up for a game of poker?"

"Where are we going to play?" Jenny asked.

"Darby can be the table," Jessica said.

"You can't make a coma patient a table," Francine said.

"Of course you can. Darby won't care," Jessica said. "Besides, if it pisses her off she can kick the cards."

That's my girl, Darby thought. *I've never been a table before, but it might be fun. God I want to scream. Let me out of this blackness.*

"We can all sit around the bed. Wait... who wants to play Darby's hand?" Linda asked pulling the cards out of the box, while Francine handed out poker chips.

"I'll play Darby's hand," Ray said.

"Oh my God. Did you see that! Aunt Darby reacted to Ray talking," Jessica said. "Mom, write it down."

Kathryn complied, and said, "Ray, say something else and see what happens."

"I've been talking to her all night. I just don't know what sparks her."

I'll tell you what sparks me, Darby thought. *It's you playing my hand. My God Ray, you have the worst poker face in the world.*

They all watched the machine, and nothing. "Well, it was there for a second and it will be back," Kathryn said. "So, who wants to be the big blind first?"

"I will," Jenny said. "But what beats what again?"

"I'm not sure," Linda said. "I know all the same color is good."

"We'll learn as we go," Kathryn said. "Did I ever tell you about our game of strip poker when you girls were off at camp?"

"You played strip poker?" Jessica said.

"Your mom, Darby, and I played," Jackie said. "It was Darby's idea. She wanted me to win some money because we were having some financial troubles."

"But how would strip poker win you money?" Francine asked.

"Exactly. We may have had a little bit too much to drink." But Kathryn knew that Darby had done what she could to make Jackie happy. They had such a fun night. Darby was always good at making them laugh.

"And then Darby did a striptease," Jackie said.

"I'm dating a woman of many talents." Ray grinned and lifted his cards. "I'm in, and will raise you two red chips."

Just look at me now.

"Darby always made us laugh," Kathryn said, calling Ray's bet. "*She* actually made the money because if I remember correctly, we stuffed dollars in her butt floss underwear."

Tears filled Jackie's eyes. "I fold," she said. "Excuse me." She got up and left the room.

"I'll be right back," Kathryn said.

When she found Jackie in the hall, Kathryn did not have to ask what was wrong. She knew. Jackie remembered every detail of that night, most likely what happened after Kathryn and Darby had left early the next morning. That was the last night any of them had with Greg, and the last night Jackie had made love with him before the accident.

"I'm sorry, Kat." Jackie sniffed. "I thought I was beyond these feelings. Somehow with Darby lying in the hospital, talking about that night, I just don't know if I can do it."

"Do you want to go home with John and Chris?"

Jackie nodded.

"Then go. We'll be fine. Darby will be fine. You go home to your men, and show them how much you love them."

"Are you sure?" Jackie asked.

"Yes, that's where you belong. Wait here for a minute."

Kathryn went into the room, grabbed Jackie's purse and ran back out. When she returned to Jackie's side she said, "Here you go. Are you okay to drive?"

"I am. Thanks, Kat." Jackie gave her a long hug.

Kathryn said goodbye, and this time when she returned to the room, the poker game was being put away.

"We voted on Darby's favorite holiday movie instead," Linda said, as she put *Elf* into the DVD player.

Once the movie began, the room turned silent. The girls sat in chairs, and laid their heads on Darby's bed. They all watched the movie, with a few laughs here and there, but there was no party spirit. How could there be? Yet the girls were strong. She was so proud of them. Together they would survive this episode in their life.

As the movie ended, Kathryn said, "Ten minutes until the count-down. Sparkling cider for anyone?"

Just hang a bottle of Jack on my IV for me.

Kathryn filled plastic champagne glasses with cider. "I think we should all make a toast for the New Year."

Linda lifted her glass, "To friends and family. I'm glad to be back, with you all."

"To Darby's health," Francine said, lifting hers.

"To Aunt Darby," Jenny said.

"To a New Year filled with Aunt Darby's laughter." Jessica lifted her glass.

Ray stood, "To the woman I want to marry and have a family with."

Oh Ray. I want that too.

"Look! Her monitor did extra beeps," Jessica said. "She wants that too, write it down!"

Kathryn wrote—12/31/2015. 11:57 p.m. *Darby will marry Ray*—and a tear dropped to the page. Then she lifted her glass.

"To the New Year. Peace, joy and happiness, and health to all. But mostly this toast is for you Darby. We love you, and we will be by your side for as long as it takes you to come back to us."

Everyone clinked glasses, as best that plastic could clink. Midnight clicked over with only one kiss, and that was Ray's with Darby. Everyone else hugged. Kathryn watched Darby's machine—nothing.

"Mom," Jessica said. "Can we spend the night with Aunt Darby tonight?"

"We won't be able to when school starts," Jennifer responded. "Please."

"I'll stay with them," Francine said.

Kathryn looked at Linda, who nodded, and then she said, "Okay then. But try to get some sleep. I think we can fit another cot in here." She turned to Ray. "I'll take you home. You need some sleep."

"I don't…"

Kathryn walked to his side and touched his arm. "We might be at this for a long time. If we don't take turns, nobody will be any good when she wakes up."

He looked at the girls, and then to Kathryn. "Okay. But I don't need a ride," he said, "my car's in the garage."

Kathryn left the room to get the cot, and when she returned the girls were painting Darby's toes. She laughed. "Remember when she gave you makeup for Christmas?" she said pushing the cot in.

"Yeah, we were... what twelve?" Jessica said.

"You treated us like babies," Jenny added.

"You are my babies." As hard as Kathryn did not want them to grow up, they managed to anyway, and with far too much pain in their lives. She moved to Darby's side, "Take care of our girls tonight," she said lifting her hand, she kissed it.

Oh God, please let me die, Darby thought. *I don't want to ruin my friends' lives. How can I be so unfair to cause them so much pain? Please God. Just take me home. Take me now.*

"Mom! Darby's machine is not beeping!" Jenny screamed.

It took a minute to register what was happening, as bells began ringing. Nurses ran into the room, shoving them out of the way, and yelling. Niman was there within seconds. Kathryn and Linda grabbed the kids and pulled them out of the room. The girls began crying and Jessica screamed, "Nooo!" She fought to break free from Kathryn, who held her tight. Linda grabbed Jenny, who was sobbing and screaming.

CHAPTER 41

KATHRYN STOOD AT the edge of the cemetery while the priest said his final words. Wind whipped hair across her face. Her eyes watered when a strand hit, and she tucked it behind an ear. At least onlookers would think she was crying. It had been two weeks since the crash, and she had cried far too many tears. No more tears for Kathryn. Now was time for action to get the bastards who did this. Jessica had been correct; this was no time to give up swearing.

The funeral had been short, and she and Jackie had sat in the back. After everyone passed, they stood and followed them outside. The walk to the burial plot was long, but it gave Kathryn time to put things in perspective, as if that would ever be possible. She was burying a chapter of her life. But with that, it opened another to figure out why this happened.

Jackie stood to her right, shivering. Kathryn tucked an arm into the crook of her friend's arm, and pulled her close to stave off the chill that she, too, felt to her bones.

"Thank you for coming with me," Kathryn said. "I couldn't do this alone."

"Of course," Jackie said.

Kathryn did not tell the girls this was the day of Tom's funeral. They did not need to attend, and, as it turned out, they did not like him. Apparently he knew that, too, and thus the grandiose gifts to win them over. Her attention turned to the group. There was a large turnout, with hundreds of Global Pilots in attendance; some wearing their uniforms, but many more without. Amongst the guests were FBI investigators, but Kathryn had no idea who they were.

They had confirmed that Tom was smuggling drugs, and all signs indicated that Darby did nothing but help him with his bags out of kindness.

The hotel subsequently stopped the pharmacist from setting up a table in the crew room. But that did not stop the process. He showed up without his table, filled orders and then delivered them in the lobby, prior to departure. Nothing changed. Crews would get a good deal on their meds in Mumbai. But then again, why shouldn't they?

The U.S. pharmaceutical system was bringing drugs in from overseas, and marking them up 600 percent, or more. The same drugs that crewmembers had access to. The retail system was a sham. If Costco could sell the same drug as a retail drugstore could, but for $500 less, there was a problem. Medicare was assisting the pharmaceutical industry in raping the government's inept drug system, among other issues. Darby was a victim of this system, and her bills were astronomical. Thank God she had insurance. But everyone paid in the long run.

"Are you going to the memorial tonight?" Jackie whispered, with a nudge.

"No."

Jackie pulled back. "But I thought..."

The last Global memorial was for Greg's plane. At the time, Jackie stayed in the hospital with Greg, and Kathryn and Darby attended the memorial. It was also when Kathryn and Darby got into their first real fight. Kathryn had been so mad, she had told her they were done and would never be friends.

Her anger, however, was not actually at Darby, it was due to the fact she had just learned of her husband's multiple infidelities. The setting tonight would be exactly the same, except without Darby. Yet, Kathryn may as well walk back in time and put Darby and Tom on the plane with Greg. No. There was no way she would attend that memorial.

"Kat, don't you think you should be there?"

"There's only one place I belong, and that's at Darby's side."

Darby had flat-lined at 1:04 am on New Year's morning. They got her heart going again, but Kathryn told the girls they could not stay. She didn't want them to watch her die. The girls cried, gave excellent reasons and then won the debate. Kathryn stayed at Linda's appartment to be within a five-minute run to the hospital. They all survived the night, and those spikes on the monitor continued.

"Is that Tom's ex-wife and kids?" Jackie quietly asked, nodding toward the opposite side of the grave.

"I'm sure of it."

"Why would he leave her? She's beautiful and all those kids…"

"I think she kicked him out. One too many affairs."

"What were you doing with him?"

"Not sure," Kathryn said, keeping her voice low. "Maybe trying to fix him? Maybe I felt sorry for him. Maybe I'm an idiot." But the reality was, he made her feel something again. He made her feel like a woman, and it felt so damned good in his arms.

"Maybe you're human."

"A malfunctioning one at that," Kathryn said. She checked her phone to see if a hospital message came through. A habit she doubted would ever be broken. She put her phone back into her pocket, and then it buzzed.

"Kat..."

"Huh?" she said, looking at her phone—John. She opened his message.

"Is that Robert De Niro?" Jackie whispered.

Kathryn glanced up for a moment, but her attention was pulled back to the message—*We found something. Call ASAP.*

CHAPTER 42

KATHRYN PARKED IN the first spot she saw on the street instead of driving into the garage, and she ran toward the hospital. Every time she saw the address over the front door of the hospital, she smiled—747. Swedish was apparently the aviator hospital, or at least an appropriate location for Darby since she loved that plane. She flew through the front doors and headed for the east elevator and pressed 'B-Cafeteria.' The elevator descended one floor.

The cafeteria had turned into their office. That way they could be close if something happened to Darby, and at the same time kept out of sight of the public. Somehow all ears in this location were tuned into only those people they loved, lying in the beds throughout the hospital.

The media had all but disappeared, and Kathryn had been thankful for that.

John was already waiting with a coffee and two chocolate chip cookies. She smiled.

"What happened?" Kathryn asked, sliding into her seat.

"First," he said, "we learned that the aircraft had a bad FADEC."

"FADEC?" Kathryn said. "Speak English please."

"Full authority digital engine control. The FADEC is more or less the brain of the Airbus engine system. It controls the engines and more or less all engine components."

"When did you become an Airbus expert?" Kathryn asked, breaking a piece of cookie off, and sticking it into her mouth.

He glanced at his watch. "An hour ago."

"A bad FADEC. So that means this was unintentional?"

"Oh, very much the opposite," he said gravely. "It was counterfeit."

Kathryn's eyes opened wide. "But how…" Counterfeit parts were not unheard of, but at a major airline like Global, that just couldn't be possible.

"There was a fake serial number on the part."

"Oh shit," Kathryn said setting her cookie down. "So this could be attributed to the airline trying to reduce expenses." She thought a moment, and then asked, "How long do you think the plane was flying with that part?"

"Not sure."

"Okay, so there are two options here. Either Global put that part into service because someone was trying to reduce expenses, or two, they put a bad part in that plane with intent for Darby and Tom to fly it."

"The second option is fairly farfetched. How would they know they would get that plane?"

"Depends. Was that part installed in Amsterdam?"

"We haven't tracked that yet, but we're working on it."

Kathryn gently tapped her spoon on the table. "Maybe it was a coincidence." Then a sobering thought hit her. "What if this was to reduce expenses, and there are more planes flying with similar parts?"

"We need to ground the fleet," John said emphatically, and then winked.

Kathryn smiled. That was always John's answer to every crash. While she knew he was half kidding, that was always his answer. But he was correct when he said, 'the only way to make sure airplanes never crashed was to never fly them.' The truth was, the world would never be accident free, but it was their job to be proactive and reduce the likelihood of failure.

"Okay," Kathryn began. "Even if that FADEC shut down the engine by itself, the pilot should still be able to fly. They are trained to fly single engine."

"Unless it shut down both engines," John said.

"Did the FADEC shut down the second engine? I thought—"

"No. But it could have." John wished that would have been the case. What he learned was far worse, and added to the complexity of the investigation.

She sipped her coffee, and then said, "Maybe you should recommend inspection of all aircraft engines anyway. Put them on notice as to the severity. We don't have to ground them, just an immediate inspection."

John nodded. "But first, let's find out how that part got into service, and when." He opened his mouth to speak, but closed it again. His eyes were dark with concern.

"What is it?" Kathryn asked.

"That other engine..."

Kathryn waited. She suspected something hit the plane, and thought it had to be a bird. Despite it being winter, seabirds still stayed close to town. Not all of them headed south. But it had happened all too fast, and John's look sent a chill through her body.

"It was a drone."

"No." Kathryn hated drones to no end, flying in the airspace with airliners. It was not if, but when, one took out an airplane. Why did it have to be Darby's? She had been fighting bureaucracy on this for over a year. She knew exactly how to solve this problem, but money won that battle.

When Tom gave the kids those gifts, he was giving them the future. But she did not want that future in her home. "Do you think someone just flew one too close? It was Christmas, and thousands of those things were gifted."

He shook his head. "There was a computer chip, of sorts. A second control device."

The enormity of that hit Kathryn's gut like a punch—not that she hadn't thought of someone using those things for harm. But that it actually happened made her nauseous. This was the next generation of threat to aviation, and to the world. The technology had been available for years to enable tiny drones to individually fly off radar, and when ready, they could swarm into both engines simultaneously. Now these damn things were going into every home.

"Do we have any indication where it came from?"

He sighed. "Too much damage. We can't see how it was programmed, where it came from, or anything relative. We only know it was present."

"We don't know who did it? Or why? Or if it were targeted for their plane specifically?" Kathryn wanted to scream. This was too much news to not be any closer than before.

John shook his head. "We'll have Tom's final toxicology reports back soon."

"Why'd they bury him before we had those reports?"

He shrugged, "I don't know, and it doesn't matter. If we need to, we'll dig him up."

Kathryn sighed. "Okay. Could the drug dealers have flown that drone into his plane?"

John scratched his head. "Perhaps. The aircraft malfunctions could have been a coincidence. Maybe they got lucky, not knowing the plane was crippled."

"But killing all those innocent people to get Tom for drugs?" Kathryn shook her head. "It doesn't make sense."

"A deal worth millions." John shrugged, and said, "More than that, the knowledge of who they were."

"Why not just take him out with a well-placed shot as he walked off the property?" Kathryn's foot began tapping under the table.

"FBI was there. They were taking him in, and they had a van on the airport property. No opportunity."

"Did they know?"

"CNN. Of course they did."

"What about all the grief the Global chief pilots have been giving Darby? Could they have flown that thing into the plane?" She tucked a strand of hair behind her ear. "I wouldn't put it past them."

"They could have. At this point, anyone could have flown it into the plane."

Kathryn sighed. "Then we have one more possibility."

John raised an eyebrow.

"I can give you three regional airlines that could have motive, and one in particular."

"An airline is not going to take out a plane of another, no matter what the competition."

"True," Kathryn said, picking at a chocolate chip in her cookie. "But a fearful employee might."

When Global steamrolled into the Seattle market, the *Seattle Times*, as well as the *Wall Street Journal*, and everywhere online shouted that the battle was on. Local airline management created fear within their employee groups, in hope they would up their game and do better. Fear filled many employees' minds at the smaller carriers.

Nobody with a right mind would ever take out a plane, but Bill has proven there were many people who were not in their right mind.

"Go on," John said.

"What if someone working on the ramp, or loading bags was listening to the fear mongers? What if they feared for their livelihood if the airline were to shut down, compliments of Global?" She scraped the crumbs into a pile from the cookie she was eating. "What if they did not intend on crashing the plane, but just wanted to do a little engine damage to cost the competitors some money, plus a scheduling delay?"

John tipped back his cup, and then squeezed it with one hand. "Nothing is out of the realm of possibility at this point."

Kathryn and John knew more than yesterday, but they were no closer to the truth. Too many different people could have flown that damn drone into the plane, and that answer might never come. But then again, there was that malfunctioning part. Were these events mutually exclusive, or was there more to this event?

She brushed her cookie crumbs onto a napkin, then wadded it into a ball and tossed it into the garbage. There was one person who could help, and he was upstairs.

RAY WAS SITTING beside Darby, holding her hand whispering something to her, when Kathryn walked in.

"How's everything today?" she asked.

"We're doing good," Ray said.

"I need to talk to you," Kathryn said. "Unofficial. But it's got to do with the crash." John had been correct in guessing Kathryn would be blocked from the case because of her connection to the victims. They never openly blamed her for knowledge of the drug smuggling, but rumors floated about the office, among them included talk of Bill. She ignored them all and maintained focus.

The NTSB allowed John to remain on the investigation, as his connection was a more distant relationship. It also did not hurt that he held one of the highest positions within the NTSB, and could do most anything he wanted. Despite Kathryn being blocked, it did not stop him from consulting her. Yet, everything she did was *unofficial.*

"Can we talk here?" Ray asked, returning his attention to Darby.

Kathryn pulled a chair from across the room, and sat beside him. Ray continued to hold Darby's hand in both of his, but his eyes fixated on Kathryn's.

"There was a mechanical problem with the FADEC on their plane."

"Do they know what was wrong with it?"

"Only that it was not FAA approved."

That's what was bothering you, Darby thought. *You knew.*

Ray's eyes moistened and he returned his attention to Darby, at the same moment her machine began a series of rapid beats followed by an intermittent alarm.

A nurse rushed in, touched the machine, and wrote something on the board, and Kathryn glanced at her watch. Once the nurse was gone, she picked up the pad, and flipped to an open page and wrote—January 16. 1445. FADEC.

"Ray, we need to talk."

CHAPTER 43

FEBRUARY 14, 2016

RAY SAT IN his office, running through inventory on his computer trying to figure out what had happened. More importantly, he could never allow this to happen again. A month had passed, and he was all but cleared. They all were. Nobody had any idea exactly how long that FADEC had been on the plane. However, records showed that a legal FADEC, with a different serial number had left his shelf and was shipped to Singapore as cargo a week prior to the crash. What happened in Singapore was out of his hands. Everyone assumed the part was swapped down there.

They had assumed wrong.

He pushed back from his desk, and stood. "God dammit!" he said, kicking his chair, sending it rolling across the room and slamming into a stack of cabinets. He had the blood of too many people on his hands. And Darby...

A knock at the door startled him, and he turned and yanked it open. His blood went cold, but he stepped aside as the man entered.

"How's business?" the asshole asked, glancing at the location of Ray's chair.

"How can I help you?" Ray asked. He hated this guy for all he had done to Darby. Ray had figured out who was behind the moving of that part, and knew this was intentional. But it was too late to do anything. He wanted to kill him for what he had done, and suspected it might come to that after all.

"Sit. Please," he said, as he sat on the corner of Ray's desk, and folded his arms.

Ray walked across the room, retrieved his chair, and rolled it within a couple feet of the desk and sat. "What do you want?"

"What's the deal with Bradshaw?"

"She's in a fucking coma," Ray shot back. "What do you think the deal is?"

"Is she going to die?"

"She's going to be fine," Ray said, trying to find conviction he did not feel.

He raised an eyebrow. "I heard she's a vegetable."

"You heard wrong."

He laughed. "Perhaps. But you fucked her up pretty bad, and killed a few hundred people in the process."

Ray jumped out of his chair and slammed a fist into his face. He knocked him off his perch, but he landed on his feet. He stumbled, touched his nose, and then looked at the blood on his fingers.

"I'm not the one you want to mess with," he said, grabbing a couple tissues from the box on Ray's desk, and held them to his nose. "But if you want to stay out of jail…"

Ray's fists balled at his side.

"Whoa, cowboy. Who the hell do you think put you here?" he said, spreading his arms.

His words as good as punched him in the gut. It all made sense. Ray had found the part, and his excuse was to wait and do nothing about it until he could find out who was behind it all. But he delayed for selfish reasons, too. Allowing that part to sit on his shelf helped him. Darby paid the price.

"That part was never supposed to go out."

"It did, and a drone finished the job."

Anger boiled. Finish the *job*? "Were you flying it?" If he said yes, Ray doubted he would leave the room walking.

He stared at Ray for a moment before answering. "No. I wasn't."

Ray was not sure if that was the truth, or the asshole knew he was walking on dangerous ground. Either way, it did not change the outcome. Darby was living in hell, and there was nothing he could do to help her. He was living in a hell all his own.

"What do you want?"

"You want to stay out of jail, and I need a favor."

"Don't you get it? I'm in prison," Ray said, placing his hands on hips. "There is nothing you can do to me that will undo what has happened."

"Then think about Bradshaw. While you're in jail, she's in a coma as an accomplice."

"They'll never believe you."

"I'm just saying, if she went away peacefully…"

"What the hell are you talking about?" Ray demanded.

But he knew. It was nothing that he had not thought about over the previous weeks, as he watched Darby's body wither into an emaciated mess. His brain swirled between the guilt for what he had done, and what the compassionate thing would be. He could give a rat's ass about the job or jail.

Today was Valentine's Day and he had planned on taking roses to her. The thought of them being on her deathbed broke his heart, but he knew that Darby would never want to live like this. This was no life. She had visited him in his dreams many times over the previous weeks, and told him as much.

CHAPTER 44

KATHRYN ENJOYED the moment of domesticity preparing a Valentine's picnic for the girls to take to the hospital. Her attention over the previous weeks had been divided between her responsibilities at work, the investigation, and the hospital. She and the twins were doing their best to survive, they all were. Getting into the flow would be the best way to explain how they were living. Just moving along from day to day.

She was putting napkins and bottles of water into a bag when the doorbell rang. She grabbed her purse and ran to answer it. After paying for their Chinese food, she set the box on the counter. Moo shoo pork was Darby's favorite. Not that having it would bring her out of the coma, but somehow it kept them connected.

Kathryn was pulling paper plates out of the cupboard, when Francine said, "Kat…"

"Hey sweetheart, have you talked to your mom?" she asked counting out plates.

"Yeah, she's coming. But…"

Kathryn set the plates on the counter. "What is it? Something wrong?" A dumb question in this house—what *wasn't* wrong, but she had to ask.

Francine looked over her shoulder and back to Kathryn. "I… I'm not sure how to say this but…" she whispered.

Kathryn sat at the table, and patted a chair. "Frankie, you can tell me anything. You know that, right?"

She nodded and sat beside Kathryn.

Kathryn feared Francine wanted to leave. Francine had been such a huge help, and she wouldn't know what to do without her. But she also did not want her unhappy. She had a life to live, and Kathryn would always appreciate the time she had given them.

"It's Jenny," she said, glancing over her shoulder, again. "She's been more moody than usual. I know with the accident and all, we're not ourselves. But she was doing really well and then…"

Kathryn reached out and held her hand, "What sweetie?"

"It's as if one day she snapped. I don't know. At first I thought it was just a bad day at school. I've talked to Jess. She sees it too, but she won't confide in either of us. But something happened."

"Maybe we can get your mom to talk to her."

"I think that would be good," she said. "But we'd have to set it up so she won't know. I think she'd freak if she knew we were plotting."

Just then Jessica bounced into the room and looked into the bag. "I'm starving. Can we go?"

"Where's your sister?"

"Upstairs, she doesn't want to come with us."

Kathryn walked to the bottom of the stairs and yelled, "Jenny, put your coat and shoes on and get down here. We're going to the hospital."

Within a few minutes, she came sulking down the stairs. "Fine."

"Don't you want to see Darby?" Kathryn asked. "Did something happen?"

Jenny folded her arms and glared at her mother. "You don't understand. You will never understand."

"Then help me."

CHAPTER 45

KATHRYN, THE GIRLS, and Linda sat in Darby's room with plates full of Chinese food. Whatever was bothering Jenny was impacting her appetite, too. How long had this been going on without her noticing? She had noticed the attitude, but did not think of it being a pattern. But now it looked like she was competing with Darby on the get skinny scale.

Maybe she was upset that Darby would not be able to teach her how to drive. Something both she and her sister had waited years to do. Kathryn said when they were fifteen and a half, and not a day earlier, she would allow them to get into the car together. That day was coming soon. Yet neither of the girls had mentioned anything about it. Kathryn stuck her fork into the moo shoo pork, and took a bite, and chewed slowly. Keeping a watchful eye on Jenny.

What are you guys trying to do, kill me? Moo shoo pork. Oh God, I might be in a coma but I can still smell. I appreciate your efforts, but I'm not sure this is the best thing.

Kathryn set her plate down and picked up her phone, and took a photo of the girls and then one of Darby.

"What are you doing Mom?" Jessica said. "Aunt Darby's gonna hate that picture."

"She's cute. She kind of looks like a Chia Pet," Kathryn said, and everyone laughed, including Jenny. Her hair was sprouting and soon they could start brushing it.

Chia Pet? That's pretty funny.

Her machine skipped a few beats, and then settled.

"I got it," Linda said, as she picked up the pad.

Kathryn mouthed, "Thank you." They had all but lost hope that those bursts actually meant anything, but it was fun to pretend she was reacting to activity. Kathryn planned on making a book of all the things that sparked Darby, after she was better. Photos would help.

"Should we get her one of those baby bows? The kind with Velcro?" Jessica asked.

"Will you guys just stop!" Jenny snapped, and then began crying.

Kathryn set her plate down, and went to her daughter's side and rapped her arms around her. As she held her, Ray walked in with an armful of deep burgundy roses—*unconscious beauty*. Kathryn smiled through the pain of her daughter.

"Hi sweetie," Ray said, touching Jennifer's shoulder. He knelt down, and Kathryn moved away. "I have something for you," he said pulling a rose out of the bouquet, and giving it to her. He then gave each of the ladies a rose, and set the remainder on the bed over Darby.

He stared at Darby for a moment, then turned toward the room and said, "Ladies, I love you all." Tears filled his eyes, and he wiped them away with one hand, and then placed it on his hip. "Darby is lying here because of me," he said extending a hand toward her. "I destroyed her life, and now I am destroying yours."

"What are you talking about?" Kathryn said. Not entirely sure if she wanted to know with the kids in the room. But she had no idea what else to say. She had hoped Ray wasn't involved. When that report closed concerning the part, she had been grateful when nothing pointed his direction. But still, she always wondered. Something tickled the back of her brain every time they talked about it. Or perhaps, it was his changing the subject.

"I beg of you. Please don't allow me to destroy your lives too," he said, wiping a tear from Jenny's cheek. "This is the day of love. Hold it throughout the entire year." He kissed Jenny's forehead, and then turned and left the room as quickly as he had come.

Kathryn's eyes widened and she turned to Linda who said, "Go!"

She left the room and chased after Ray. The door to the elevator was closing and she stuck a foot in and stopped it. Sliding inside she said, "Cafeteria," and pressed the button. He folded his arms. When the door opened at the lobby level, he did not get off. Kathryn was ready to run after him if he did.

Within no time they were sitting in a booth with hot chocolate in front of them.

"Darby loved chocolate," Ray said, more to himself than informing Kathryn of something they all knew.

"Why is this your fault?" she finally asked, not giving him time to back out.

Ray began from the beginning and told her everything. Everything except for the name of the person who moved that part into the system by installing it on an airplane. Ray had been warned that if his name was ever mentioned, Kathryn's girls were as good as dead. Ray believed him.

"Darby didn't know what was bothering me, but she knew something was. She was going to help me solve it after the first of the year." He placed his hand on the top of his cup and flattened it.

He sighed, and looked into her eyes. "She was going to make me have a New Year's Resolution."

Kathryn smiled. Darby always made her make resolutions, too.

"I don't know what to say," she said, surprised, but not shocked. She, too, knew something was up. Just because there was no proof in Singapore, there were too many signs pointing to Ray.

However, she was grateful the case was closed. She never wanted to believe that Ray was part of this. More than anything, she knew Ray loved Darby. This was almost too much information.

"They need to lock me up," he said, with a sigh.

Ray was already in prison. Kathryn saw that every time she watched him with Darby. But Darby reacted more to him than anyone. Right or wrong, Darby needed Ray, and putting him behind bars would do nobody any good. It would only bring more pain.

"Ray, you did not do this to Darby." She took his hands in hers. "She was flying that plane just fine without an engine. What you did was wrong, but you did so much right." Kathryn hesitated to find the right words, and then continued. "I don't know what I would have done in your place, either." She breathed deep. "But we will find out who put that part into service, and make them hang."

He sighed and turned his hands, now holding Kathryn's. "So, there's been a lot of speculation. Do you think that drone was flown into that plane on purpose?"

"Appears that way. But we need to figure out who owned it."

"But if the plane had been solid..."

"If it were on purpose, then an aircraft with two engines would not have survived. They would just fire another drone at the other engine," Kathryn said. "But one thing I do know is that you did not hurt her."

"Uncle Ray," Jenny said, and Kathryn and Ray jumped, dropping hands and turning toward her.

Kathryn had no idea how long her daughter had been standing there. She slid out of her seat, and all but pushed Jenny in, and sat beside her—more to block her daughter from running.

"What is it, sweetie?" Ray asked.

Jenny's tears began to flow again, and Kathryn's heart broke for her daughter. She put an arm around her, and pulled her close. They sat that way for what felt like an eternity. Jenny's tears subsided and when she gained composure, she sat upright. Ray handed her some napkins, and Jenny accepted them and wiped her eyes and blew her nose.

Jenny looked between Kathryn and Ray. "Mom, I'm so sorry. Uncle Ray, you didn't do this to Aunt Darby, because I did."

CHAPTER 46

PRESSING THE ACCELERATOR, she cleared the yellow light before it turned red. Kathryn was on her way home to meet John. She had left the girls at the hospital with Ray and Linda. She had no idea what Jennifer had been going through the previous few weeks. That poor girl, thinking she was to blame.

Kathryn sped down her street and pulled into the driveway. John and his team were already there waiting. She turned off the car and John was at the door, opening it for her.

"I hope you're right," he said.

"Jenny's drone flew off on its own," Kathryn said, rushing to the front door. She fumbled with her keys as she attempted to unlock it. "Jenny had been upset for losing it, but when they got back to the house, we were watching the news..." Kathryn pushed the key into the hole and turned the lock.

"Where's the other one?" John asked, opening the door.

"Girls' room. Jessica's closet."

Kathryn ran into the house, and then up the stairs and down the hall. John followed. Inside the girls' room Kathryn pulled open Jessica's closet door, and there it was. John slipped on his gloves and pulled the machine out of the closet. He carried it to the kitchen.

"There you go, guys," John said, setting the drone on the table. "Do your magic."

Kathryn breathed deep, and walked to the living room. She stared out the window with her hands on hips, drumming her fingers at her sides, wishing she were wrong. Wondering if this search would just lead to more questions with no answers.

John touched her shoulder, and she jumped. "I have tea," he said.

Kathryn turned from the window, and a steaming cup of tea was on the coffee table. She moved to the couch and lifted the cup of warmth. "How long will it take?"

"Maybe thirty minutes."

She set the cup on the table, and grabbed her purse. She dug for her phone and when she found it, sent a text to Linda—*We need an hour. You okay?*

Linda replied—*We're doing great. Text when we're clear to bring the kids home.*

Preliminaries done, Kathryn sipped her peppermint tea and settled in for the wait. "Jenny had been having problems, and I was clueless. I had no idea why she'd been upset. But apparently when she heard on the news that a drone had done it, she knew it was hers that hit Darby's plane."

"Why didn't she say anything?" John asked, sitting beside her.

"Same reason Ray didn't. Punishing herself, I suppose."

"This doesn't make sense," John said. "That thing flew at Tom's plane. Why?"

Kathryn shook her head in exasperation. None of this made sense. "Maybe he didn't know there was a device in the drone. Maybe he was a pawn."

"How could he not know?" John asked.

"This has *Bill* written all over it," Kathryn said. "Tom went to see him. What if Bill set this up without Tom knowing? What if Bill set up the gifts? Besides, Tom didn't have money to buy those drones."

John shook his head. "I don't think so." He sighed. "Tom's toxicology report showed he overdosed, and his heart stopped."

"On what?" Kathryn asked. When had John learned this? More importantly, why hadn't he told her?

"Tom had some anticholinergic drug and high levels of antidepressants in his blood."

"I'm not surprised that he was on antidepressants, but what's that anticholi stuff?"

"Antihistamines that block the brain's neurotransmitters." Then in a monotone voice he said, "This drug can lead to dry mouth and nose, flushed skin, dilated pupils, inability to urinate, mental issues, seizures, arrhythmia, high blood pressure, and coma." He took a deep breath and added, "But they do allow you to eat your favorite foods without heartburn."

Kathryn laughed. "Don't think that doing a commercial about the drug, is going to get you off the hook for not telling me about this."

"I'm sorry. I simply forgot. He may have just combined the wrong dose, and it caused his heart to seize."

"Did he have Provigil in his system?"

"No."

"So an antidepressant and antihistamine cocktail did him in?"

"Looks like it," John said. "Combining drugs, even legal, can be lethal. More than likely this was a result of his normal stupidity. You guys approved pilots to fly with antidepressants, but if they mix them with the wrong thing without knowing, bye-bye captain."

The FAA allowed antidepressants. But Kathryn was not sure that was the best thing, due to dosing issues with international flying, time zone challenges, and consistency.

"Darby always said she would rather fly with someone *on* antidepressants than someone who *needed* them," Kathryn said.

"I suppose."

"John, what the hell is going on?" Kathryn asked. "Drug smuggling, overdosing pilots, and drones taking out airplanes. Suicide pilots flying into mountains. A missing triple-seven. And chief pilots who are worried about a safety book." Kathryn put her hands to her face, and shook her head. When she dropped them she added, "I would laugh if I didn't want to cry at the thought of Darby lying in that hospital."

John crossed his legs, and watched her. "How's she doing?"

"She hasn't changed. But she's still spiking throughout the day."

"Sorry I haven't been there. I just…"

Kathryn reached over and touched his hand, "I know."

She squeezed his hand and then lifted her cup, and took a sip. She wasn't sure if she wanted to find out that Jessica's drone had a control device. It would only move them closer to unanswered questions. It would also leave so many more questions of fear and regret.

"Why doesn't the FAA mandate a TCAS system on every drone?" John asked.

"Oh, don't think I haven't tried." Kathryn rolled her eyes.

UAS (unmanned aircraft systems) most commonly called drones, would be the next big aviation threat. She knew it, and there was a fix. Hundreds of thousands of these aircraft would be flying within the next few years. These were airplanes and they needed regulatory compliance, and operator training. But as of now, anyone with a little bit of money could get one.

"There should be a system enabling drones to fly an escape maneuver," Kathryn said. "I thought, anytime it got close to another aircraft it could divert." She tucked her legs up onto the couch, and pulled a blanket over her lap to ward off the chill. "Someone with power and money is fighting the TCAS system in drones, and shut down my recommendation."

"Hmmm." John folded his arms. "But any mandates, from registration to TCAS systems, won't matter if someone decides to use them for harm. They'll just uninstall the system."

"You're right," Kathryn said, nodding. "But it would keep the innocent mid-air collisions at bay."

"That it would."

"Mr. McAllister," a voice said, from the kitchen. "Would you mind coming in here?"

Chapter 47

KATHRYN MOVED THROUGH the metal detector, paying extra attention to every process and procedure. She waited in the lobby for Warden Filmore. This was the last place she had wanted to be, but when they found that control device in Jessica's drone, she had to know if Bill was behind it. Both John and she had forgotten that Chris had also received a drone. But as it turned out, his did not have a device. Thus, clearly indicating a personal attack on Kathryn and her girls.

She waited well over a month to allow the NTSB to do their thing, whatever that may have been. As far as the drone was concerned, there were only two suspects and she was about to visit one.

April Fool's Day was an appropriate day to visit her ex-husband in prison. She was tired of being the fool, and was about to take control of the situation. Despite her hatred for this man, he had brought into her life the people she loved most. So the Bill experience was not all a waste. But he was also systematically taking those people she loved away, one by one.

Kathryn had told Jackie she was going to Walla Walla, but made her promise not to tell John. When they found the tracking device in Jessica's drone, John had told her she could not be involved, even unofficially. Whatever they found, she could tarnish the case. But this was personal.

She could not have John know what she was doing.

When the warden approached, Kathryn said, "Film, good to see you again."

"Kat," he said, shaking her hand, and holding a bit longer than last time. That was exactly what she hoped for, and she smiled warmly at him.

"Can we talk in your office?"

"Certainly, please…" he said, extending a hand. They walked to his office and he closed the door.

"How's Bill been doing?"

"Same. Charming everyone." The warden sat on the edge of his desk. "But there's something off about him."

"He's lethal," Kathryn said. He wasn't telling her anything she did not already know. The question was not *what* was off about him, but what *wasn't* off about him.

Film lowered his voice, "He makes me ill. When that Global plane went down, the smug look on his face, all but froze my blood. I've been around here a long time, and have seen everything. He's the worst kind of evil."

Kathryn nodded. "I need a favor."

"Anything."

"Can you get the prison doctor to put him on a heavy dose of antidepressants?"

The warden folded his arms. "If you think it would help," he said, with a grin.

"I know it will." Kathryn locked eyes with Film. "It would be best if he didn't know."

"Consider it done. Now, what else can I do?"

"Would it be possible to meet him in a regular room, so I can buy him a Pepsi?"

The warden raised an eyebrow and then said, "I can get you a room." He hesitated, warily assessing her. "Kat, be careful with this one. I know you were married to him, but you were one of the lucky ones. Don't push that luck."

Kathryn knew the dangers of locking up a brilliant, but sociopathic mind in a cage, with nothing to do but think. That was a lethal combination. Somewhat like forcing a pilot with a safety mission to sit at home on reserve. The brilliant mind could never be turned off. The only difference between the two were the outcomes—one found ways to improve safety, the other always led to destruction and loss of life.

In no time, she was entering a room with tables and chairs. No other visitors or inmates were in the room. Vending machines lined the walls. She sat and waited for Bill.

Within minutes he was escorted into the room.

"Well, why do I have this pleasure?" He said.

"I need your help."

He raised an eyebrow and set his cuffed arms on the table.

"Turns out that the drone that hit the Global plane had some additional control device."

"Hmmm," Bill grunted. "What about the boyfriend?"

"He was smuggling drugs, but turns out he had a heart attack. I suppose it was from stress."

Bill grinned.

"You've always been so compassionate," she said, glancing at the Pepsi machine. "Want one?" she asked, pulling a credit card out of her purse.

And there it was—a spark of pleasure, and he flashed his eyes to the guards. The Warden had said Pepsi was something Bill had not had to drink since he arrived three years earlier.

"Why the shift from bitch?" he said, eyes narrowing.

"Oh, I'm still a bitch. And the sooner you die the better my life will be. But I want information. Consider *this* a bribe." She turned her attention to the guards. "Guys, do you mind if I buy our guest a Pepsi?"

When they shook their heads no, she stood and walked across the room. She inserted the credit card and pressed the Pepsi button and the plastic bottle dropped. Then she pressed Diet Pepsi, and another bottle dropped. She opened one of the bottles as she returned to the table, and handed it to Bill.

He eyed her warily. Bill was anything but a fool. Yet his biggest mistake had always been to underestimate her. She sat, and stuck her credit card back into her purse. Then she twisted the lid off, and took a sip, watching him pull a long drink on his Pepsi.

"So what do you want?" he finally asked.

"I want to know how you did it?

"Did what?"

"Put a tracking device in the girls' drones. More importantly, how did you know they would be flying them when Tom and Darby's flight was landing?"

"Babe, I'm not sure what you're talking about?" He winked, and then put the bottle back to his lips and emptied it.

"Was it a coincidence it hit their plane? Or was this just another way to see if you could crash more aircraft?"

His eyes went cold. "Drones are the next level of terrorism, and what are you and the FAA doing about it?" He belched loudly. "Nothing. You think that the FAA's raising the mandated flight hours is helping safety? It's bullshit!" he bellowed, slamming the empty bottle on the table.

A guard quickly approached and took it from him. The other guard's hand went to his gun. Had the bottle been glass, it would have shattered.

"You think that regulation is not part of the bigger plan? As soon as the FAA induces a pilot shortage, then you'll be forced to allow airlines to reduce the number of pilots out of *necessity*."

He was right about everything. The FAA mandated 1,500 flight hours for a pilot to take the airline transport pilot test to be able to work for an airline. Yet the FAA determined that the number of hours of training at the airline did not determine quality performance. So they relieved airline training requirements from a mandated number of hours to a train to proficiency model, thus reducing training expenses for the airlines. However, the FAA *increased* the number of flight hours required to get *to* the airlines. There was no consistency in their thinking.

"I don't disagree," she said. "But they'll never allow drones to fly passengers." Sadly, she did not sound convincing, even to herself because that technology was already in the works.

"You are a fucking idiot," he spat, leaning forward. "They're replacing pilots with automation. This NextGen crap is all in preparation for an entirely automated aircraft. Killing pilot jobs altogether."

"Crashing planes is not the way to control the industry," Kathryn said. "Innocent people will die, like Darby." Kathryn assessed him, trying to find the words that would pull his heartstrings. "Bill, the girls could have been on that plane."

"The law of unintended consequences is not always a bad thing."

CHAPTER 48

THREE-DOZEN HELIUM BALLOONS filled the hospital room, floating above with strings hanging down like a jungle. The twins were eating chips and salsa. Kathryn had smuggled in a thermos of margaritas, and Jackie and Linda held plastic cups with ice, while Kathryn filled them. Darby wore a sombrero that Kathryn had cut the back half off so she could wear it in bed. Her hair had four months of growth and was flourishing with all the nutrients in the liquid that was pumping into her veins. But she was white, and looked like a ghost.

Darby was also unable to sustain weight as her muscles were shrinking before their eyes, despite the daily exercise routine. Kathryn participated in moving her arms and legs in attempt to keep everything alive. But she never noticed any difference. Still, Kathryn enjoyed the connection.

"Happy Birthday," Ray said, walking into the room carrying a cake with one candle.

"How old is she?" Frankie asked.

Darby's monitored spiked. *If any of you tell, you're toast.*

"Frankie, we never discuss Darby's age," Kathryn said, picking up the pad of paper, she wrote down the experience.

"Mom, she can totally hear what we're saying," Jenny said, sitting on the bed beside her.

I hear it all sweetheart. I'm here.

"I think so, too," Kathryn said. But in reality, she was not so sure. Especially after what Niman had said. The reactions on her machine were random. Granted, they often occurred when something was said about Darby. But she also reacted when the guy was emptying the garbage, or when nothing was occurring at all, and Kathryn was just sitting there crying silent tears. But they needed hope, and Kathryn would never allow that to waiver.

"Why does she care about her age?" Frankie asked, looking confused and holding out her glass for a drink.

Linda's eyes widened. "What are you doing with that glass?"

"Mom, I'm in college. *Seriously?*"

Linda laughed. "Half a glass, and you're not driving!"

"I never do."

Kathryn laughed. Oh, she would be facing those days with the girls. She leaned down and whispered in Darby's ear, "I need you here to help our girls survive their teenage years. I'm going to be a monster."

"What are you saying?" Jessica asked, holding out her glass.

"Nothing good," Jenny answered. "Darby didn't respond."

Kathryn poured water into Jessica's glass with a glare of warning.

"Jeez mom, I was kidding."

"I hope so," Kathryn said, and then theatrically rolled her eyes.

"You're such a Darby," Jackie said, with a laugh.

"No matter what, Darby will always be with us," Kathryn filled her glass. She lifted it and said, "To Darby," and they all toasted. "Now, we just need to get her butt out of bed, and to the party."

"Happy Cinco De Mayo," a nurse said, entering the room.

"Thanks, Mary," Jenny said. "And, it's Aunt Darby's birthday. She says birthdays are to celebrate life. So, we're celebrating."

"There is life," Kathryn said. "And Darby... we are drinking margaritas and eating chips in your honor because you *are* alive."

Yeah. In your dreams. I'm not alive. I'm nothing but a body that can't talk. Can't cry. Can't tell you how much I love you. And then you are seriously putting me through hell. Moo shoo pork on Valentine's Day, and tequila on my birthday. Seriously? If I didn't know better, I'd think you're trying to kill me!

"We should hang a bottle of tequila on her IV," Ray said.

Now you're thinking. I knew there was a reason I loved you.

"She always said, 'tequila makes your clothes fall off'," Jackie said.

"And she proved that." Kathryn smiled as she sipped.

The room fell silent as Ray lit the candle. Then they all sang happy birthday. When they were done, Ray blew out the candle and everyone clapped. Eyes were moist, but smiles sincere. The reality was, as long as she stayed alive, there was hope.

"Is there a party in here?" Niman asked from the door.

"Heard we have holiday cheer?" Kathryn asked, walking over and giving him a hug.

"I hear nothing. I see nothing," he said, in an embrace. "I came to see our girl."

Niman had been relocated to Seattle for Darby's case, yet despite no change in her condition they allowed him to stay because the good folks at Swedish overloaded his schedule. But he checked on her often, despite other duties.

Kathryn, Linda, Jackie and the kids got into a rhythm all their own. The days flowed together, as one day rolled into the next. The only two people that had yet to visit Darby were Chris and John.

Each had their own excuses with underlying reasons. Kathryn did not push.

Kathryn's phone buzzed and she pulled it out of her pocket. *Speak of the devil.*

John—*Call as soon as possible.*

CHAPTER 49

KATHRYN RETURNED JOHN'S text with a message that she would call him in 10 minutes. Then she attempted to return her attention to the party. But her mind was in the NTSB office, and with John. She missed that life, mostly because she had been wrong about the FAA. Providing closure for families was much more fulfilling than beating her head against the wall. Thinking she could stop accidents from occurring was futile. Not with people like Bill, or the pilot managers at Global...

"Earth to Mom!" Jennifer said.

Kathryn turned her attention to her daughter, and then Jackie said, "Was that John?" When Kathryn nodded, she added, "Go call him, we're good."

Kathryn glanced at the others, and everyone stared her way. Everyone except Darby.

"I'll be right back."

She rushed out of the room, took the elevator to the ground floor and walked out the front door of the hospital. These days, the cafeteria became the meeting place out of necessity only. With Spring in the air, daylight and fresh air was not only appreciated, but a requirement. She pressed speed dial and walked down the sidewalk toward a bench.

"What did you find?" Kathryn asked the moment John answered. Anxious for any detail that would take her away from the hell that had become Darby's life. She glanced up to the hospital as she sat on the bench.

"I received a call this morning from my counterpart at the FAA. You just got clearance to do what you do best."

"Which is?" Kathryn said, with a laugh. "Being a pain in the ass?"

"That, too," he agreed. "I've got you back on the case..."

Oh my God. Kathryn placed a hand to her chest. She could not believe it. "What happened? How?" It had been months since she had been prevented from stepping a foot on Global property. The home of what she suspected was a major source of the problem.

"I'm not exactly sure. But something tells me there is more going on there than I previously suspected."

Kathryn smiled, and said sarcastically, "Really?" She had been telling John for months they needed to get the investigation within the walls of flight operations at Global. He always had a reason why they were not going that way.

"Point taken," he said. "I never disagreed with you. I just couldn't open those doors because of your connection to both pilots."

"Both pilots?" Her eyes narrowed. "One of those pilots has a name. It's Darby." John had yet to see her. Now he couldn't even say her name. But more than that, lately he had been detached... or secretive, more evasive. Something. She could not put her finger on it, but time would tell. It always did.

"When can you start?" he asked.

"Last month."

He laughed. "Stupid questions are my new thing."

"Do you have anything specific?" Kathryn asked, thinking out loud, "Or am I free to go where I want?"

"You are free to roam about Global as you see fit."

Kathryn laughed. Two jokes within 30 seconds were out of character for John since the accident. But she had no time to deal with John's mood swings. She had to find out what the hell was going on at Global. She suspected, but proof was all about the data. Big data.

"Have you read Darby's book yet?" Kathryn asked, as she stood. Darby had printed a copy and given it to all of them for Christmas. Her agent had authorized the pre-editions. They were moving forward with publication, despite Darby's condition. "John?"

"Yes. I've read it."

Kathryn smiled. "Speaks volumes, doesn't it." Then she realized that was the exact reason why John was able to get her into Global. He read the book, and put in a good word. The FAA was not required to take recommendations from the NTSB, and most often they didn't due to high expense to the airlines. But if what Darby had written had merit, there would be minimal expense involved, beyond time spent improving processes. "Was that a case study on Global?" John asked.

"More or less. I'm thinking more." Kathryn stood and walked toward the street, to calm her excitement. Now she could go behind the walls of Global, in an attempt to fix the issues at hand. The source of many industry problems.

"Do you think Patrick read it?" John asked.

"Not sure, but I will send him a copy tomorrow morning."

"I wonder if he has a clue what's happening in flight ops?"

"I'm giving him the benefit of the doubt, and saying no," Kathryn said. "With a company that size, the CEO must enable managers the freedom to do their jobs. He had no reason to doubt them."

"He's still responsible for everything that goes on within his corporation."

"Of course. And I don't relieve him of his responsibility," Kathryn said. "It's what he does after he knows the truth, that will answer many questions."

CHAPTER 50

KATHRYN GLANCED AT her watch. She had been waiting 45 minutes in the Global headquarters lobby. Her briefcase resting on her lap, she held it tightly. *Get a grip*. Nobody was going to steal her briefcase, and if they did, she had copies of everything at the office. John had a backup set too, as did her boss.

Breathing deep, she set the evidence on the floor and stood, bringing blood back to her legs. Then she walked to the window. A Global A330 was on short final at Oklahoma City airport. Just prior to the big bird's touchdown, she closed her eyes as visions of Darby's plane took hold. She took two calming breaths and opened her eyes as the wheels touched the runway. Each time it got easier.

Glancing back at her briefcase, she was not quite sure what to do. She returned her attention out the window, as the plane exited the runway. It had taken two weeks to gain access to all records, and four weeks to sort through two years of records.

Global legally could destroy everything prior to two years, and they did. This process was another indication that legality trumped proactive learning. Data was important, and gave answers to everything. But if that data were destroyed, none of it could be used in litigation. Despite what pilots thought of their FOQA and ASAP data being de-identified and classified, when an accident or incident happened, and the case went to court, it was all open and on the floor.

FOQA data was part of an airline voluntary safety program designed to improve safety through the use of automatic reporting of flight data. Whereas ASAP data was composed of errors or deviations reported voluntarily by pilots for the same purpose—to improve safety. Both sets of data were supposed to be used to identify and proactively correct deficiencies in operating practices. Yet destruction of data beyond the legal two-year point missed the point of using data. Retention of data to identify patterns was essential.

Kathryn had given a month of her life to searching through documents, visiting Darby, and giving her girls the attention she thought they needed. The truth was, they did not need her beyond her being a shuttle service. With Francine living with them, she had taken up the slack on driving them around. Francine also began teaching them how to drive.

At fifteen, the girls were living their life without her, and never missed a chance to point out that she was never home, or always tired. Not that they involved her anyway. Jackie didn't have the same issues with Chris. Instead, he complained that she was always in his business. Yet Kathryn was sure he enjoyed the fact that he never had to do anything in the house.

She glanced at her watch. These guys were wasting her time.

Kathryn sighed. She wasn't sure if Darby's accident had changed their family dynamics, or if this would have occurred anyway, as a natural growth process with teenage girls. Kathryn had always thrown herself into her work. The truth was that Darby lying in a coma had changed them all.

She glanced at her watch again—55 minutes. Now they were just pissing her off.

She turned, facing the room, and half sat and half leaned on the windowsill, folding her arms. Today she would be meeting with the Director of Flying—Odell, Director of Flight Operations—Wyatt, the manager of Flight Operations—Clark, and Hughes, a Regional Director—alias Darby's go-to guy.

Wyatt and Clark were in the same positions today that they were in 2012, when the big Global FAA fiasco occurred. Hughes was new to the party. Odell was another story.

Odell had been the chief pilot who put that letter in Darby's file. At the time, he blamed those above him when he said, "They made me do it." But he subsequently moved up. Apparently at Global, those who followed orders were well rewarded.

Furious at what she had found, the best she could do was to fine the airline. But that would not solve the problems. The problems had to be removed. Unless she could prove that the director of flying, Odell, had something to do with the accident, and Wyatt and Clark were intentionally not following SMS mandates, there was not much else she could do.

Shitty management skills were not illegal, but they could cause equally as many problems as a sociopath. Yet what she had learned was nothing short of...

The door opened and Odell stepped into the lobby. Kathryn drummed her fingers on her arms, with clear intent to show her displeasure of flying to Oklahoma City and being kept waiting. This was a move she would not have done for a secretary, but this man deserved no less.

"Mrs. Jacobs?" he asked.

She glanced around the lobby, as if there could be anyone else that might be Mrs. Jacobs waiting an hour for a meeting, and then said, "That would be me. And who are *you*?"

His face turned red as he replied, "Director Odell."

"Oh yes," Kathryn said, walking toward him with an extended hand. "Sorry about that. The extra pounds and hair loss look good on you." She shook his hand firmly.

His mouth opened and then closed. Then he said, "We're waiting for you in the conference room."

She followed him down the hall and into the same conference room that she and Darby had lunch with the CEO, Lawrence Patrick, only three years earlier. She walked to the chair Darby had sat in, and touched the back. Kathryn fought hard to keep the emotion out of her eyes and would take Darby's seat for strength.

Kathryn set the briefcase on the table, and shook hands with Wyatt, Clark, and then Hughes. All the players were at the table. She had requested the Director of Training, and the Manager of SMS, too, but Wyatt said he would prefer to do the preliminaries with the lead managers and they would communicate results to the rest of the team.

"Do you mind if I record this?" she asked, sitting.

"Of course not," Wyatt said, exchanging a glance with Clark.

Kathryn snapped open her brief case, pulled out her recorder and placed it on the center of the table and pressed *record*. She had learned if she did this early enough, before they began talking, they would forget the recorder was there. If she had not been employed with the FAA, she wouldn't have asked. As long as one person knew they were being recorded, that meant her, she could have recorded without any of them knowing.

As she pulled out copies of her report and set them on the table in front of her, the door opened behind her. Clark's expression of surprise, followed by Wyatt, Odell and Hughes all jumping to their feet, brought a grin to her face. Kathryn did not have to turn around to know who was standing behind her.

She stood, and turned toward the guest, and extended her hand. "Thank you for joining us."

"Good to see you again, Kat," Lawrence Patrick said, with an air of familiarity. "Thank *you* for the invite." Clark shot daggers her way. Point given and well taken. She had asked Clark to invite the CEO, but Clark said Patrick opted out and would expect a briefing afterwards. Apparently he never extended that invite.

"I'm glad you could make it," she responded.

"I'm sorry to be late," he said, assessing the room. "What did I miss?"

"We have yet to start," she said lightly. "Gentleman, in light of our new guest, thank you for keeping me waiting for an hour."

Odell's red returned. Wyatt sat, but this time in a chair to the right of, the head of the table. Clark stared blankly at Kathryn, and sat without removing his eyes. Hughes looked oblivious. She turned her attention to Mr. Patrick, who took his place at the head of the table.

"Gentlemen, we are here today to review problems within the walls of Global that appear to be contributing factors in the December crash."

"A drone took out that plane," Odell said, and then flashed his eyes to Patrick. Patrick held his eyes on Kathryn.

"Yes, but a crash is never one thing." She handed a report to each of the men in the room as she continued, "This is a copy of the report, with supporting documentation."

Wyatt was the first to open the cover, and his eyes narrowed. Odell's face began to turn colors again. Clark opened his file, and scanned the first page without expression. Hughes opened the folder and flipped pages without reading.

Patrick's eyes, on the other hand, narrowed. "Please, continue."

CHAPTER 51

ONCE EVERYONE WAS settled, after fidgeting with their copies, Kathryn opened her folder. She had no need to look at it, as she had written the report, and memorized it. A report that would shock the hell out of Patrick. She trusted that he truly believed his airline had a safety culture with free flow of information. He was wrong. Darby's crash was nothing short of a culmination of culture issues. To hell with the drone.

"In alignment with a SMS, or I should say out of alignment, Global has some serious issues."

"With all due respect," Clark said, "SMS is not mandated until January of 2018. We have two years to comply."

"True. But the problem is, for a safety management system to work, the airline must have a safety culture. Therein lies the problem with Global. You *don't* have one."

Patrick looked up from the document. His full attention was on Kathryn.

"We're going to step back in time, to when Check Airman Alan Jones showed up to the simulator 15 minutes prior to a training event, subsequently played on his cell phone during that checking event instead of observing the pilots, and then proceeded to falsify training records—"

"I'm sorry to interrupt, but Darby has had three check rides since then, you can hardly blame that check for her performance," Odell said. "Besides, there is no record of that."

"First, I have documentation from Darby's files. Second, the relevance is, there have been no processes put in place to assure that what happened in that check ride would never happen again. Third, while that check airman was removed from training during the time you were moving the training department to Oklahoma, he was subsequently hired as a line check airman."

"He wasn't…" Clark glanced his way, cutting Odell short.

"Either one of two issues are at play here," Kathryn said. "Either he was rewarded for what he did in that simulator event, or there is no information-sharing between simulator training and line training." Kathryn hesitated to let that sink in, and then added, "I'm still debating which is the lesser of the two evils—a few corrupt management pilots, or an entire airline with a broken information system."

"You can't say that," Odell snapped.

Hughes' head bounced back and forth, as if he were watching a ping pong game, and landed on Patrick when Odell said she couldn't say that, as if Patrick were the referee and would give the answer. Kathryn wanted to laugh at the humor of antics, but instead she turned her attention to Mr. Patrick.

Patrick leaned back in his chair and folded his arms, and nodded for her to continue.

"SMS demands processes for hazard identification. Subject matter experts, SMEs, are essential to identify hazards to mitigate risk," she said. "Experience is obvious."

"Your point?" Clark said.

"My point, Captain, is that you hire inexperienced pilots in positions that demand experience. With Captain Armstrong gone, you had an opportunity to put a pilot with 30 years of international flying experience into that position. He was an A330 and A350 check airman, line check airman, simulator instructor, 747-400 check airman, type rated on the Boeing triple seven, and he wrote the training program on 787. You had the opportunity to have someone who had more experience than everyone in this room combined. Instead you put an MD-80 captain into that position and made him responsible for the entire wide body international fleet."

This might not be the way to start a meeting, but the outcome would depend on what they would do with the information. She needed these pilots to hang themselves, as her hands were more or less tied. So she pulled the pin, threw a grenade, and waited to see what they would do.

Kathryn's previous boss, Tom Santos, had killed Armstrong. Armstrong was unqualified for the job also, but that wasn't the reason he was murdered. Kathryn smiled. Not that killing incompetent pilots was the new FAA methodology for problem solution, but it could be effective.

She had talked to Patrick back then about filling that position with experience. Yet nothing had changed.

"How the hell can he identify hazards without knowledge or experience? He can't," Kathryn said.

Not only were non-qualified pilots placed in management positions, but after two years these pilots were replaced with another inexperienced pilot. Getting a new mind into the position was a positive. But their current process was that as the inexperienced gained on the job training, to where they may be effective, they were replaced with another inexperienced body.

"Next," she said. "Recency training requirements are in place because pilots are sitting on a reserve system, or not flying due to long-haul flights with multiple pilots onboard. But your training setup is nothing short of a joke."

"Excuse me?" Wyatt said, glancing from Kathryn to Patrick.

She may be stepping over the line with opinionated commentary, but she needed to push some buttons to see what surfaced. She only hoped she was not pushing too many at once, and that none of them were Patrick's.

"You're bringing pilots from Seattle and requiring them to report at their body clock time of 2 am. That is not the time to learn anything. Your instructors spend sometimes less than 15 minutes per pilot during their recency, doing the minimum."

"We comply with all requirements," Clark said.

"Perhaps," Kathryn said, tapping her pen on the table. "But compliance and doing the minimum does not define a safety culture."

When Odell opened his mouth, Kathryn held out an opened hand and said, "Please. Allow me to continue." She took a breath, and glanced at the paper. "Point three. The month of the crash, Darby Bradshaw not only flew an international trip, but she was scheduled the following day for her recency at that 2 am hour. She was fatigued and then sent out the following day on a trip into another operating theater."

"This is ridiculous," Odell snapped. "Our schedulers are in complete compliance with FAR 117."

Anger fueled Kathryn's next statement. "Were you FAR 117 compliant when your schedulers called her on her day off in New York, and forced her on a trip with an inverse assignment?" This was personal. She stood, and with both hands on her hips said, "They deadheaded Darby from New York, through Oklahoma City, to Seattle, with 45 minutes to report for a flight to Hong Kong."

Kathryn placed her hands on the table, glaring into Odell's eyes, and said, "She had been awake for over 30 hours! Then with one night's sleep, there was a flight from Hong Kong back to Seattle, and then off to training, followed the next day by another trip."

"If she signed the release, then I suspect she would be liable for any of what you say, despite the scheduler's part in the equation," Wyatt said, folding his arms over his girth.

"I'll give you a hundred human factors studies as to why pilots would take a flight under similar circumstances. But the bottom line is, she had not more than a three-hour nap due to the hour the pilot scheduler called. The best I can figure is she had been awake for 21 hours before she signed that release."

"And this negates her responsibility how?" Clark asked.

"Being awake for 21 hours is equivalent to .08 alcohol level," Kathryn said, calmer. "Not unlike the person who swears they will not drink and drive, after the first beer they *cannot* think clearly enough to maintain that resolve."

Wyatt shifted in his seat, and said, "Our pilots can cancel a flight any time they see fit."

"Bullshit!" Kathryn snapped. "Your manager of scheduling told Darby's indoctrination class there were *only* four reasons a pilot could cancel training. One of which was fatigue—"

"There you have it," Odell said. "She could have called in fatigued."

"He also said, and I quote," Kathryn read from the report, "'But don't ever call in fatigued at Global. That is the *other* F word.'" Kathryn's anger boiled. "And do you think after all the crap you've pulled on Darby, that she would feel confident that she would be supported if she turned down a flight? This gentlemen, does not constitute a safety culture."

Kathryn closed her briefcase with a slam and everyone jumped. Everyone except Patrick. She clicked it secure and set it on the floor, and then picked up her packet, turned the page, and stared at it. She was not reading, but calming her emotions. This was why they had not wanted her on the case. She was too emotional. But the reality was, emotions were becoming a thing of the past. She was just pissed. Furious that this bullshit was going on in 2016!

"And what about dispatchers that argue with captains, encouraging them to take a broken aircraft because it's legal? The hell with safety. From what I see," Kathryn said, followed by a deep breath. "There's not one department at Global that has a safety culture."

"These are some serious allegations," Mr. Patrick said.

"Yes sir, they are. And each event is documented."

"Half of them by notes," Hughes, said. "That does not constitute legality."

"You're wrong," Kathryn said. "But despite notes, I have records that fall within the two-year limit for record retention."

"But—" Odell said.

"Captain, I have pages and pages of current documentation," Kathryn said. "For example, five months ago you sent a first officer who had been on an Airbus for 17 years to training on the Boeing. This was a first-time Captain checkout, and you gave him a flash drive to learn the plane. Then you reviewed the test so he could pass it electronically. Not to mention, you paired him with a new-hire for simulator training." She glanced at the list on her report. "Then you had him sit for 6 weeks before you assigned him his line training to go out the day before Christmas, in the worst weather of the year. Not to mention two weeks prior he began calling, and emailing numerous times to get an extra simulator session before he flew."

Kathryn spoke for two hours covering a list of issues that violated a safety culture, presenting examples, and identifying the many factors that could have impacted Darby's flight. Global's policy of locking a supporting pilot out of the flight deck if there was a medical issue in the cabin was nothing short of ridiculous. The other first officer could have helped in those final moments. The company had increased the crosswind landing limit from 20 knots to 40, prior to training all pilots. Darby had yet to complete that training, despite her just returning from her recency training. The winds were every bit of 40 knots on the day of the crash.

As if Darby reached from her grave of solitude, her book *Fight For Safety—Inside the Iron Bubble*, provided Kathryn with insight to issues that she had no idea had been going on within Global's walls. She used Darby's book as a map that told her what to look for, and where to find it.

"Captain Odell," Kathryn said. "It was brought to our attention that you had Darby pulled into the chief pilot's office to reprimand her for her book."

"I did no such thing. I... I just told her she couldn't use the name Coastal and put a photo of a Global plane on the cover."

"Why not?"

"What do you mean why not?" He glanced from Wyatt and Clark back to Kathryn. "Copyright laws."

"Hmmm, it could have been exceptional marketing for the airline."

"I think you've overstepped your bounds," Odell said. "Is the FAA in charge of our marketing department now?"

"I was going to ask you the same thing. Since when does the Director of Flying have control over marketing?" Kathryn's eyebrow raised and she said, "You also ordered Darby to never contact corporate communications, and subsequently ordered her to bypass her chief pilot and report directly to Hughes." Kathryn tapped her pen on the table. "Someone directly under your command."

"What does this have to do with anything?" Odell said, glancing toward Hughes.

"Exactly what I've been wondering," Kathryn said, scrutinizing him. She stood and walked to the opposite end of the table from where Patrick sat, and stopped.

Turning to the group she said, "Your manuals are not consistent with each other, and in error. Your instructors are training what works in the simulator and disregarding safety of flight. Your FOQA data indicates you have serious training problems, and your fixes are nothing short of reactionary Band-Aids. And yet…"

She hesitated, and then placed both hands on the table and leaned in. "You have taken it upon yourself to block Darby from following procedures that were set up for the entire employee group. You put her under a microscope. You harassed her. Selected her out, and then Odell forced her to remove any reference to Coastal Airways. Why?" Kathryn sighed, and then more to herself than the group she said, "How far would you go to remove her permanently?"

CHAPTER 52

KATHRYN RETURNED TO her seat, and assessed the room. She sighed—deliberate and loud. There was definitely something in Darby's book that Odell did not want the world to connect to Coastal or Global. Perhaps it was both airlines. More than likely, he did not want the world to know that he was connected to that book and the many issues.

"How far would you go to remove Darby?" Kathryn asked, again, this time staring directly at Odell.

"This is bullshit," Odell said, a little too loudly. His face turned crimson once again, and he glanced at Patrick whose eyes flashed his way and back to Kathryn.

"Let's talk about that letter you put in Darby's file," she said, directly to Odell. "Not only do you change policy, but you don't follow your own policy. You stuffed a letter in Darby's file under nothing but threat. 'Threat and error management' does not mean managing by threat. You couldn't even take accountability for it, instead you said, 'they made me do it', and promised Darby it would be out of her file in three years."

Kathryn poured herself a glass of water, and took a long drink before she continued. "Gentlemen, please reference pages 22 through 30," Kathryn said. "Odell falsified a letter to threaten

Darby. These pages also include support from the newspaper to show that her blog post was never published. A letter from Airbus Industries and a Global check airman, attested to the accuracy. And as far as her sharing training secrets, she was not only *not* trained for high altitude recovery, but she had never received stall training either."

Kathryn was more than pissed. They had placed a letter in Darby's file, manufactured with lies, to scare her. This airline did not have a safety culture, and the reason that nobody would speak out against any of them. They were afraid.

"Gentlemen, there is only one reason that flight operations has a do-or-die chain of command policy, and that's because—"

"Excuse me," Mr. Patrick said. "But we have an open door policy."

"With all due respect, your company may have an open door policy in writing," Kathryn said, "But flight operations has its own set of rules in many areas. The chain of command is one of them, and is another conflict of a safety culture."

Patrick looked from one pilot to the next and then said, "Is this true?"

"No sir, it's not," Wyatt said.

"Captain Wyatt, as you read the report, you will see numerous references about the chain of command with emails from a couple of the people in this room." Kathryn sighed, and turned her attention to the CEO.

"Mr. Patrick," Kathryn said. "I don't need to tell you that a Safety Management System and a safety culture depend upon open and just communication." She tapped her pen a couple times on the table, before she spoke, again. "You know, I tried to get a grip on why Darby called her book the *Iron Bubble*. Then it hit me.

Nothing penetrates an iron bubble, and nothing escapes. If your boys keep everything isolated from you, then you have no idea what is really going on within your company.

"That bubble is shiny, and looks good. But it reflects everything going on outside the organization, not what's happening within. To the innocent observer, all they see is a reflection of what is happening externally, yet nothing gets out from the inside."

"I had no idea any of this had been occurring," Wyatt stated.

"Neither did I, sir," Clark added.

"I, uh… uh… uh…," Hughes said, "I didn't know any of this."

Odell folded his arms and shook his head. "I've been playing your game, to move to where I can do some good," he spoke directly to Wyatt and Clark. "But I'm tired of this. You both have set this culture in place, and it's time we change."

Kathryn began to laugh. Was Odell really turning this against his superiors? Granted, they were part of the problem, but *everything* Odell did was for two reasons—power and money. "I'm sorry sir," she said regaining her composure. "It's just that…"

She set her briefcase on the table, and opened it. Then placed her copy of the report inside. "I will be submitting my recommendations when I return. I suspect some heavy fines, bad publicity, and if nothing is changed, you will see another crash. Unless…"

"Go on," Mr. Patrick said.

She studied him for a moment. "Unless you change this culture," she said, with a wave of her hand toward the men sitting at the table.

"We can make that happen," Wyatt said, and Odell and Clark's heads nodded in agreement.

Kathryn looked at the management team and smiled as the thought of the Three Stooges flashed before her eyes. Only there were four. She turned to Patrick and asked, "Have you ever done any remodeling before?"

He nodded. "There was a time."

"Well, we both know that you can paint over dry rot and mold, but it does not solve the problem. When structural integrity is in doubt, you have to break down the walls. Rebuild. Put up new sheetrock. And then use a ton of primer *before* you paint. Decorating comes after the hard work."

Kathryn glanced at her watch, and said, "You have a major remodeling job to do."

She had two hours to make her flight. Exhausted, she was looking forward to the flight home and seeing her girls. She had done all she could here. Picking up her briefcase she took one more deliberate look at Captains Wyatt, Clark, Odell, and Hughes, each with a smug expression all their own.

She shook her head slowly and then looked directly at Mr. Patrick. "Lawrence," she said. "You have to get rid of the dry rot."

Chapter 53

KATHRYN SAT IN John's office and waited for him to finish his phone call. He held up a finger indicating it would be just a moment. She had nobody in her office she trusted to share her thoughts with, and she needed to bounce some ideas off someone. That had always been Darby's job. While she and Darby continued that relationship, it had turned one sided, and Kathryn needed a friend to talk to. John had turned into that friend.

As it turned out, the emergency exits on Darby's plane were functioning properly, yet there was no conclusive reason as to why they were not opened after the accident. No videos existed of life inside the A330 inferno—rumors and speculation were never validated. All the same, Kathryn had authorized an investigation into flight attendant safety procedures at Global. Jackie said she was taking time off to be with Darby. Truth be told, she had quit because of the door issue.

Kathryn smiled as John rolled his eyes at the person on the other end of the call. She did not mind waiting for him.

She had just returned from seeing Bill again. They had shared another Pepsi, but she learned nothing new. However, the visit was not a complete waste of time. The Warden assured her that

Bill was taking his meds, and high doses at that. There were times she felt sorry for him, and this last visit was one of them. But she reminded herself that he was evil in the worst way. The thought of her daughters being a positive unintended consequence of a drone hitting an aircraft fueled her every motivation to see and stop him.

"Thanks for coming," John said, after he finished his call. He stood, and walked around the desk, and they hugged.

"My pleasure," Kathryn said. "With the wedding plans and all, I know you're busy."

He nodded and returned to his seat. "What do we have?"

"Everything. But not a damn thing." Kathryn had never felt more helpless, or perhaps she was impatient for results. "May I?" she asked, picking up a pen.

She wrote as she spoke. "We have the bad FADEC, but not necessarily the cause of the crash. However, the reason that part made it into the system was a result of trying to squeeze too much out of employees to make ends meet, compromising safety... We have the drug connection so there was motivation to get rid of Tom. And we know a drone hit that plane."

"But, we're no closer to finding out who programmed those drones." John leaned back, and folded his arms.

"I think it was Bill." Kathryn knew the world would never be safe until he was buried 20 feet under. "I'm not sure we'll ever have proof that he had anything to do with the drones, or if a disgruntled employee did it. But combine that missing plane, and the pilot who flew into the mountains... time will tell, but I'm just saying..."

"Any news about Tom's finances?"

"His ex-wife was very helpful. He had no money in the bank. He was trying to get out of debt with the drug deal. Looks like this was the first time for that. He was a womanizer," she said, blushing, "and a bad investor. The drug deal was just another gamble that went south."

Kathryn had no idea what she had seen in Tom. And yet she knew what kept her coming back for more. He had been the first man that touched her since Bill, and more than that, he had made her feel wanted.

"At least he left his ex-wife with an insurance policy. Then again, so did Linda's husband." Kathryn shook that thought from her mind. "But, I don't think he had anything to do with the drones," she said. "Other than giving them to the girls."

"I want to know where he got them," John said.

"Me too." Kathryn doodled *China* on the page. "You know, a lot of flight crews buy drones overseas because they're cheap. Imagine if the Chinese government installed cameras, recording devices, or worse, mechanical controls to take over the aircraft."

"A nightmare for U.S. security," John said. "What about Global?"

She wrote *Global* on the paper. "I received word this morning that they fired Odell, Clark, and Hughes. I suspect they need to keep Wyatt in place so they have someone who knows what's going on." Kathryn tapped the pen for a moment. "I don't have proof, but I still think that Odell could have had something to do with those drones."

Ray knew more than he told. Kathryn just didn't know what that might be. But he was very short when any mention of Odell came up.

"How would Tom get them from Odell?" John asked.

"They worked for the same company. He could've easily put them into his hands."

"Why? And how would he know the kids would be flying them the same time Darby's plane would be landing?"

"You're right. He wouldn't. That's why this goes back to Bill. He's the only idiot who would take out a planeload of people," Kathryn said. "As he said, he just got lucky."

She had told John about Bill's comment 'if the girls had been on the plane'. He assured her that Bill was just trying to get her riled. Kathryn knew better. His dead eyes spoke volumes. She hoped the antidepressants would help to dull his brain.

"So the only thing we know is someone was able to put a device in a drone, so they could control it." John leaned forward, resting his arms on his desk.

Kathryn nodded. "Until we know where they came from..."

"I've got my team working on it," John said. "We'll find something."

"FAA's mandating registration of all drones," Kathryn said. "But unless we have inspection processes in place, we still won't know what will be flying in our airspace."

They sat quietly for a moment and then John changed the subject. "Are we any closer to finding that missing plane than we were six months ago?"

"Not yet. And I'm not convinced these are isolated cases," Kathryn said. "Nothing new about the pilot who flew into the mountain either."

John shifted in his chair, and then gave her that look. The one that said she had better be sitting. "Kat, we need to mandate psychological evaluations for pilots. That guy was sick. Tom needed help. I think that the missing plane was pilot action. Then there's Bill. I just can't see another way."

"It's a waste of time and money," Kathryn said. She doubted they would ever agree on this point. "Even in the worst case, it's difficult for doctors to identify mental health problems. It would be better to allocate those resources to training. Mental problems are not causing the FOQA data."

Flight Operational Quality Assurance data, was essential in showing what the aircraft was doing and how pilots were operating it, but not *why* the pilots were doing what they were doing.

"Perhaps," he said. "Now what?"

"Pray nothing else happens. Get ready for the wedding. We wait for Darby to come out of the coma." Kathryn assessed John as she mentioned Darby's name. "Speaking of which, are you sure you are okay getting married in the hospital room?"

"That's what Jackie wants. I love her. So… yes."

"Have you talked to Chris about it?"

"We talked, and he agreed for the same reason. He's a good kid."

Jackie and John planned a wedding on August 9th. Jackie was adamant that she wanted Darby to be part of it. Kathryn was not so sure that was good for Darby. But as the months passed, Darby's reactions to events were fewer. If Darby knew what was happening, it would break her heart that she could not be standing beside her friend. It would also break her heart to know she may never live the same experience.

"It will be a beautiful wedding," Kathryn said. "Wherever it is."

John's eyes moistened. "I wanted to wait for Darby to come out of her coma, but…"

"But waiting, you may never get married."

He nodded. "This somewhat seals the deal, that we believe she's not coming out of this."

"Not true. You can't stop life," Kathryn said. "That would be the last thing Darby would want. And she *will* come out of this, it hasn't even been a year."

"I know. It just feels wrong to be so happy with her lying there."

"There's nothing more right than you and Jackie getting married. The wedding in the hospital room, well that's another story."

John laughed. "She's your friend, you talk to her."

"I tried," Kathryn said, and then she glanced at the paper, and the word—*Global*. "Not to change the subject, but if Odell didn't have anything to do with taking out that plane, he still hated Darby. And now he's lost his job. What if…?"

"I'll have security stationed outside her room."

"Thank you." With one worry off her plate, Kathryn stood and said, "Well, I better let you get back to work." She headed toward the door. As she reached for the knob, she stopped and turned toward John. "You know, Darby poured her heart and soul into that book over the previous three years. All she ever wanted was for things to change at Global, and to improve safety."

"She did an excellent job, and change is happening."

"I know. Because of the crash, I suspect this will be the most-read aviation book in history. Change will occur worldwide," Kathryn said. "She got her wish."

"Kat…" John's eyes narrowed and grew dark. "Is there *any* possibility that Darby could have done this on purpose to create that change?"

CHAPTER **54**

KATHRYN STUCK THE brush back into the bottle, and closed the lid. She lifted Darby's hand and said, "Red, white and blue, sweetheart," and then she blew on her fingers. "You've got the most beautiful hands in the hospital."

I hope they match my toes. You've never been one for nail fashion.

Kathryn set her hand on the covers and moved to the bottom of the bed with supplies. Once she was set up, she lifted the covers and began painting Darby's toes. Kathryn could not shake John's words of Darby's part in the accident.

"Darby, I know there is no way you did this intentionally." She stroked red on the big toe and skipped the next two, and then touched the brush to the fourth. "We're going to have to clip these beasts again," she said, as she painted.

"I've been out to see Bill, again." She closed the red bottle and picked up the white.

Stay away from him Kat.

Darby's machine spiked a couple beats and Kathryn jumped. She set the bottle of polish down and grabbed the pad of paper. There had been only eleven events for the month of June. They were definitely reducing. Kathryn added the event with a July 1st time stamp.

She turned the page. During the month of May, there had been forty, and Kathryn read the list. Then she turned to April, and then March. "Oh my God," she said turning the page, back to February. "Darby, you *are* listening."

Six months and you've just figured this out?

"If you can hear me, make your heart jump again," Kathryn said, and waited. Nothing. "What if I told you that I was going to paint your toes black for July 4th?" Nothing.

Seriously? Like black would really upset me. I love black. And black toes are so in.

Kathryn opened the bottle of white and continued to paint Darby's toenails. Perhaps Niman was right, and she was just not ready to let Darby go. Perhaps when she did, Darby would move peacefully into the light, or wherever one went after they died.

Kathryn's faith in a higher being was wavering. How could there be a God, when so much horror occurred in the world? She was not sure. All she knew was that she would *never* let Darby go.

Once finished with her toes, Kathryn put the bottles of polish into a bag, and then stuck it into her purse. She pulled a chair beside the bed, and began to brush Darby's hair.

"Your hair grew back beautifully," Kathryn stroked. It grew quickly and was still red, but thicker than ever. "You've got twelve inches now," she said pulling the brush through, "I'm thinking we might have to give you a haircut soon."

It's Auburn! And don't you dare cut my hair. All right, this is it. Pull the plug and let me go someplace. Anyplace but here!

Carefully lifting Darby's head, Kathryn brushed the back. When finished, she set her head gently on the pillow. "You're beautiful," she said, setting the brush on the nightstand. Then Kathryn leaned forward and kissed Darby's forehead. "I'll be back tomorrow sweetheart."

Kathryn set the pad of paper on the windowsill. There was no doubt in Kathryn's mind that Darby was with them and she could hear. If only she could prove it, she would get Niman back on Darby's case. But why couldn't she react on command? There had to be a way.

She lifted her purse, and threw it over her shoulder as she walked toward the door. Kathryn turned the knob, but hesitated opening the door. She looked back at Darby, and said, "I'm thinking about getting back together with Bill."

The hell you are! I'll kill the bastard before I ever let that happen!

The machine beeped wildly as Darby's blood pressure spiked.

CHAPTER 55

AUGUST WAS WITH them before they knew it, as John and Jackie's wedding day had arrived. Kathryn had just finished putting flowers in the arch, set in front of the window in Darby's room. She was surprised that it fit. It was as if the room had grown to accommodate the event. Yet her mind had been playing tricks with her as of late.

If she didn't know better, Bill was drugging her again during her visits. But there was no way that could be happening. She had been concerned that early Alzheimer's was setting in. It was probably just stress. She scheduled blood tests for the following week to find out what was happening. Days had a way of flying by and she couldn't remember any of them. She remembered key events, meeting with John, investigating the airline, and holidays. But the normal stuff was lost on her. Even her daily visits with Darby were rolling into one event.

"Mom, that looks really good," Jennifer said, as she and Jessica stuck tiny flowers in Darby's French braid.

Kathryn glanced at the arch and for the first time, she really noticed it. "Thank you. I think Jackie will love it." She stepped down off the chair and turned her attention toward the girls.

Jessica had braided Darby's hair to the side of her face, and laid it on the pillow. They added makeup. Tears welled up in

Kathryn's eyes. "I still remember when Darby gave you makeup for Christmas," Kathryn said.

"Yeah, and we thought you were going to blow a gasket," Jessica added, with a laugh.

Kathryn remembered that night well. The night that Darby had learned Global was no longer running traditional recurrent training where they brought pilots into the training center. That was the day they began allowing pilots to teach themselves the planes they would be flying—Chapter 5 in Darby's new book.

Darby's machine did a double-quick beep and Jessica said, "Look. Aunt Darby reacted to us talking about the makeup!" She grabbed the paper and wrote the event down.

Makeup? Or was Darby reading Kathryn's mind? Kathryn sighed. *Get a grip Kat.* Weddings were always stressful. But this event would only be their circle—she and the girls, Chris, Linda, Niman, Francine, and Ray.

"Okay, I think we're done," Jennifer said.

Jessica rolled her eyes, "I hope so. We're out of flowers." Kathryn gave Jessica a look of warning not to start the bickering today. Message was received with a nod, and Kathryn smiled.

"Okay ladies, we have four hours until the wedding. We'd better get home and get ourselves ready."

"Darby, I want no playing outside and ruining your hair and makeup," Jennifer said, and kissed her cheek.

Jessica glanced at her mother, and Kathryn shook her head. She knew something smart was going to come out of Jessica's mouth to insult her sister.

Instead, Jessica said, "See you soon." She kissed Darby's other cheek.

FOUR HOURS LATER Jackie and John stood under the arch, with the minister standing in front of them. Chris stood to John's side holding the ring. Kathryn had set chairs in rows at the end of Darby's bed. Linda, Niman, and Francine, were in a row in front with an empty chair for Chris, and she, Jessica and Jennifer were behind them. She glanced at the empty chair to her right, surprised Ray was not there. But the real surprise was the number of hospital staff that stood behind them, filling the room, and blocking the doorway.

This was John's first time in the room, but Darby's staff knew Jackie and loved her. She and Kathryn had taken turns, morning and night, checking on Darby. Jackie always managed to bring cookies, or flowers, or did something nice for the nurses and assistants. She did it because she was grateful for all they did for Darby.

Kathryn smiled at her friend, who looked more gorgeous than she ever thought possible. Instead of discouraging the hospital wedding, Kathryn finally understood. Jackie's wedding in the hospital was her closing one door and opening another. She had thought her life ended in a hospital room when Greg died, and that she would never love again. Now she was giving her heart and life to another, and she wanted to not only have Darby share it, but in a way, she wanted Greg to know it was okay for him to move on.

Moving a tissue to her eyes, Kathryn dabbed underneath, so not to ruin her makeup. Jackie had told her that when she came to see Darby, she could feel Greg was with her. She needed to release him, and showing him she was moving on would be the only way she could do that. This conversation had been in front of Darby. July 21st, the event was documented in Darby's journal.

Jackie was saying her vows, when movement behind Kathryn caught her attention and she turned. Ray was squeezing between the people and he sat beside Kathryn. She reached over and touched his hand. Glad that he arrived, she was not sure that he would make it. He had told her that he planned on proposing to Darby. She had said, "Well maybe we can have two weddings."

He had laughed, an uncomfortable laugh, "I think that's like marriage rape. She kind of has to say yes." If she hadn't known before, she knew then, that those two were perfect for each other.

The next few minutes were surreal. John leaned in to kiss the bride. Ray reached up and touched Darby. The sun shone brilliantly through the window. Warmth filled her soul. And Darby's machine beeped multiple extra times. Kathryn looked from Darby to the machine, and then back to the blinding light coming through the window highlighting Jackie and John. The most beautiful glow filled the room. And then there was silence.

CHAPTER 56

KATHRYN STOOD OUTSIDE the prison. She gripped her purse, and looked to the sky. There was no other way. She glanced at her watch. In exactly three hours she would be on a plane, headed back to Seattle. This would be her final trip to Walla Walla Prison. She would never see Bill again.

Kathryn entered the prison. "Hi Frank," she said to one of the guards.

"Nice to see you again, Kat," he replied.

She placed her purse on the x-ray machine, and then walked through the scanner.

Film was waiting for her, with arms folded. She grabbed her purse, took a deep breath, and followed him to his office.

"How was the wedding?" he asked.

"Beautiful."

"And Darby? Anything new?"

"No," she said. "But, I know she hears us. Nobody believes me, but now it's as if she knows what I'm thinking too, and who is in the room." Warden Filmore had become more than her link to Bill. He had become her friend.

"How are you feeling?" He asked pulling a chair up beside her. "Have you gone to the doctor yet?" He handed her a glass of water.

Kathryn nodded. "But they couldn't find anything." She drank her water, finishing the entire glass. She had told him about her losing days and he listened, and that she was planning to get blood tests. He had told her not to worry, that he was sure it was just stress.

She would miss him when she stopped visiting. There had been more than one time when she questioned whether she was using Bill's visits to see Film. But today would answer that question.

"Have you seen any change with the meds?" She asked.

"Nothing noticeable."

"Are you sure he's taking them?"

"Yes. We're putting them in his food."

"Good." Kathryn nodded. "I guess I should go see that sociopath."

"What's today's goal?"

"I need to find out if he had programmed those drones."

"Same. Same," he said.

Kathryn smiled. "More or less."

The skies had been quiet since Darby's crash. But it felt like the calm before the storm. She had to know today. But if he wouldn't talk today, he never would.

"We're getting nowhere, and someone put those devices in the machines," she said. "He's one of two people who had access to Tom."

"Well, let's get you in there to find out," Film said.

As he walked her down the hall she said, "I wish we could give him one of those truth serums."

"You might not be prepared for what comes out of his mouth," Film said soberly. "Here you go." He opened the door and she walked into the room.

Kathryn walked over to the table where Bill was already sitting, and said, "Hi." The guards stood back and watched. His arms were bound in front of him as always. Kathryn sat, and placed her purse in her lap.

"I want to know if it was you who was responsible for those drones." She was getting tired of whatever the game was that he was playing.

"Of course you do." He narrowed his eyes and watched her. "Where's my Pepsi?"

"In that machine." Kathryn nodded to the side of the room. "I want an answer."

"What the hell does it matter if *I* did it or not?"

During her last visit, she had learned that Bill was more against drones than she would have imagined. Unreasonably so. Maybe they had something in common after all. She knew one way to get him to talk—push every button.

She raised an eyebrow. "Of course it matters," she said. "Drones are the future, and there's nothing that a drone can't do, that a pilot could."

"Fuck you!" Bill spat. "I know exactly what you're doing with this NextGen bullshit. It's nothing more than a test bed for pilots validating automation to remove them from the cockpit."

"It's the future," she said flatly. "What does it matter to you anyway? You're never getting out to fly a plane again."

"What does it matter?" Bill's face reddened, and his eyes grew dark. "It matters because you're taking pilot jobs!"

"Bill, get over it. You've never given a damn about the industry," she said with a wave of her hand. "You've only been about power, money, and control. You were never anything but another management pilot politicking for a position of power. The only difference was, you were on the union side. You're all climbers."

"At least I stood for something," Bill said, followed by a smirk.

"Your point?"

"My point? You can't stop me, even behind bars."

"Did you do this?" she snapped. "I want the truth."

"You can't handle the truth."

"Did you put those devices in the drone?"

"You're damn right I did!"

She knew it. Kathryn breathed deep. She also knew there was only one solution to ending this hell. She slid her chair back and pulled out her credit card, stood and then threw her purse over her shoulder.

"Looks like you've been gaining some weight. Want a Diet Pepsi today?"

"Fuck you," he said, but he still glanced at his gut.

She walked across the room, stuck her credit card into the machine and pressed regular. When the machine popped the bottle out, she removed it from the machine and opened the lid and repeated the same action, but pressed diet, for herself. She stuck her card back into her purse, and grabbed the pills.

When her bottle fell to the catch, she turned toward the machine and dropped the pills into Bill's bottle. They fizzled nicely, as they dissolved in the soda. She pulled her bottle out, and stood. She walked back to the table, and handed Bill his drink.

By the time Kathryn sat, and opened her lid, he had downed the first half of his bottle and belched.

Kathryn held her bottle toward Bill and said, "When you get to hell, tell them I sent you."

HER FLIGHT TOUCHED down in Seattle, ninety minutes after she had left the prison, and Kathryn turned on her cell phone. Four messages popped up—one from John, two from Jackie, and another from Film. She listened to them as the plane taxied toward the gate. They all shared the same information. Bill had died from cardiac arrest ten minutes after her flight departed.

Waiting for her departure had been the longest wait of her life. She was afraid if she didn't get out of town, she never would. Kathryn closed her eyes. The FAA was working toward proactive measures for aviation safety, more so than reactionary, and she was fully committed to that concept.

CHAPTER 57

HE STOOD in the dark, staring at Darby's bed. Darby hoped this was just another nightmare. They were becoming more vivid with each passing moon. The days were getting shorter, the dark became darker. Either she was drifting further into the hole, or her friends were not visiting as much. But they would never leave her side.

She felt his breath, and the room grew cold.

What the hell are you doing here? Darby tried to scream, but no words ever escaped. Her heart felt like it would burst out of her chest.

Bill pulled a hand through her hair. "I'm here to take you for a ride."

But... you're in prison.

"Not anymore," he laughed. "Kathryn released me."

You can hear me?

"Of course," he said, sliding a finger down the side of her face and under her chin. "You're as dead as I am."

Leave my room. Now.

"I'm not going anywhere, without you," Bill said. He spread one hand over her throat, and the other he grabbed a handful of cords going to the wall.

Please leave. Please. I don't want to die. I can't die.

"Sometimes we don't have control over what we want," Bill said, as he simultaneously squeezed her neck and yanked all the plugs from the wall.

"Stop!" Kathryn screamed, sitting upright in bed. Her heart was racing and she was soaked in sweat. She turned the clock on her nightstand, so that she could see the time—1:54 am.

She climbed out of bed and called the hospital, and requested to be connected to Darby's nurse's station.

When the nurse answered Kathryn said, "Marion, this is Kat. Will you check on Darby?"

"I just came from there, and…"

Kathryn closed her eyes and said a prayer. "Is she okay?"

"She is now. About five minutes ago that machine of hers was beating wildly, and lasted a good two minutes. I sent a message to Dr. Niman."

"Has anyone been in there?"

"At this hour?" Marion said surprised. "Not a soul."

Kathryn asked her to document the event, and check on her through the remainder of the night. Then Kathryn wandered downstairs and into the kitchen. She made a cup of tea, sat at the kitchen table, and cried.

That dream had been too real. Bill had been gone for a month and a half now, and he had been visiting her dreams almost nightly, walking through her home. Stopping at the girls' room but never going in. This was the first time she saw him visiting Darby.

Kathryn was growing more fatigued as the days went on. They said Bill's heart attack was natural causes and nothing ever came of it. Film had called once, and asked if she wanted to visit a couple of his other inmates. She forced out a laugh, but Film never said anything more.

After Kathryn finished her tea, she climbed the stairs and crawled back into bed. But sleep never came. Before she knew it she could hear the girls in the kitchen making breakfast.

She climbed out of bed and wandered downstairs.

"Holy cow Mom," Jessica said. "You kind of look like the living dead."

"You sure do," Jenny concurred, looking at her closely. "Is this your Halloween costume?"

"I thought you were going to be Cat Woman," Francine said.

"I'm going for the living dead Cat Woman look," Kathryn said, as she poured herself a cup of coffee.

"You okay?" Francine asked.

Kathryn nodded, "Nothing that caffeine can't fix."

After she kissed the kids goodbye, she called her office and told them she would be in late. Then she put on enough makeup to hide the dark circles, but that made her look worse. Then she thought about going as the living dead, being it was Halloween and all. Assessing herself, she decided that was exactly what she would do.

She wiped the makeup out from under her eyes. Then she pulled on black slacks, followed by a black turtleneck and added white powder to her face. Then she slid bright red lipstick over her lips. Life was pretty pathetic when you looked better without a costume on Halloween.

She returned downstairs, refilled her coffee cup, and sent Jackie a text—*Meet me at the hospital in 45 minutes?*

Jackie's reply—*Yes. Everything okay?*

Kathryn typed—*It will be.*

CHAPTER 58

KATHRYN SAID HELLO to the security guard as she passed him, and walked into Darby's room. Jackie was already sitting beside Darby.

Jackie stood as Kathryn entered. "Kat, you look like…"

"I know," she said waving a hand. "It works for today."

"Are you okay?" Jackie pulled a chair up beside hers, close to Darby's bed.

Kathryn glanced over her shoulder and back at her friend. "What time are the nurses scheduled to come in for rounds?"

"Not until ten thirty," Jackie said.

Kathryn walked over to the door, looked out, smiled at the guard, and closed the door.

"Kat, you're scaring me," Jackie said.

Me, too.

Kathryn sat beside her friends and held each of their hands and tears filled her eyes.

"Whatever it is, it's going to be okay," Jackie said, squeezing her hand.

"I know. But…"

"Tell me."

"I poisoned Bill. I forced the heart attack."

Jackie's mouth opened, but nothing came out. Darby's machine beeped three fast beats, and then settled back into the regular rate.

"Did you see that?" Kathryn asked, wiping her eyes. "Any mention of Bill, she always reacts." She wasn't crazy.

"What do you mean you killed Bill?" Jackie whispered.

Kathryn told her how she planned the entire thing, and she selected September 11th for the day of his death to never forget.

"But the problem is, I see him every night. He wanders my house."

"Bill's in your house? Like a ghost?" Jackie asked.

"Not literally in my house, but in my dreams. I'm watching him. He never does anything but is just there. Until last night…"

Kathryn blew her nose, and then she continued. "He came here."

"To the hospital?"

"Yes. And he talked to Darby."

"You're having nightmares because of the guilt you feel."

"But it was so real. And he pulled those plugs out of the wall and put his hand over Darby's throat." Kathryn's eyes widened. "Look, bruises!"

Jackie's eyes widened. "I'm sure there's a reason," she said, gently touching Darby's neck.

Kathryn jumped from her chair, and opened the door and said, "Fred, has anyone been in this room during your shift besides the regulars?" Fred was one of the evening guards John had stationed for Darby, and one of the more conscientious ones, too.

"Well," he began and scratched his head, and wandered into the room. "Early this morning, uh… an hour after I came on duty, I stepped into the restroom and when I came back there was some pilot in there."

"A pilot?"

"Yeah. I saw movement so I opened the door and this guy was just like standing there. He pointed beside the bed. So I asked who he was and he said that he was a pilot who had flown with Darby and wanted to see her. He seemed nice enough."

"Did you check his ID?"

"Yeah."

"Who was it?"

"I don't know. I looked at the picture and that it was a photo of him, and it said Global across the top."

"If you see him again, hold him and call John and me immediately."

"I will," he said. "Is everything okay?"

Kathryn nodded, "Yeah, fine." He stepped outside, and she closed the door.

Nothing was fine. Kathryn was a murderer. She would be locked in nightmare hell with Bill haunting her, and some pilot was trying to kill Darby. Odell, no doubt. It had to be him, pissed that he no longer had his management position. But why didn't he finish the job?

"Kat, don't tell anyone else that you killed Bill. Well, maybe Linda. But only because you need to talk to her to get rid of the nightmares. This will stay between us. I will never speak a word of it."

They won't get anything out of me either.

"How can I live with what I did?" Kat said. "I killed the girls' dad."

He was nothing but a sperm donor. You did good!

"He threatened their lives, more than once. He put some mechanism into drones to take out planes, while he was in prison.

He's killed hundreds of people. Bill deserved to die!" Jackie stood and placed her hands on her hips. "I'm sorry, Kat, but I can't feel empathy for him. You did the world a huge favor."

This is the best Halloween ever. Bill's a real friggin' ghost. It doesn't get better than this!

Kathryn was surprised by Jackie's outburst, but that was exactly what she needed to hear. "But, I just can't keep having these nightmares. I need sleep."

"Maybe now that you told us," she said, patting Darby's hand, "they'll go away."

"Perhaps."

Just then the door opened, and the nursing staff came into the room. Kathryn and Jackie stood to the side while the nurses busied themselves with feeding tubes, and then began cleaning her up. Jackie turned her back, pretending to look out the window. Kathryn watched as sheets came off the skeleton of a body. Darby always did like Halloween the best out of all the holidays.

And I've yet to be a skeleton, so this is a first.

Kathryn pulled her phone out of her purse, and texted John— *Darby had a "pilot" visitor this morning around 7 am. Can you pull security tapes and get a visual?*

CHAPTER 59

KATHRYN WAS UP early frosting the girls' cake to hide it before they awoke. This was their sweet-sixteen special day, and she had nothing planned for them. It just kind of snuck up on them all. Thank God this was a weekday, as she would plan a party for them on the weekend. She finished the last stroke of frosting.

She carefully lifted the cake to the table—a princess castle, just like when they were six. She was adding candles, 16 for each of them, around the edges. She was sticking the last candle in when…

"Mom," Jessica said.

Kathryn jumped. "What are you doing up so early?" It was 5 am.

"I couldn't sleep."

"Neither could I," Jenny said from the door.

"Happy birthday girls." She spread her arms and they both came in for a hug.

"Mom," Jessica said, and looked at Jennifer, who nodded. "We both decided that we don't want to celebrate our birthday this year."

"But—"

"Mom, it's just not right without Aunt Darby," Jenny said. "She was so excited on our last birthday because of this one. She's been waiting for our sixteenth birthday for… sixteen years."

Jessica pulled up the barstool and said, "It's not right, and you can't change our minds."

Kathryn watched them closely. She was not sure if this was a bad sign. Or this was normal? Could she force them to celebrate their birthday? That would be no celebration. She needed Linda.

"What about the DMV today?" Kathryn asked. That would clearly show their mental state.

The both looked at each other and said, "Hell yes!" in unison.

"Aunt Darby would be disappointed if she awoke and we weren't driving," Jenny said.

Kathryn laughed. They would be just fine. "Can we still eat cake?"

"Can we have it for breakfast?" Jessica asked. "It's really beautiful."

"Darby always said, 'life is short, eat dessert first'," Jennifer said.

"I think she would be happy to know we were starting this day out right," Kathryn said.

CHAPTER 60

KATHRYN SAT AT Darby's bedside, holding her hand. Nobody could explain where Darby's bruises came from, but they had since healed. That pilot was Neil. He didn't want Ray to see him, so he snuck in late. He was sincerely paying his respects. Kathryn's nightmares had all but stopped. Bill was gone. Darby slept peacefully. And it was Thanksgiving.

"I failed you Darby," Kathryn said. Tears filled her eyes. She had so much to be thankful for, but she could not find the joy. Not this year. She wiped her cheeks.

"Bill programmed the drones, but hitting your plane was an accident."

She stood, and smoothed and tucked in Darby's blanket.

"Your book is still on the *New York Times* best sellers list," Kathryn said, as she fluffed her pillow. It had been for months now. "Global is making some serious changes. For all it's worth, your accident was not in vain."

Marketing was using clips of Darby's accident for advertising, and sales were skyrocketing. Kathryn hated that, but the reality was that the more people who read the book, the more chance of change industry-wide. "You've already put three million into the swear jar for the kids' college."

Darby had started that jar, and they had joked she would be able to pay for college. "God, I wish you could be here to enjoy your success." Kathryn wiped another tear, and glanced at her watch. Jackie was hosting Thanksgiving dinner at her house, and she had 45 minutes until she would be considered late. They all agreed to keep this dinner out of the hospital.

"Hey you," Ray said from the doorway. "How's my love doing today?"

"She's good," Kathryn said. "Are you coming to dinner?"

"No. I'm going to stay here." Ray picked up Darby's hand and turned it over, and kissed her palm. He sat, and placed her hand on his chest. Tears filled his eyes.

Kathryn touched his back and said, "I know." She walked across the room and lifted her purse and coat. She stepped to the door and stopped for a moment.

"Happy Thanksgiving my love," Ray spoke quietly to Darby.

Happy Thanksgiving, Ray. Please don't give up on me, I'm coming back.

"I will never give up on you, baby. You're my life. My love. My every dream. I am so thankful that you came into my life." He set her hand down and stood. "Why, God?" he whispered, and then he saw Kathryn watching him.

He shrugged. "It's not fair," he said. "We didn't have enough time together."

Kathryn dropped her coat and purse on the floor and went to him. She spread her arms and he fell into them as he choked out a sob and then cried. She just held him, patting his back and allowed his tears to flow, and hers followed.

There was nothing she could say. No words could take the pain and injustice of it all away. She knew how he felt, but then, again, maybe she didn't.

"We can't give up hope," she said. "Annie Shapiro awoke after thirty years."

Ray pulled back and wiped his eyes. "I'd wait fifty."

"Then that's what we'll do," she said. "I'll bring you a plate in a few hours."

He gave her a nod, and then returned to his seat. "Hear that sweetheart? We don't have to cook *or* clean tonight," he said lifting her hand, he kissed it.

Don't ever let go, Ray. Your love will pull me back to your world. I know it. I feel it. I will hang on and I won't make you wait fifty years.

CHAPTER 61

KATHRYN WAS DEEP in thought scrutinizing Global's new training program. God, she needed Darby to help her with this. She tapped her pen on the desk, then opened Global's flight ops manual, and turned a few pages until she found what she was looking for. They still had so much work to do. She glanced at her watch. The girls would be out of school for their holiday break in twenty minutes.

They were going to get Darby's tree, and decorate it tonight. She shut down her computer, then closed the manuals and pushed away from her desk. She stood and pulled on her coat, and then headed for the door. Glancing back at the room, she wondered why she spent so much time at this office. A lot of good it did for Darby. She turned out the light, and closed the door, then walked to her secretary's desk.

"I'm calling it a day. If anyone needs me, will you tell them to call?" she said with a wave of her phone.

"I'll do that," Betty said. "Have a good weekend."

"Thank you," Kathryn said, "you, too." She turned and headed for the elevator. She stepped inside and a chill found a way inside her coat. When the doors opened, she walked out, and all but ran into John.

"What are you doing here?" she asked, surprised.

"Coming to talk to you."

She looked at her watch. "I've got to get the girls in fifteen minutes." They both passed their driver's tests, but had to share her car. She wished she could help them more.

"This will take just a minute." He stuffed his hands into his pockets. "I'll walk you to the car."

"That doesn't sound promising."

"We've cancelled the guards outside of Darby's room."

Kathryn stopped before they got to the door, and turned toward him. "Why?"

"The case is closed."

"What? You can't close the case. It hasn't even been a year."

"I know it's faster than usual. But we have everything. Bottom line is, this was just a shitty bad fucking day."

"But Darby…"

"She's going to be safe. Odell moved back east to manage some corporate airline. Clark's enjoying early retirement in Hawaii, and Hughes is flying the line. We just can't justify the expense."

"So now what?" Kathryn asked, fighting tears. Closing the case was like giving up on Darby. She knew the day would come, but never imagined so soon. "What will your report state?"

John sucked a deep breath. "Pilot error."

"God dammit John!" Kathryn snapped. "That's what you always say. It was scheduling, training, fatigue, mechanics. Was it pilot error that she didn't have any engines? Oh, definitely it was pilot error that Tom had a heart attack. Whose error was it that he was taking drugs?"

"Probably his."

"Point taken." Kathryn said, folding her arms. "But, Darby did everything she could to land that plane safely."

"We don't know that."

"Yes we do!" Kathryn headed for the door. This conversation was done. Darby did everything she could and nobody, especially John would ever implicate her in that accident. She was a victim of the worst kind.

John yelled after her, "Kat!"

She waved a hand and kept walking, and slammed into the door to open it. Once outside she ran to her car. She started it up and backed out of the spot before John could reach her. But he never emerged from the building. She put the car into gear and stepped on the gas and drove out of the parking lot. She slammed her palm onto the steering wheel multiple times and said, "Damn! Damn! Damn!"

CHAPTER 62

KATHRYN AND THE twins carried the box into the hospital. They mutually decided to get Darby a fake tree. Mostly because Niman had told the girls, via Francine, that real trees were not allowed on her floor due to germs, bugs and whatever else they drug in. Not to mention the fire hazard when it dried, and needles would end up everywhere.

They found a fake eight-foot fir and it was going to be the most beautiful tree anyone ever saw. They also cleaned out the shelves of colored lights, found funny ornaments and tinsel. Once on the elevator, Jessica pushed the button and they headed up to the 13th floor.

"Looks like you have a project ahead," the evening nurse said.

"We do!" Jennifer answered. "It's going to be beautiful."

As the girls approached Darby's room, Jessica asked, "Where's the guard?"

"John had to cancel him."

"Why?"

"Budget. And it looks like there's not much more they can do. She's safe. The nurses are watching and we'll be here more since you're out of school."

"Aunt Darby!" Jennifer said, running into the room. "We are done with school for Christmas break. And, we're decorating your tree." She dug into the bag and pulled out an ornament and said, "Look at this. Santa is flying a plane! I think it might be an Airbus, but you can't really be sure."

"Why would you think that's an Airbus?" Jessica said.

"Because it has those winglets on it."

"Boeings have those, too."

"Who cares," Jennifer said. "I think it's your airplane, Darby. So... we'll just believe that."

"'Tis the season to believe," Kathryn said.

"Hi, ladies," Niman said, from the door. "Are you Santa's helpers this year?"

"More or less," Jessica said, busily pulling everything out of the bag and lining it up on the windowsill.

"I'm thinking you probably need some cookies and cocoa for this project."

"Oh yeah!" Jennifer said. "Darby, would you like a cookie? Oh, I know... get her a candy cane and we can stick it in her mouth."

Now that's the best idea I've heard all year. The holiday phallic symbol. Not just for Santa.

"You got it. Two hot chocolates, four cookies, and one candy cane," he said, writing the order on his prescription pad. "Just what the doctor ordered."

"Niman, that's awfully nice," Kathryn said.

"Would you help me?" he said, with concern etched in his eyes.

"Girls, we'll be right back."

Kathryn followed him in silence. He fidgeted the entire way, and attempted at small talk. Kathryn knew something was wrong. When they arrived at the cafeteria, he said. "Grab a seat. I'll get us some coffee."

This could not be good. Kathryn sat as he ordered. He paid for the cookies, cocoa, candy cane, and two cups of coffee, and then said to the clerk, "I'll be back to get the chocolate in a moment." He brought the coffee to Kathryn, and sat at the opposite side of the table.

He handed her some cream and pushed the sweeteners her way. She poured cream into her cup, and added a packet of yellow powder.

"Is everything okay?" she asked, worried about Linda and Francine. She was not sure if she could handle one more event in her life.

He shook his head. "I have been ordered to recommend a disconnect."

"What?" Kathryn said. Her heart found its way into her throat. "What do you mean?"

"She's not getting better," he said, reaching for Kathryn's hand.

She pulled it back and put it in her lap. "No. You cannot pull the plug on Darby."

"We have to honor her request. We found a copy of her will. She doesn't want to be kept on life support."

"You went through her house? This is not right!" Kathryn said. Tears began streaming down her face. "No. You can't do this."

"Her will was mailed to the hospital."

"But…"

"I asked Ray if he sent it. But he was as upset as you are now." Niman pulled a hand through his hair. "Who the hell would send that?"

"Who would have access to her house? None of us want to pull the plug on Darby. You can't do this!"

"Does she have any relatives that can stop it?" he asked.

"Nobody."

"I don't know what to tell you," he said. "We may have no choice."

Kathryn's mind whirled. She was the problem solver. She could figure this out. But how? She could take her to another hospital. "I could apply to be her legal guardian! Then I would have the decision."

"Yes." Niman sipped his coffee. "That might just work. I wish we had thought of that a year ago."

"I'll do it first thing in the morning."

"Tomorrow's Saturday. But you can fill out the form on line. I'll make some calls and see if there is any way to expedite it."

"Do Linda and Francine know?"

"Linda does."

"Can we keep this quiet from the girls?"

"She said that would be the best idea, too."

"Okay. Cocoa and cookies. We have a tree to decorate and I have a Darby to adopt."

They filled the girls' cocoa cups, and headed back to the room. Kathryn forced herself to think positive thoughts the entire way. Darby would love this story best, when she awoke and found that Kathryn was legally her mom. That would show her for acting like one of the kids more often than not.

When they arrived back at the room, the tree was standing. The lights were hung and glowing.

"Wow, you girls are fast!" Kathryn said. "How did you do this?"

"We weren't fast. You were just gone forever," Jennifer said.

"Where'd you go, the North Pole?" Jessica asked, eyeing her mother.

Kathryn smiled. "Maybe." She handed the girls their cocoa and cookies.

Jennifer set hers on the ledge and she unwrapped half a candy cane and slid it into Darby's mouth. Then placed an elf hat, tilted upon her head.

"Jess, get your butt over here. We need an Aunt Darby shot with both of us." She handed her phone to her mother.

Kathryn stepped back and took a photo of her three favorite girls. She wiped a tear from her cheek.

"You okay mom?" Jessica asked.

"Oh yeah. You know how the holidays make me emotional," she said. "But I think I need to be in this shot too."

She handed the phone to Niman, and leaned over the bed with the girls. Her smile never felt more forced. Investigation closed. Pull the plug on Darby. And all in one day. Holiday joy does not get much better than that at Swedish Hospital.

CHAPTER 63

KATHRYN HAD FILLED out the paperwork online over the weekend, and then the first thing Monday morning she found her way to the courthouse. She paid the fees, and applied for guardianship. The system was backlogged with cases, and the clerk said that it could take up to four months for a decision. Kathryn tried to explain for medical reasons that Darby needed a guardian, now. But that didn't matter.

Exasperated, she stormed out of the courthouse. Ray was standing on the steps waiting.

"What'd they say?"

"Four months," Kathryn said, and sat heavily on the step. "But we don't have four months. We can't let them pull the plug. How the hell did they get her will anyway?"

"Someone broke in and took it."

"Are you sure?" Kathryn asked. "Who would do such a thing?" But deep down, she knew.

"I wasn't sure. I've been going by every few days to water her plants, and last week the back door was unlocked. I thought maybe I left it open. But then I found an upstairs window open too. Her filing cabinet was askew. I thought someone climbed in the window, took something out of the filing cabinet and walked out the door. I called the police."

"Did they investigate?"

"They asked if anything was missing. I told them I didn't know."

"So they did nothing?" Kathryn sighed.

"Nothing. I thought that maybe someone pulled a credit card number. I called the bank, but nothing ever came through."

"Odell. I know it was that asshole," Kathryn said. "Who else would give a damn?"

"Can we petition the hospital to wait four months?"

"That's exactly what we'll do."

"Then we have nothing to worry about," Ray said.

CHAPTER 64

KATHRYN SAT ON the windowsill, Jennifer and Francine sat on one side of Darby's bed, and Jessica sat on the end. Jackie, John, and Chris sat in chairs by the tree, and Linda and Niman were by the door. Ray sat in a chair beside Darby. *Santa Baby* played over the stereo. They all talked quietly, enjoying each other's company.

Darby had always talked about room parties in Tokyo. Now she lived them daily. Her life had become one big room party. Kathryn lifted the pad of paper. Two weeks had passed and Darby hadn't made one indication that she was aware of anything. It saddened Kathryn to no end. Her friend was slipping deeper into the darkness.

Niman told her that the hospital would be willing to delay the option, as long as insurance covered the room. She and Ray dug through the policy, and learned it would end on January 31st. A life comes down to an insurance premium. She would be damned if they would kick her out. Global would be footing this bill. She had told Niman as much. Now she had to make sure it happened. But her bank account had money, and so far it was untouchable.

Over three million dollars from her advance, combined with book sales, sat in a trust fund for the girls, who were minors. They could not touch it until they were eighteen. But she would find an attorney to see how they could change those terms. How ironic the money a person earned would be legally tied up and the system could allow them to die.

Jennifer braided Darby's hair, and Jessica's head lay on Darby's legs. The girls would be lost without her. Hell, they all would be lost.

"Any New Year's resolutions?" Kathryn asked to nobody in particular.

"I'm going to get straight A's" Francine said.

"You got them this year," Jessica said.

"How'd you know?"

"I looked at your report card."

"Jess!" Kathryn said. When had her daughter become a peeping Tom?

"Don't Jess me," she said. "If stuff is laying about, I can't help but look. Actually, I was really just looking at what classes you were taking."

Francine smiled. "It's okay. But if you read my diary, you're toast."

"You have a diary?" Jennifer asked, eyes lighting up. "Did you write anything about Brad in it?"

"Brad?" Linda said.

"Does a girl have no privacy?" Francine said, with a lightness Kathryn loved. "Brad is my business, and nobody else's!"

"As long as it's not monkey business," Linda said.

"Mom!" Francine blushed. "Enough about me."

"I'm going to adopt Darby," Kathryn said, to save Francine from any more talk about Brad. That broke the discussion in one swoop.

The girls sat upright, with eyes wide.

"What?" Jennifer said.

"You're adopting Aunt Darby?" Jessica asked. "She's going to be our sister?"

Kathryn nodded. "She needs a guardian to make medical decisions for her."

"Medical decisions? You're going to pull the plug?" Jennifer said. She started crying. "You can't do it mom! Please, Mom, no!"

"Jess. I'm doing this to keep her alive. Someone broke into Darby's house and found her will. It clearly stated she did not want to be kept alive on life support. They sent it to the hospital."

"Who would do that?" Chris asked.

"I can only guess. But I'm fighting it. If I can become her legal guardian, we can keep her alive."

The room fell silent, and on cue *Silent Night* played in the background. Kathryn had no idea the kids would think her adopting Darby would be to cut her off life support. But they, too, must have been thinking about it, with that immediate reaction.

"Look! It's snowing," Jessica said. "Aunt Darby, we're going to have a white Christmas."

"What if she doesn't want to be kept alive?" Jackie finally said. "I know you don't want to hear this, and maybe this is not the right time, but..."

"Please don't say that." Kathryn had asked herself that same question, too many times to count, but the answer was always the same. Darby would want to live. "When she signed that paper, she never imagined that her body would be perfect, but she would be in a deep sleep. I'm convinced if there is a chance, she would want to live."

"I just keep remembering her a year ago, tonight," Jackie said. "This was the last night we all saw her. Now, look at her. I'm not so sure."

"I saw her the next morning," Ray said. "I should never have let her go to work."

Jennifer said, "Seriously Ray? You think you could ever tell Aunt Darby what to do?"

"Good point," he said with a wink.

"Remember how tired she was that night?" Niman said. "She had been awake for so many hours. How the hell could they put her on a plane?"

"Well, she's had a year of sleep," Jessica said, "and I, for one, am ready for her to wake up."

"We all are sweetheart," Kathryn said. "How about we make a holiday toast for Darby?"

John lifted his glass, "To health, happiness, and a long life."

"To a very long life," Kathryn said. "Nothing will take Darby away from us."

CHAPTER 65

DECEMBER 25, 2016

CAPTAIN GEORGE WYATT walked quietly through Kathryn's house, and up the stairs. Bedroom doors were closed. The house was silent. The time was 0300. He had been there many times over the years with Bill. Before that bitch had thrown him into jail, that is. Now Bill was gone. But there was nothing that he could not handle on his own. He and Bill had been a team, and they had orchestrated a plan that would take down an industry. He in management, and Bill with the union—together there was nothing they couldn't do. Now he had to go solo.

He headed back down the stairs. Halfway down a board creaked, and he froze. He counted to 120 and then continued his descent downstairs.

Bill and he had some great plans. The Middle East and those psychotic radicals were becoming of great use. Divide and conquer, distract and destroy. Wyatt had an entirely new revenue source. Perhaps with Bill gone, he was better off. He actually didn't need him, and that would mean he could keep all proceeds.

But Kathryn Jacobs was a pain in his ass. He had held onto his job only because he was the highest in command. Because of the chain of command policy, that he had no idea existed, nothing ever got to his level. He pleaded ignorance, and Patrick believed him. You live a lie for so long, everyone will want to believe it.

Unfortunately, Patrick was micromanaging flight operations and forcing him to clean up the training department. One by one his training managers were being replaced with experienced pilots, and all from the Coastal side of the house. *Fuck them all.*

He knelt at the Christmas tree, and set the box on the ground. He clicked open the lock, and lifted the lid. A pressure-sensitive flashlight clenched between his teeth illuminated the contents. He located the package and carefully lifted the explosives. He set the small box on a branch at the bottom of the tree and pulled the wires out and draped them onto the floor.

As he lifted the knife from the box, a board squeaked from a room above and he froze, releasing pressure on the light. He folded over, ducking below the stream of light that was shining through the window from the streetlamp, and hid in the dark. After two full minutes of silence, he went back to work.

Squeezing the light once again, he sorted through the various cords. When he found the master that would be plugged into the wall, he moved precisely two feet back from the plug itself. He sliced open the plastic exposing wires. He pulled them free and cut through both wires. He stripped the plastic and took one and twisted it to one of the wires that was laying on the floor. Then he did the same to the other.

He pulled a roll of electrical tape from the box and wrapped the wires. He stuffed his handy work into the tree, and placed the cord that Kathryn would plug into the wall onto the floor by the outlet. She would come down the stairs, plug in the tree before the kids awoke and "*Boom!*" he whispered. Kathryn would be finished. If the kids got out or not, was nothing but a side effect.

Wyatt put his supplies back into the box, shined the flashlight over the floor to assure nothing was left behind. He glanced at his watch. Two more stops, and the holiday clean up would be complete.

WYATT PULLED ON his white coat and walked into Swedish Hospital through the Emergency entrance. This was the only access without an ID check. He had been visiting the emergency room numerous times over the previous week and when the clerk saw, him he would say, "Merry Christmas." She would smile and return the greeting. She would recognize him, and assume he belonged with the white coat. Recognition. Therefore he belonged.

His plan worked impeccably and he walked through the emergency room without question. Patients waiting in rooms moaned and called for help from behind curtains. Christmas morning was the perfect day, as there would be minimum staff, the most junior ones at that, and everyone would be distracted due to the holiday. Somewhat like airline operations, air traffic control, and the entire emergency support system—*Christmas next year would be spectacular.*

Wyatt found the elevator, pressed the button to the 13th floor and waited forever for it to arrive. He had taken a side trip to Ray's driveway and sliced his brake line. When lover boy received the news that Darby was gone, he would jump into his car, not notice the fluid all over the cement, and rush to the hospital. Flying down the Seattle hills with no brakes, he would be with Darby sooner than later. It was the least he could do—give them a Christmas together.

The door opened on the 8th floor and a guy wheeled in a laundry cart. Wyatt looked straight ahead. The elevator stopped on the 9th floor, the man left with his load, and the elevator continued.

He grinned at the thought of this entire fucking group joined together, burning in hell for eternity due to their interference.

It took great crafting to get Darby on that flight, schedule that particular plane to be waiting in Amsterdam for her, and then have the kids play with their drones that he had given to Tom. He knew that telling Tom about the drugs, and who to contact for the loan, was a no brainer. Same with the kids flying their drones. He just tracked them, and when Darby's flight was on final he activated them.

The FBI being at the airport was a positive distraction.

His only failure was to not remove the twin drone. Reports were vague and he thought they had both gone into the engine. Regardless, that didn't matter. He was just lucky that Ray hadn't mentioned his name. But then he gave Ray the perfect out with an indication that the FADEC was installed in Singapore, and he gave himself an insurance policy by threatening to kill the twins if Ray said anything to anyone.

When Odell told him that Ray had that part on his shelf, he used that information the best way he could—blackmail. The idea of using that part was nothing short of brilliant. Yet he had no idea what would actually happen on the plane if he did. All he had to do was pay a mechanic a few extra Euros to install it, in Amsterdam, and hope for the best. But sadly, that poor bloke ended up in an accident. Wyatt did not have to pay a corpse.

The door opened and he stuffed his hands into his pockets and walked toward Darby's room.

CHAPTER 66

FRANCINE'S ALARM WENT off and she jumped, and silenced it. It was 4 am and she and the girls had a plan. The night before, which was not more than four hours earlier, everyone agreed that nobody was allowed out of their rooms before 9 am, because they had all been up so late. But she, Jess and Jenn wanted to do something nice for Kathryn.

The room was cold, but Francine pulled on her robe and crept into the girls' room. "Hey you two, you ready to do Christmas the right way?"

"Oh God," Jessica said. "Whose idea was this? Kill me now."

Jennifer jumped out of bed. "Jess, get up. We can go back to bed after everything is ready." She pulled a sweatshirt over her head, and stuck her feet into slippers.

"Okay. Okay." Jessica rolled out of bed and pulled on her robe. "Where are the presents?"

"I've got them in my room," Francine whispered.

"Whose idea was this?" Jessica asked, again.

"Yours," Jennifer said. "The best you've had all year."

"Grrr," Jessica said, sticking her feet into her slippers. "What are we doing again?"

Francine giggled. She loved these girls and was glad to have sisters. "We are filling stockings, putting presents under the tree, baking fruit cake and making a pot of coffee."

"When Mom comes down, she's going to be so surprised," Jennifer said.

Together the girls went to Francine's room and found the gifts, and they each carried something down the stairs. Francine set her stack on the floor under the tree.

"Why don't you guys set up the gifts and stuff the stockings, I'll start in the kitchen," Francine said.

"Okay. Let's get this party going and light up the tree," Jessica said, grabbing the chord.

CHAPTER 67

GEORGE WYATT WALKED into Darby's room and smiled. He walked to her side and said, "I would leave you in this hell, if I knew you would never come out of it."

"Merry Christmas doctor," a voice broadcast behind him.

"Merry Christmas," he said and walked to the other side of the bed and picked up the pad of paper for a distraction. As he turned the pages, he realized what this was. There had been no reactions for all of December. Either they stopped writing, or Darby had stopped responding.

"You're making rounds early," she said, changing one of Darby's bags.

"Promised the wife I would be home when the kids awoke."

"That's nice," she said, hooking up the new bag. "Well, have a good one," she added and rushed out of the room.

Wyatt had been watching this room for weeks and this was a new person. Holiday staff. He smiled. And she was busy, too. He glanced at his watch—0405.

"Well my dear, I would love to say I'm sorry to see you go. But I just can't do that."

He stood for a moment still contemplating the best way to do this. If he pulled the plug, the machines would beep outside, immediately. The midnight staff was never responsive, but he couldn't take that chance. No, the best way would be a pillow over her face. By the time she was dead, the machine would beep, and he could stuff the pillow back where it belonged.

Stop you bastard! Please no. Someone help me.

Wyatt glanced over his shoulder and then pulled the pillow out from under her head, and placed it over her face. She did not move, and the only indication of her death would be the machine. He waited.

Darby gasped for air. She fought wildly. Please God no! And then the girls were standing there in the light, and Darby ran toward them.

Darby's machine flat lined and the machine sang out—music to his ears. Alarms burst out from the nurses' station waking the entire floor. He lifted her head and stuffed the pillow under it.

He began a modified CPR, and was in the process when the doctor on staff burst into the room with cardiac pads. "You've got it doctor," he said. "She just stopped breathing."

Within seconds Darby's shirt was ripped from her body and electronic pads were placed on her chest, and zap! Nothing. They did it again. And again. Wyatt stood outside and watched until the doctor called the time of death. He turned, and headed for the elevator, making sure his face would not be seen on camera.

CHAPTER **68**

DARBY SCREAMED AND sat upright, throwing the pillow off her face, as her alarm cried from the nightstand. The wind howled from beyond the pane. Her heart raced wildly and she grabbed her phone. Silencing the alarm first, she then clicked to the calendar—December 25, 2015.

She climbed out of bed, pulled on her robe and ran to the window. Visibility was no more than a quarter mile. Snowdrifts piled high everywhere, as far as she could see. At least a foot of snow dumped through the night. Ray's car was in the driveway, but only a dusting was on his car. She ran to the top of the stairs.

Santa stood at the bottom holding two Venti-sized Starbucks. "Merry Christmas!"

"Oh God, I love you!" she said, with tears streaming down her face, as she ran down the stairs two at a time.

"I'm hearing that a lot these days," Ray said, with a smirk. "I'm thinking it's the hat."

She grabbed him and hugged him tight. She could not stop the tears. That nightmare had been far too real, and her fear was that nothing was beyond her chief pilots' doing at Global. She was living a nightmare.

Her body shook violently.

"Honey, what's wrong?" he asked, setting the coffees on the table. He wrapped his arms tightly around her and said, "Yes, I risked my life heading out into this weather, but you're worth it, and I survived..."

"I... I just had a really tough night," she said with her cheek pressed to his chest. "It was so real."

"You were pretty active last night," Ray said. "Kept me awake most of the night."

Brushing tears from her cheeks she asked, "You stayed?"

"Of course. But as much as I wanted to play with you, I let you sleep."

"You can play with me forever," she said.

"I plan on it." He kissed her forehead, and then said, "Now that step one is complete—caffeinating my sweetheart, we need to get some food in you."

She took his hand and followed him into the kitchen. He pulled out a chair for her, and she slid in, and tucked a leg up under her. She wrapped her arms around herself to stave off the chill.

"What went on in that beautiful mind of yours?" Ray asked, dropping slices of bread into the egg mixture. "There were moments I thought you might kill me." He placed a slice of bread on the grill, followed by two more slices, and then dropped bacon into a frying pan.

"I had a nightmare that was so real, and everything the chief pilots are doing worked into my dream, and then some." Tears filled her eyes.

"Then some?"

Darby told him what happened, from the drugs, to the drones, and that they were trying to kill her, as he cooked breakfast.

"Here you go sweets," he said, placing a plate in front of her. He set another plate for himself on the other side of the table, and sat. "It was just a dream, and they can't hurt you."

Her attention was on the gift sitting on the windowsill—a small box wrapped in gold with a matching bow on top. "I'm not so sure." Tears filled her eyes again, as she returned her attention to him.

"Look what they've done so far," she said. "I have my own chief pilot to report to. They're censoring my book. They've blocked me from talking to marketing. They forced me to take a trip that violated FAR 117."

"What they are doing is bullshit," Ray said.

Darby sighed. "This is beyond bullshit. This is nothing short of ridiculous. I'm just not sure if these guys are stupid and can't see the ramifications of their actions, or if they know and don't care."

The industry blamed pilot error as the cause of airline accidents and incidents. However, if a root cause analysis were conducted results would indicate that pilots made errors due to a systemic problem of inadequate training, complements of an FAA 'train to proficiency' concept. Pilots should be trained to competency. They ate their breakfast while Darby told Ray the rest of her dream. Everything except for the fake FADEC, and Ray listened intently.

"Sweetheart, it was a dream. Everything's going to be fine," he said, reaching out and touching her hand.

"Perhaps," she said, and sipped her coffee, working to calm her heart. "But this was all part of it. You. The hat, coffee and the exact same breakfast…"

"I'm that predictable, huh?" He raised an eyebrow. "And this was a nightmare?"

"No, this was the good part." Darby smiled. "This was the best part." She glanced at the box. "But, all I'm saying is that I am never taking that much melatonin again."

"How much did you take?"

"Apparently too much."

Ray tipped his glass of orange juice and finished it. Then said, "I didn't tell you, but Joel and I went to 13 Coins for dinner the other night. He grabbed me as I was leaving the office."

"What did he want?"

"For me to tell you not to publish your book."

"See, I knew it!" Darby said. "I have one question. Does that problem we were going to solve after the first of the year have anything to do with a bad part on the shelf?"

Ray's mouth opened, and his color drained from his face. "How did you...?"

A chill found its way into her body, and then Ray told her what happened at work. While the situation was different than her dream, the issue stemmed from pressure at work and lack of a safety culture. The truth was, that nobody was safe as long as the current flight operations management team existed at Global.

"I've got to call Kat," Darby said.

She dialed Kathryn's number and when she answered Darby asked, "Is your tree turned on?"

"Merry Christmas to you, too," Kathryn said. "And I'm not sure how 'excited' my tree is, but, yes, it's illuminated."

Darby laughed. "Okay. Good. But do not let those girls fly their drones today."

"In this storm?" Kathryn said.

"You've got a point."

"Darby... Are you okay?"

"I couldn't be better," she said. "I love you. I love the girls. Merry Christmas! Hug everyone."

Darby hung up and Ray asked, "What time do I need to get out of here, so you can get ready for work?"

She held up a finger. "One more call."

Darby dialed crew scheduling and punched in her code. The phone rang and rang. When someone finally answered, she was placed on hold. She drummed her fingers on the table while she waited. Finally a voice said, "Crew scheduling, how can I help you?"

"This if First Officer Bradshaw, pattern 1225."

"Yes?"

"I'm calling in fatigued."

"You can't call in fatigued."

"So they say. But I am. I'm not fit to fly today. That cross-country excursion wiped me out. Followed by bounces at 2 am yesterday morning. There's a raging storm in Seattle, and I have not flown for eight months. I can't do this, not today. I'm beat. I had a shitty night's sleep, and we owe passengers more than this."

"I'm reporting you to the chief pilot."

"Wish him a Merry Christmas for me."

"But I don't have anyone to take the trip," the scheduler cried. "You have to do it."

Darby yawned as she glanced outside at the whiteout. "We should never fly on the wings of luck."

"But—"

"Merry Christmas. I'll call you when I'm rested."

Ray's mouth dropped open, and then it worked into a smile. "I don't know what's got into you, but I like it." Ray kissed her hand. "You're my hero."

"I'm no hero. But I am going to start practicing what I preach," Darby said, lifting a piece of bacon. She pointed it at him. "We might not be able to change things overnight, but I can stop being a hypocrite and telling others how to operate safely, while I'm willing to put myself on a plane when I am clearly not fit to fly." She stuck the bacon into her mouth, and said. "I'm exhausted."

"Then we should get you back to bed," Ray said, with a grin.

"I want to open my present first."

"What present?" Ray said, glancing at the box with a grin.

"Don't play with me. I'm fatigued, and dangerous."

He slid the gift across the table. She wiped off her hands and lifted the lid and her mouth fell open. She looked up at Ray and back to the box. "What the…?"

He grinned.

She pulled two folded tickets out from the box. When she unfolded them, her eyes widened. "I can't believe you did this!" and yelled, "Go Hawkeyes!"

Darby removed two tickets on the 50-yard line for the 2016 Rose Bowl game, holding them high she said, "Iowa will kill Stanford!" She looked at them again to make sure she was reading them right and it wasn't a joke, and then said, "I love it! I love it! I love it! This is the best gift you could have given me!"

EPILOGUE

SEPTEMBER 9, 2016

DARBY FILLED BOTH Ray's and her cup with champagne punch. They were celebrating Jackie and John's wedding at the Normandy Park Cove. Memories of the memorial for Greg, and all who were lost on that flight, were being replaced with new memories of hope, life and dreams that only a wedding with a pregnant bride could bring. Jackie was three months along.

Jackie quit her job in flight attendant training to focus on her growing family. But she already had one foot out the door. There were too many problems that she did not have the energy to battle.

The truth was, the first time an accident occurred and the flight attendants were unable to perform the proper procedures, due to fatigue and confusion because of the many aircraft they were responsible to learn, things would change—a reactionary method of safety. How the airlines would apply safety management systems to flight attendant training and procedures would be an interesting process to watch.

Stepping up to Ray, Darby handed him a cup of punch. "Here you go," she said, and then leaned in and whispered, "I spiked it."

"Thank you sweetheart." He kissed her on the cheek.

"Aunt Darby, hurry!" Jessica said. "Jackie's going to throw the bouquet!"

"I'll be right there," Darby said. She had not allowed the girls to fly their drones until John's team had inspected them. After they were cleared, she took the girls to register them with the FAA, and signed them up for a drone course at a Highline Community College. She also loaded the B4UFly app into their phones.

"Congratulations on your book," someone said, stepping up to Darby.

Her book sat on the best sellers list for six months, and was still holding. She had sent a copy to Global's CEO, Lawrence Patrick, upon its release in February. She was subsequently invited to a meeting with Wyatt, Clark, and Odell, as well as the head of SMS and the director of training, to discuss significant issues.

Wyatt, Clark and Odell were removed from their management positions, and replaced with experienced pilots with leadership skills. The fleet training captains were also replaced with experience.

History dictated management pilots were to have type ratings in order to bring flight experience into the office. Yet as the airlines grew and the airspace system became more complex, pilots held management positions without management experience and could not handle the complexity of the job. Global was changing that paradigm, and now all managers were required to take management and leadership courses. Such a novel idea.

To make matters worse, as aircraft became more complex those pilot managers no longer held piloting experience to understand the automated aircraft. They also spent all their time in the office, and lost sight of the flight line. They were just empty suits attempting to manage a system that was nothing like *anything* they had ever experienced in the military, or anywhere else.

"You better go get that bouquet," Linda said.

Niman shook Ray's hand. "Good to see you."

Linda and Niman moved to Seattle and both took full-time jobs at the University of Washington Hospital, and Francine stayed in Iowa. She was having way too much fun being away from Mom.

"Can you hold my drink?" Darby asked Ray. "I've got flowers to catch."

Ray disclosed what was going on in his department, and he was relieved of his management position and put back on the maintenance line, but neither he nor Darby cared. He was a top-notch mechanic and loved his work. With a regular schedule, they had more time together and often took trips in his airplane. They both signed up for glider camp, and would be starting next month.

Darby headed toward the patio that Bill had stood on so many years before—once upon a time when he was a king. In his own mind anyway. As far as she knew, he was still rotting in jail. The pilot who had flown into the mountain was found to have been mentally ill, and sadly his doctors had known about it, but never notified the airline. The industry was rumbling about mental health regulations, and it would only be a matter of time until the aviation industry saw a change in that arena.

They had yet to find the triple seven, thus that mystery prevailed. Darby suspected it had crashed into the ocean, and one day clues would be pulled up by a fishing boat, and questions would be answered. She suspected a hijacking, but there was no proof without a body.

Speculation of that plane safely landing somewhere, and rumors of a conspiracy took hold. But the reality was, another Boeing 777 with a check airman sitting in the right seat, and a captain who had just been trained (and who would have been the best he ever would be fresh out of training), were unable to land on a clear day with a 12,000-foot runway—they had crashed short of the runway.

Darby also sat in the jumpseat with a check airman and new captain once, where death appeared imminent. The terrain warning wailed and neither pilot reacted until Darby shouted, 'Speedbrakes!' The difference between her flight and the plane that crashed short of the runway was that she spoke up, thus they did not inadvertently fly into the ground, too.

Kathryn and Tom's relationship died a natural death. As it turned out, he had gone to ask Bill permission if he could date Kathryn. What the hell was he thinking? Darby did not have to say she was happy they broke up. Her happy dance gave that away. The last thing Kathryn needed was another project. She needed someone who would take care of her, and spoil her to no end.

Darby stood for a moment and grinned at her friend, who was oblivious to the potential of new love. Kathryn was talking with Richard, a new inspector at the NTSB, and good friend of John. She was giggling like a schoolgirl, and had spent most of the wedding with him. Time changed everything.

"Kat, come catch the bouquet," Darby shouted. She hated pulling her away from that devastatingly handsome man, but Darby suspected that he would wait for her return. There was something in the eyes that told all.

The ceremony had been beautiful. Darby danced and laughed well into the evening, celebrating with all the people that she loved. While the Hawkeyes lost the Rose Bowl, she and Ray had the best time ever.

Sports were a lot like life. If a person played it safe, the other team would always walk all over them. The Hawkeyes made it to the Rose Bowl because of hard work, dedication, and doing what it took to be the best they could be. Yet they played safe in the big game. If Darby could have given them their pre-game pep talk she would have said, "You've done all you can to get here, with nothing to lose and everything to gain. Play fearless, and strong." Words that she told herself often in her pursuit of safety.

She gave a wave to Ray, and did a little happy dance. Then returned her attention to Jackie. Darby had work to do.

Jackie yelled, "Here you go!" and threw the flowers.

They went flying through the air. Darby jumped high, and caught the bouquet, and then held it up and yelled, "Score!" Everyone laughed.

Ray was standing off to the side smiling.

ACKNOWLEDGMENTS

BRINGING A BOOK to life takes a team. Especially when the author is as airline pilot, who is also in the midst of working on a PhD, flying around the world, and playing with grandkids. This team has been phenomenal, and I am ever so grateful for them all. They are the only reason this book made publication in early 2016. Thank you all!

Carol Singleton began this journey with reading *Flight For Control*, and editing *Flight For Safety* 'after' a rush to market. This time she got Flight For Survival before it went to print, and proceeded to give me her time and energy, over the holidays, to make this book a reality. Carol has been working in the aviation industry for many years, and continues to be the heart of flight operations at a major airline. More than that, her son is a pilot working his way up to that dream job. Carol's passion is one of support for aviation safety, and she has a phenomenal ability to edit with motivation for the safety of all.

Nathan Everett is my go to guy for his talent, with an eye for perfection. When I contact Nathan, I never know where in the world I will find him. Literally. But wherever that is, he is always willing to help. His talent and assistance in bringing this work to life, was perfectly timed. He is a master of publication, and is always willing to work my projects into his schedule. If you want to publish a book, Nathan can help you make your dreams come true from editing to full publication and anywhere in between. elderroadbooks@outlookcom.

Pat Kassner, my mother, received the first copy of *Flight For Survival* hot off my printer for her Christmas present, along with a copy of Strunk and White's, *The Elements of Style*. She is one of those people who has a master eye for the written word, and has read many of my technical papers. She had commented that she wished she "remembered the rules." So… I gave them to her, with my novel, along with a job. However, I took that gift back and she was presented with the clean copy, for the final read at the end of the day. Also, two of may favorite Darby statements came from my mother.

Kayla Wospschall is my middle daughter and the designer of my book covers. Her talent never ceases to amaze me. She recently illustrated our first children's book: *I Am Awesome, the ABCs of Being Me.* This book is amazing. All proceeds go to her non-profit startup: The Children's Museum of Central Oregon, where hands on learning focused on STEM education is the focus. If you want more information email her at kwopschall@gmail.com.

Dick Petitt, my husband of 34 years, not only read this book, but as I fed him first draft chapters he kept asking for more. His love of the story exceeded the speed of my writing. He read, edited, and gave me great feedback throughout the entire process. There is no greater support system than my husband.

John Nance, Chris Broyhill, Eric Auxier, and **Leland Shanle.** I am honored to have these captains, and best selling aviation authors, give me their valuable time to read and endorse *Flight For Survival.* Especially during a time when they are all in the middle of projects of their own.

BOOKS BY KARLENE PETITT:

AVIATION THRILLERS. A TRILOGY…
UNTIL BOOK FOUR MAKES IT A SERIES.

Flight For Control
Flight For Safety
Flight For Survival

MOTIVATION:

Flight To Success, Be the Captain of Your Life:

> *"When you fly toward a dream*
> *embraced by passion in your soul,*
> *the clouds art, the sun shines and*
> *the rainbow guides you to*
> *your deepest desires."*

CHILDREN'S:

I Am Awesome, The ABCs of Being Me:

I can be an Astronaut
because I am Awesome.

Stars shining bright,
up in the sky.
I want to fly to the moon,
And ask them why.

KARLENE PETITT

An international airline pilot
who is type-rated and has flown
and/or instructed on the B747-
400, B747-200, B767, B757,
B737, B727, and A330. Petitt is
a 37-year veteran of flying, and
has worked for Coastal Airways,
Evergreen, Braniff, America
West Training, Guyana, Tower

Air, Northwest Airlines, and currently flies an Airbus, A330, for
an international airline. Based in Seattle Washington, she is the
mother of three, grandmother of seven, holds MBA and MHS
degrees and is working on her PhD in Aviation, with a focus on
safety.

KARLENE IS AVAILABLE to host aviation discussion groups, join book
clubs, or speak at your meetings.

Please email her at Krlene.Petitt@gmail.com to schedule
your next event. And check out her blog for more writings at
KarlenePetitt.com